Praise for Tricia Goyer

"I can always count on Tricia Goyer to draw me into her story world. She deftly writes characters I can root for right to the very end. Treat yourself to a great Goyer read!"

Robin Lee Hatcher, bestselling author of *Even Forever* and *All She Ever Dreamed*

"Tricia Goyer once again has crafted a beautiful tale of sacrifice, hope, and second chances. *Beyond the Gray Mountains* swept me into the heart of Montana, and Ben and Marianna's story kept me turning pages far into the night. A riveting story of a musician, a woman struggling to find the balance between her Amish upbringing and her new freedom in Christ, and the God who makes all things new."

Tara Johnson, author of *Engraved on the Heart, Where Dandelions Bloom*, and *All Through the Night*

"Tricia Goyer has a talent with creating characters that take you inside the Amish community in a unique way. Bridging the English and Amish world with a reality that is refreshing, you will enjoy this series."

Martha Artyomenko, Avid Readers of Christian Fiction

Beyond The Gray Mountains

BIG SKY AMISH || BOOK ONE

TRICIA GOYER

"The Lord your God is with you,
the Mighty Warrior who saves.
He will take great delight in you;
in His love He will no longer rebuke you,
but will rejoice over you with singing."
Zephaniah 3:17

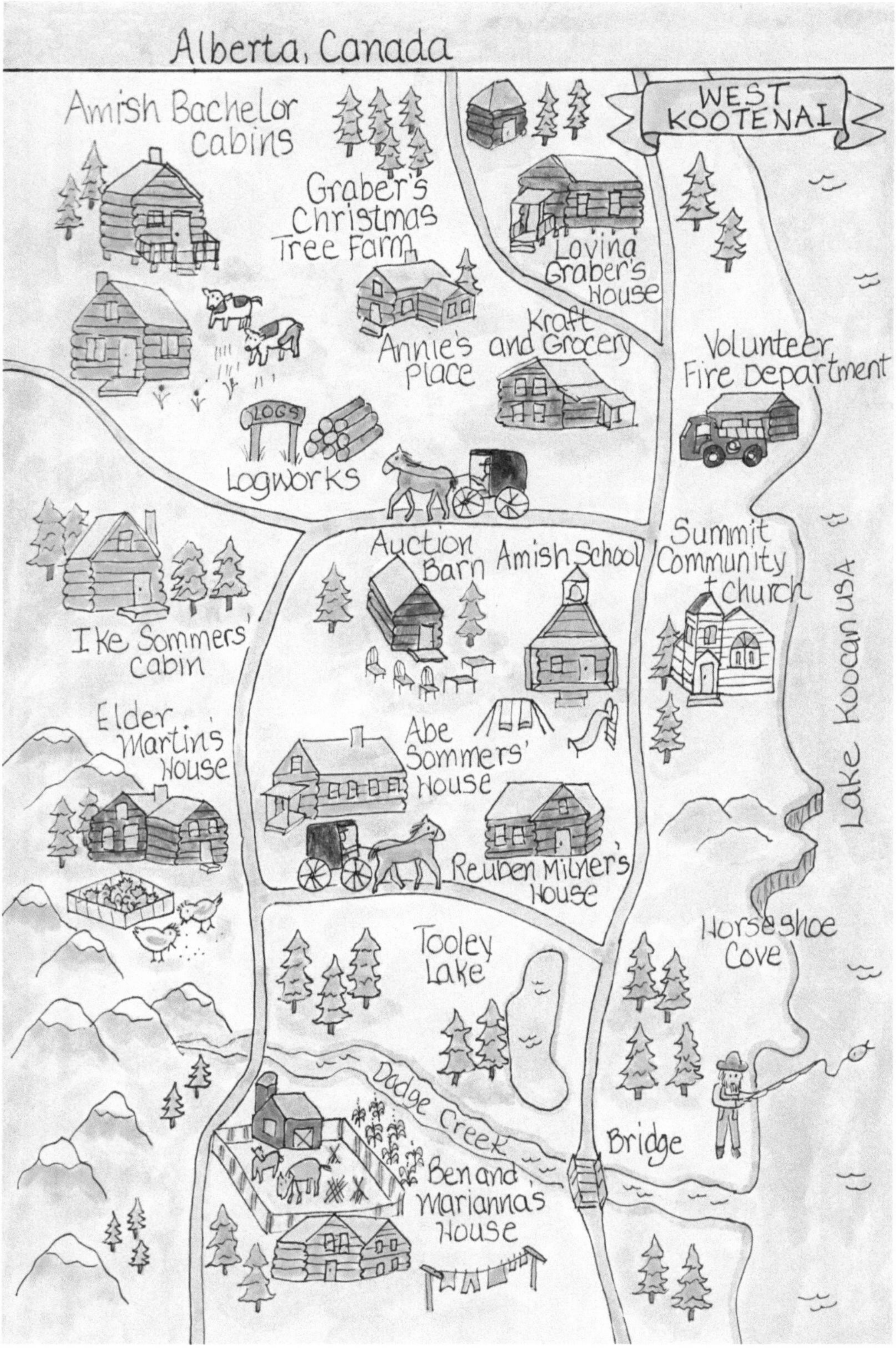

Alberta, Canada

WEST KOOTENAI

Amish Bachelor Cabins

Graber's Christmas Tree Farm

Lovina Graber's House

Annie's Place

Kraft and Grocery

Volunteer Fire Department

LOGS

Logworks

Ike Sommers' cabin

Auction Barn

Amish School

Summit Community Church

Lake Koocan USA

Elder Martin's House

Abe Sommers' House

Reuben Milner's House

Tooley Lake

Horseshoe Cove

Dodge Creek

Bridge

Ben and Marianna's House

Chapter One

Saturday, June 24, Kalispell, Montana

"How hard can it be to plan one wedding?" Marianna Sommer mumbled to herself as she strode down Main Street in Kalispell toward the dress shop—the *Englisch* dress shop. The warm spring breeze blew softly, ruffling strands of light-brown hair that, for most of her life, had been neatly secured under her *kapp*.

But no longer.

On one side of Marianna paced her friend Annie Johnson, wearing her typical jeans, flannel shirt, and cowboy boots. In her mid-forties, Annie was the owner of the Kootenai Kraft and Grocery. Along with providing a location where one could buy anything from bulk flour and garden seeds to fencing and fishing supplies, Annie was also known to provide a listening ear and a boost of moral support. And this was why she'd offered to take Marianna and her mother dress shopping today.

Marianna had never attended an Englisch wedding, much less planned one. Yet now that she was marrying Ben Stone—the handsome musician with his dark hair, bright blue eyes, and easy smile—many changes would be taking place.

Starting with choosing a wedding dress.

Mem padded on the other side of Marianna in a typical Amish dress, apron, and kapp. She walked with her head lowered and shoulders slumped. She crossed her arms over her chest and uncrossed them as if she didn't know what to do with herself. It was partly because Mem didn't have baby Joy on her hip. Yet Marianna also knew this wasn't how Mem had planned her life. First, losing her oldest two daughters years ago in a buggy accident, and now, having Marianna marry an Englischer. Every Amish mother dreamed of her daughters growing up and following in her footsteps. For Mem, this wouldn't be so.

Lord, help me to get through this with peace...marrying the man I love yet also honoring my family and Amish friends. Was that even possible?

"We've planned many weddings," Mem said, answering Marianna's musings. Mem quickened her pace just slightly to keep up with Marianna's steps. "At least we can plan the same food...that's something both the Amish and Englisch can agree on, *ja*? Who wouldn't want fried chicken, potatoes, and pie? Surely no one would disagree about that."

A chuckle spilled out of Annie's lips. "Has my vote." Annie sniffed the air as they neared the dress shop on the corner. "And do you smell that? There's a place just across the street that makes the best burgers... after we find the perfect wedding dress, of course."

A wedding dress...this is really happening.

Had it only been a few months ago when the sweet realization blew in with the hints of spring that Marianna was truly loved by her Creator God not because she was Amish, but because she was His child?

She'd opened her heart to so much more God had for her, including the gift of Ben Stone. She'd never dreamed of marrying an Englischer, much less an acclaimed music artist who was just as comfortable singing in front of tens of thousands of people as he was in the remote Montana community they both called home.

More tourists than locals filled the sidewalk today. They'd come to visit Glacier National Park, hike on local trails, and camp. Many also liked to stroll the idyllic downtown of Kalispell with its false-front wooden-and-brick buildings, reminiscent of the Old West, cowboys, and cattle drives.

Along the sidewalks of Main Street, families and couples walked by, snapping photos of the western brick storefronts, antique light posts, and large hanging flower baskets. The fragrant flowers filled the air with a sweet, floral aroma.

One young couple pointed to Mem as they walked past. Marianna remembered the looks, yet now she wasn't included in their inquisitive glances. Wearing a simple blouse, long skirt, and sandals, with her hair falling in soft brown waves over her shoulders, she no longer reflected her Amish roots.

Annie paused at the bridal shop. With a broad smile, she opened the door and ushered Marianna inside. Marianna turned to welcome her mother in. Mem paused her steps, frowned and glanced up and down the sidewalk as if checking to make sure no other Amish person spotted her, and then she tentatively followed inside. Seeing Mem's hesitation caused Marianna's heart to pinch, and all the uncertainties about the wedding swirled around in her mind again.

They entered the shop, and she immediately noticed the large chandelier that cast glimmering beams of light on the dress racks running down both walls and along the back. Beautiful gowns hung neatly, each covered with lace, pearls, and sequins. Romantic guitar music played on overhead speakers, reminding Marianna of the moving melody Ben had played the first time she'd heard him at the Kraft and Grocery. Soft and lilting, romantic and captivating.

The store smelled of lavender and vanilla from a candle burning, and while the mood was set for customers to enjoy the moment, heat rose to her cheeks as she imagined Ben playing more songs like this for her in their home as they started their life together. *I'm really doing this. I'm marrying Ben Stone.*

"Well, well, look who we have here!" A voice broke through Marianna's thoughts, and a woman with a crown of blonde curls hurried toward Marianna, taking both hands and offering a squeeze. "Marianna Sommer, right? I'm Julie, the owner of this shop." She looked to Annie and then to Mem. "And from what I hear, this will be an extraordinary wedding."

"Yes, that's correct," Marianna responded, her one phrase answering both questions.

Julie tilted her head and narrowed her gaze. "Beautiful brown hair, gray eyes. A classic beauty." She released Marianna's hands. "I have some dresses I think will fit perfectly. Let me grab some and set up a dressing room."

The woman moved toward a rack near the back of the store. Within a minute, Julie had returned with five or six dresses slung over her arm. Marianna's jaw dropped at the number of them and the shine of the fabric and pile of ruffles.

"Ai, yi, yi." Mem shook her head as she looked around. "Such a fancy shop with so many trappings of the world. I know you are Englisch now, but do you think you will find something here? I mean, just look at that one. No sleeves?" Mem pointed to another with a low-cut sweeping neckline. "Do they want to attract nursing babies to their wedding? Who would wear such a thing?"

"Mem, please." Heat again rose to Marianna's cheeks. "You're right. I'm Englisch now, but it's not as if I'd wear something like that."

"I'm sorry, Marianna. It's just that I did not realize these are the choices we have. Maybe there is another shop?"

Placing a hand to her neck and releasing the sigh she'd been holding in, Marianna glanced over at Annie. "I don't want to try on too many dresses. And nothing too fancy or revealing. But of course, you know that."

Annie placed a hand on Marianna's shoulder. "I mentioned that on the phone, but I'll tell Julie again just in case."

With hurried steps, Annie approached the shop owner. They talked for a moment, and then Annie motioned to a simple white satin dress on a dress form.

Julie frowned slightly, but then she nodded. "Let me just hang these dresses in the dressing room, and I'll get that one off the form."

Julie moved to the fitting rooms, and Marianna shook her head and took a step back. Then she glanced at her friend. "I don't know, Annie. I'm not sure I can do this."

Even though she was no longer wearing Amish clothes, she still felt Amish. Would she ever be able to face a day when she knew the right thing to do? How to act? How to be?

Marianna looked at Mem. Her lips were pressed tight, and her face was pale. Mem moved to sit in a plush chair. Seeing the way Mem clenched her hands on her lap caused anxiety to tighten Marianna's chest. Marianna took another step away from the dressing room, unsure if she could try on those dresses.

Annie rushed to her side. "It's all right. You don't have to try on any dresses you don't want to, but I think you should at least try one on," Annie's voice cooed, more maternal than Marianna had ever heard it. "Just see what it looks like. Check to be sure you don't want to wear an Amish dress after all."

"I don't." The words spouted from Marianna's mouth, yet she spoke with more conviction than she felt.

Annie pulled her into a side hug and gently led her to the dressing room area. "I know it's hard now, but just think about what this is all about. You're marrying Ben. You're going to be his bride. God has brought you together. A few changes are to be expected."

A few changes?

Taking a deep breath, Marianna motioned for Mem to follow, and then she took tentative steps forward. Even as she followed Annie to the dressing room, Marianna wondered if she'd ever get used to the changes. As far as she was concerned, her marriage would distance her even more from the Amish world she knew as she started a new life with Ben. As long as she wasn't asked to go on the road with him or get too involved with his music or fans, things would work out fine.

Reaching the dressing room, Marianna realized that Mem hadn't followed.

"Mem, are you coming?" Marianna looked back over her shoulder.

Her mother still sat in the chair and forced a timid

smile. "Go ahead. See if there is anything you like yet. If so, then come and show me."

"Of course." Marianna returned to the dressing room and her breath caught. Her shoulders tensed and the skin on the back of her neck prickled. *It's just a dress,* she told herself. *And just a marriage to an Englischer to follow.*

~

SATURDAY, JUNE 24, SOUTH BEND, INDIANA

BEN STONE TRIED NOT TO SQUINT AT THE lights as he looked at the lunch crowd across the small auditorium, which wasn't too far from where he'd visited Marianna in Shipshewana where she'd grown up. He strummed his guitar, thankful it was a small venue today. One more show to mark off the list. He'd be on to the next thing on his agenda after just a few more songs to play.

Dozens of phones were fixed on him, recording his performance. His heart ached as he sang, thinking of his bride-to-be, Marianna.

You're nothing alone. You're everything together.
Aches all fade when someone helps you weather
the hard times,
Come fill my heart, come fill my life—
Every warm cabin
Needs a good wife.

My granddaddy told me, 'If you wanna be whole,
Son, find a good woman who fills up your soul.
Whose smile brings sunshine, whose laughter rings true—
'Cuz son, life ain't nothin' 'til you do.'

Then came the day I looked into your eyes,
I knew Granddad's words were heartfelt and wise.
Your smile, your laughter proved my granddad knew
A thing or two about life.

Ben closed his eyes as he strummed and pictured Marianna. Soon he'd be home. Soon she'd be his bride, and they wouldn't have to worry about living two separate lives anymore. His heart swelled with longing, thinking of her maybe even coming on the road with him. It would be mighty fine to look out in the audience and see Marianna's face. Her smile.

Once the set was finished, the applause rose, and Ben gave one last quick wave before he stepped off the stage. His manager, Roy Knight, waited with a broad smile, along with a man Ben didn't recognize. Yet from the man's perfectly tailored designer suit, shined dress shoes, and air of confidence, Ben knew this wasn't a typical groupie who waited in hopes of getting a selfie, handshake, and autograph.

"Ben, I'd like you to meet Mitch Chapman. Mitch

is that tour promoter I was telling you about. He flew in today to hear you sing—"

"And you didn't disappoint." Mitch stretched out his hand.

Ben quickly shook it, forcing his brightest smile as a truckload of boulders settled on his chest. He hadn't mentioned the possible tour to Marianna yet, thinking it best to bring it up when he was back home. "Glad you enjoyed the show, Mr. Chapman—"

The man's handshake was firm and confident. "Please call me Mitch."

"I'm glad you enjoyed the show, Mitch. But I thought we already had a meeting set up in a few months." *After the wedding.* And after he'd had a chance to break the news to Marianna about going on the road next year.

Mitch's eyebrows arched, and he shrugged. "You know what they say. 'Nothing is more expensive than a wasted opportunity.'"

Ben laughed. "Yes, I've also heard the phrase 'Happy wife, happy life.' You know I'm getting married in three months, right?" He narrowed his gaze at Roy, even though his words were directed at Mitch. "Marianna isn't one I picture wanting to be on the road with me full-time." Ben rubbed his brow and laughed. "She'd hate the fame, the attention...and I want our first year of marriage to be special."

"Of course, who wouldn't want that?" Mitch reached forward and squeezed Ben's shoulder. "And you don't have to worry. It's all been explained to me.

The best songs are written by those in love or those facing heartbreak. Let's go for the man in love, don't you think? I'm looking at no more than twenty locations. I'm sure your new wife won't have a problem with that. She does know she's marrying a rock star after all, right?"

Chapter Two

SATURDAY, JUNE 24, KALISPELL, MONTANA

"I don't know, Annie. I'm not sure I can do this." Marianna's stomach twisted in knots as she stepped into the dress, letting its silky, cool fabric slide over her frame. For someone who'd been told all her life that God forsakes the proud, putting on this fancy dress went against everything she'd known to be true.

"Can't do what? All you're doing is trying on a dress, right? It's not like you're roping a calf." Annie chuckled and winked. "Now, that I'd like to see."

Once the dress was on and she glanced in the mirror, Marianna sucked in a breath. She'd never considered herself an exquisite beauty—it would be wrong to do so—but tears filled her eyes as she eyed her reflection.

The creamy, smooth fabric fit her perfectly. The high collar and long sleeves were exactly what Marianna wanted. And even though Ben had said he'd marry her if she wore a gunny sack, she imagined the sparkle in Ben's eyes when he saw her wearing this dress.

It wasn't too tight or loose, but it highlighted her thin waist and reminded her of an elegant swan. The style was simple and timeless. She felt beautiful, truly beautiful, for the first time in her life.

Could she walk down a church aisle in front of family and friends in such a manner? More than that, could she be the wife Ben deserved? Could she step into his world without altogether rejecting the old? And should she?

As Marianna tilted her head and contemplated the dress, every rule against such things filled her mind. Satin...and so form fitting. Indeed, this was just too much.

"If you lift your hair, I can do up the buttons." Annie pushed her long, blonde ponytail over her shoulder. Her words were slow, hesitant, as if she expected Marianna to jump out of the dress and back into her plain blouse and skirt any moment.

Taking a deep breath, Marianna reached her hands behind her, took hold of her locks, and twisted them upward into a bun as she'd done a thousand times. She held it there, allowing Annie access to the buttons. Before last year she'd only worn her hair up under a kapp, but then she'd met Ben. She'd not only fallen in love with him, but Marianna had also fallen more in love with God, who loved her if she didn't follow the Amish ways—something her heart still struggled to believe at times.

Annie let out a low whistle as she worked on the pearl buttons. "Thirty buttons, would you believe that?"

Marianna gazed at Annie's reflection in the mirror—her deep green eyes and heart-shaped face—taking confidence in her friend's smile as Annie peered over her shoulder. Was it only a year ago when Marianna had arrived in West Kootenai, Montana, and found herself wrapped up in Annie's warm hug?

On that first day in their new community, Annie had welcomed Marianna's family into her store, feeding them a hot meal of a breakfast casserole and homemade cinnamon rolls. Sitting down that day with Annie and Ben, their driver, had been the first time Marianna had eaten a meal with Englischers. And no matter how much she'd tried to keep Ben and Annie at arm's length, they had pursued a friendship with her. A soft smile curled on Marianna's lips. No, Ben had done more. He had pursued her heart.

Annie took a step back, and her ponytail swung with her movements. Marianna released her own hair, letting it cascade over her shoulders.

Eyeing Marianna in the mirror, Annie let out a low whistle and planted her hands on her hips. "My, you look lovely. What do you think? Do you want to step out and show your mem?"

Marianna's gut tightened into a knot, and she instinctively placed a hand on it. The satin felt soft under her fingertips. "I don't know, Annie. My mother's waited a long time to have a daughter marry, and this isn't the wedding she's waited for, to be certain."

With a gentle sweep of her hands, Annie pulled Marianna's hair back behind her shoulders. "Listen, Mari. I know your mem—your parents—still grieve your two sisters who were lost, but that doesn't mean they feel any less joy in your marriage to Ben. Even though he was the last person your dat wanted you to be with at first, Ben has won them over. His love for God and you—well, what parent wouldn't want that for their daughter?"

Marianna wasn't sure about Annie's statement, but she didn't want to argue. Mem and Dat had seemed to approve of Ben when they'd first returned to Montana from Indiana. Yet as the months passed, both seemed to pull back. Maybe because the reality of an Englischer becoming their son-in-law had become real? Would Marianna adding Englisch traditions into her wedding along with the Amish ones cause them to resist even more?

"I'm still not sure..." There was so much she wasn't sure about. She knew she loved Ben and that she loved God too. And that she did not need to conform to Amish traditions anymore. Still, every rule she'd been taught battled for a place in her mind.

Lord, I just want to do what's right. I love Ben, but I need to know...am I doing the right thing?

Her fears went deeper than the wedding. She worried about the marriage too. *How can our two lives merge into one? And what will he expect of me?*

If she didn't have to get too involved in his music, then all would be well. She would focus on living her life with the Ben she knew in Montana. Then she'd just do her best to cope when he was away performing on the road.

Annie's brows folded and her lips pressed into a thin line. "Don't you think it's beautiful? Or we can try another one if you like. I'm sure there are more plain dresses."

Marianna fingered the satin where it tucked around her waist, curving to her frame. She'd never worn something that showed off her body in such a way. Was it wrong that she *did* like it?

"Yes, it's lovely, but a satin dress? And so form fitting?" Marianna smoothed it down over her hips next, seeing how it fell perfectly to the floor in her reflection. "I think we have different ideas of plain. It's so fancy. This shiny fabric, I just don't know. I'd always imagined myself in a pretty periwinkle blue dress, coming to my groom with hordes of servers surrounding me. And I haven't even looked at the price tag. I'm afraid to."

"It's simple and elegant, beautiful. And the price isn't much compared to most others in the shop." Annie lightly placed a hand on Marianna's shoulder. "Besides, Ben already called ahead and told Julie he'd pay for any dress you choose. You should have seen her smile when she told me. It's an honor for her, too, you know. I bet the fact that Ben Stone's bride chose a dress from her shop will bring in new business."

Ben Stone's bride. The words replayed in Marianna's mind. And even though she'd tried not to pay attention to such things, she knew the tabloids had already reported on the September wedding, just three months away. How many hearts would be broken to discover their favorite musician would be married, and to an Amish woman, no less?

I'm not Amish anymore. Yes, it's hard to realize that.

To her, it wasn't his fame or even his music that she had fallen in love with. It was his heart. His kindness and faithfulness. After many hard years seeking fame and fortune and coming up with an empty soul, Ben had found God. Now he clung to Him with everything he had. That's what made Ben the man she loved. The man she wanted to spend her life with.

Goosebumps danced on her arms as she remembered that day over a year ago when she'd picked up his guitar and he'd wrapped his arms around her to show her some chords. Now Ben had chosen her. She could look forward to being wrapped up in those arms for the rest of her days.

Marianna's head dipped slightly. She touched a soft hand to her breastbone and turned to face Annie. "Yes, I'd like to show Mem. It might be hard, but I think she'll like this dress. It's so simple compared to the others in the shop. So beautiful too."

Annie nodded and took Marianna's hand, leading

her like a mother would lead a child out of the dressing room area.

Mem looked out of place sitting on the tufted high-back pink chair. Her hands were folded on her lap, and she seemed unsure of herself, especially since seven-month-old Joy was being babysat by Eve Peachy for the day. Without a baby to distract her, Mem fidgeted and glanced around. And even though Mem often read the Englisch Bible with Dat and was growing in her relationship with God, she lived as an Amishwoman, still wearing her plain dresses and kapp. Dat, too, still wore his Amish clothes, with long-sleeve shirts buttoned to the top, long beard, and flat rimmed hat. While their hearts were changing, it hadn't impacted their Amish lifestyle or their simple ways.

Mem's eyes fixed on Marianna as she stood before her. "Why, Mari, you have so much beauty but look different too." Mem touched her cheek. "It doesn't look like you."

"I know I look different. But do you like it?" As simple as the dress was, Marianna's stomach knotted thinking of the buttons on the back. She'd face Mem's reaction to that when she turned. But first, she had to know...did Mem approve even the slightest?

"What do you think?"

A smile started to curl up Mem's lips, and then her chin lifted, and she set her jaw firmly. "What do I think?" Mem opened her fisted hands and grasped the arms of the chair as if wishing to push herself up and stalk out. "What do I think?" She breathed out, and her voice was much softer. "As a child, I was always drawn to fancy—" Mem paused. "To lovely things. It is a lovely dress. I can say that much."

Marianna's heart longed for Mem's approval. It was a familiar feeling from her childhood. Even then, she knew her mother could never actually approve. The fact that Mem had even come to this dress shop to watch her daughter try on Englisch dresses would be considered worthy of church discipline by some. Marianna could imagine their words. *You approve of your daughter dressing like an Englischer? Marrying outside the Amish? Leaving our ways for a musician, of all things?*

And then, "Surely Marilyn and Joanna would have married godly Amish men, God rest their souls..."

The familiar thudding pounded Marianna's heart like a woodpecker striking diseased wood, watching pieces flake off with each blow. But instead of crumbling under the belief that she had to take her sisters' places, Marianna squared her shoulders. She *was* marrying a godly man.

"It is lovely, isn't it?" Marianna turned to the mirror in the sitting area near Mem, forcing herself to look at her reflection with eyes of love and not of duty. "I do believe you are right, Annie." Marianna heard the softest gasp as Mem, no doubt, saw the buttons, but she urged herself not to be bothered by it. She turned back around and looked at her friend. "I believe this is the perfect dress for me." Its beauty reminded her of all God's wonderful transformations in her life—and all He'd continue to do.

Hearing Marianna's words, Julie rushed to her side. "I am so glad you love it. This gown is truly stunning on you. Should we also try on shoes and a veil?"

Marianna looked at Annie. Her mouth slacked. She'd already made this one decision. How could she ever make more?

With a dismissing wave of her hand, Annie stepped forward. "I know you have some lovely things to show us, but let's save that for another day, shall we?" She placed a hand on the shop owner's shoulder. "Why don't you measure her for alterations, and we'll consider those other things when we return to pick up the dress. Don't you think that's a good idea, Marianna?"

Marianna nodded, and when Julie left to get her notepad and measuring tape, Marianna reached for Annie's hand and gave it a squeeze. "Thank you. You always seem to know..."

Annie chuckled. "It's not as if I'm a mind reader. What you think is pretty plain on your face most of the time. While I think you've made the right decision about the dress, I don't want to push things. There is plenty of time to plan this wedding, plenty of time. Let's not get so caught up in the small details that you miss out on the joy of being engaged to the one and only Ben Stone."

Chapter Three

Saturday, June 24, South Bend, Indiana

"So here he is in the flesh, the one and only Ben Stone." The podcast host flashed a broad smile and reached her hand across the table in his direction. Behind the woman, high windows provided a stunning view of the city skyline.

Ben set his guitar on the guitar stand next to the guest's chair and reached for her hand. One more interview to check off. One day closer to home. *I can do this. Put on the charm and remember what you're doing this for. Who you're doing this for...sweet Marianna.*

A scent of soft floral and citrus filled the room. Fading sunlight tinted the woman's blonde hair with streaks of gold.

"I'm Stacy. Glad you could come in today." Her broad, white smile welcomed Ben, and her hand felt soft to his touch—not like the rough hands of those who knew a hard day's work. She was just the type of woman he used to be drawn to, model-perfect and confident. But not anymore. Not since meeting Marianna.

Ben ignored the woman's plunging neckline on her silk blouse and gave her a firm handshake. "Thanks for having me. It's great to be in Indiana." He'd been all over the country the past few weeks, yet Indiana brought back memories of his time here with Marianna. Roy had set up his media tour to promote his newest song release, "My Favorite Hello." Ben would have declined if he didn't need to finish the expansion of his cabin in preparation for a wife. A few weeks of promotion and small concert venues would provide just enough money to finish the new addition.

Ben's smile broadened but not because the woman's hand clung to his a little longer than necessary. He smiled knowing he only had to do a few more of these gigs before he could get back to Montana. More importantly, get back to the woman he loved.

Ben adjusted his jacket and sat in the studio chair before the microphone. Traffic had caused him to run late, and he hadn't had time to look up information about the host or the program, which he usually did. It helped to prepare for where the conversation might go. However, lately, all the hosts had been most interested in his engagement—even more than his new song climbing the charts.

He put on his headset as the intro music was already playing, and he leaned toward the mic. Stacy slid on her headset, smoothed her long hair, and held up ten fingers. He nodded. They'd be live in ten seconds. The time ticked off, and Stacy leaned into her mic.

"Welcome, friends, to *The Stacy Cannon Show*, where I give you the down-low on all the latest entertainment news by digging deep with your favorite artists. Today I have one of my favorite artists here in my studio." Stacy's eyes fixed on his. "Ben Stone is a name that has become popular on the airwaves over the last two years. I was privileged to know Ben even before one of his popular songs hit the radio." Stacy laughed. "And by the worried expression that just crossed his face, I guess Ben has no idea what I'm talking about."

Ben's heart pounded a triple beat. Immediately his mind raced, trying to place her face, her name. He didn't remember her from school or the music world. A tense knot grew in his stomach, and he bit his lower lip. He closed his eyes briefly and sent up a quick prayer that she wasn't one of the groupies he'd only known for a night. He regretted so many things touring with his band in those early years. All the women in all the cities was one of them.

"I would say it's great to meet you, Stacy, but I suppose we've met before." He tried to keep his tone light. "I will say it's great to be here. It's a beautiful afternoon in South Bend."

"Oh, you're wiggling in your seat, Ben, and I'm trying to decide. Should I give you a hint or let you squirm for the next thirty minutes?" Stacy hit a button on the computer in front of her, and a laugh track played.

Ben searched for a way to turn this conversation. An idea came to mind. He snapped his fingers. "I've got it. Did you ever go to Richardson Springs Summer Camp? I think it was the fourth grade when I had a crush on a girl named Stacy, and I let her have my Push Pop."

Genuine laughter spilled from Stacy's lips, and her face softened. "I like that, but I'm not that Stacy. I'll give you a hint. We went sledding, and you dated my best friend for a while."

Like a movie flashing onto a pull-down screen, a memory of his first time in Montana filled his mind. Roy had invited him up to produce some new music. That's when he met Roy's daughter Carrie, and their romance took off fast, but then—just months later, when Ben hit the road—their relationship burned out just as quickly. And yes, he remembered now. A much younger Stacy had been staying with Carrie that December.

A smile filled Ben's face. It was almost as if the mic had disappeared. "Oh, I remember. It was our first time in Montana, and as California kids, we almost froze."

"We did freeze." Stacy chuckled and brushed a curl of hair from her cheek. "And then I fell in that tree well." She shook her head. "I had no idea the warmth of the trees melted the snow around them, making perfect holes for people to fall into."

"Which was the inspiration for one of my first songs, 'Falling for You.'"

Stacy's fingers hovered over her computer. "I was hoping you would say that." She clicked a button on her keyboard, and Ben's voice came through his headphones. He smiled as he listened to his younger self crooning about true love, something he'd had no fathom of at the time.

They continued chatting, talking about Ben's older music compared to his newest songs. Ben relaxed in his chair and enjoyed the conversation until the tilt of Stacy's head and a twinkle in her eye told him that she'd succeeded in getting his guard down. "Well, I know we can be expecting some new music from you now that I hear wedding bells are coming soon. Finding the girl of your dreams has already produced some great songs."

"Yes, that's true. A beautiful woman and a wedding. And I couldn't be more grateful."

"Well, congratulations. And since I helped to inspire one of your first recordings, I came up with some ideas for future hits." Stacy slipped an index card from under her keyboard and held it up to read. "How about these. 'He Thinks Her Bonnet's Sexy.' '50 Shades of Hay.' 'Let's Make Whoopie Pies.' Do you think any of those will work?"

Silence followed, and Ben wished he had a laugh track button to hit to break the awkwardness. Heat rose up his neck. It took everything within him to remain in the chair. "I have to say you're very creative."

"I think all our listeners out there probably get the references, but for those who don't, do you want to share why the titles include bonnets, whoopie pies, and hay?"

"I don't mind sharing that I've fallen in love with the most wonderful woman. And yes, she formerly was part of an Amish community." Ben gripped his hands on the arms of the chair, preparing for the following snarky remark.

Instead, Stacy relaxed in her seat. "I imagine you couldn't find a more perfect woman." Her voice softened. "Honestly, sometimes I wish I could leave this busy world, you know, and live a similar life. Montana is beautiful, and at a slower pace...well, isn't it what we all dream of?"

"It is beautiful, and I'm looking forward to getting back."

"Then I won't keep you, but for our listeners, let's take this show out with your last hit, 'Every Warm Cabin Needs a Good Wife'...which is exactly what our friend Ben Stone will soon have. Check out Ben's music wherever music can be downloaded or sold. Until next time, I'm Stacy Cannon."

Ben nodded and picked up his guitar. This was the easy part. No matter how bothered he was by the interviews, everything turned right again with the guitar in his hands. His fingers moved on the strings, and he took a breath and leaned in.

Entered my cabin, all warm from the fire,
Muscles were achin', worn out 'n' tired
From hard work like Granddaddy did—
Ever' day of his life.

Got my cabin deep in the woods
But need somethin' more to call it all good
To fill the aching hole in my life—
'Cuz every warm cabin
Needs a good wife.

Across the table, Stacy smiled as he sang. When he was done, Ben returned the guitar to the stand. He felt weary from the interview, as if he'd just been in an air boxing match, dodging and ducking with all his might.

He removed his headset, thinking of Montana, of getting home, of being with Marianna in a place where their relationship wasn't a media spectacle. And then maybe taking her on the road with him. A sweet peace settled over him at the thought of doing these types of interviews with Marianna sitting in the corner, watching him with a soft smile.

Stacy pushed back the mic and slipped off her headset, setting it on the polished table.

He expected Stacy to look pleased by the way she'd made him squirm in his seat. Instead, she sauntered to his side of the table and cast a sheepish smile. "Hey, I hope that was okay. My producer came up with those song titles. I thought they were creative."

Ben stood and shrugged, gathering up his guitar.

"They were. I'll give you that. Better than questions about me turning in my truck for a buggy or asking if I'm going to grow a beard, which Amish men do after they get married."

She crossed her arms over her chest and nodded. "And really, what you want to talk about is your music. I get it." She opened the door to the studio and led him into the adjoining room.

Ben placed his guitar back into its case. "I understand, but it makes me more ready to get home where we can live in peace. Where there are no media to bother us."

Stacy's jaw dropped, and she shook her head. "Oh, I'm sorry to say I don't think that will happen. Even Montana isn't far enough away."

He snapped the clasp on the case shut and straightened up. "What do you mean?"

"Have you talked to Carrie lately?" The look in Stacy's eyes told him she still did—and that he wouldn't like what she had to say.

"No, why?"

"She's in broadcasting now, working as a reporter out of a news station in Missoula, Montana. I'm surprised Roy didn't tell you."

"Roy and I don't talk about his daughter. You know, after I broke her heart. We keep business about business."

"I hate to be the bearer of bad news, but the word's leaked about your wedding date in September. Paparazzi are already booking spots up that way.

Someone told Carrie he tried to rent a helicopter to do a flyover, and three different companies have already been booked for that weekend."

Ben felt his knees weakening. He settled back into his chair as dread hit his chest like a rockslide. "Why in the world would they do that?"

"Have you looked at all the online sites? The news that gets the most hits stays in the prominent spot. Someone got a photo of an Amish woman up in those parts—you can't even see her face—and it's getting a lot of attention. I mean, think about it. One of their favorite artists is marrying an Amish woman. What's that wedding going to be like? Is there going to be a rock band and buggy rides? Will she wear a white dress and one of those Amish bonnets?"

Ben rested his guitar case on the floor and then lowered his head into his hands. Ever since he and Marianna had returned from Indiana and started their relationship, they had worked to create their own path. Marianna did her best to still respect her family and their heritage while also seeking God for this new and different lifestyle. He, too, had worked to not overwhelm her with all the elements of his career. The internet was as new and foreign to Marianna as it would be to anyone from the earth being asked to colonize Mars. Marianna understood his calling to perform—and even appreciated his music. Would she even consider a life filled with tabloids, entertainment news, or social media when her life was so far removed from that?

Stacy stepped forward and placed a hand on his shoulder. "Are you all right?"

Ben brushed it away. "All right? It's about the same as if you'd just told me that aliens are invading and targeting the people I love and my community, because that's basically what this is."

Stacy raised her hands as if in surrender. "Hey, hey, now. Don't shoot the messenger. Forget I said anything. Maybe I shouldn't have told you, but at least now you can be prepared." Sadness tinged her voice. "And thanks again for the interview." She moved to the door, ushering him out.

Ben stood again, brushing his hair off his forehead. "Listen. I'm sorry. I didn't mean to take it out on you." He grabbed his guitar case and moved to the door. "And actually, I should thank you. The last thing Marianna would want is a media spectacle. At least now we can figure out another day or a new plan."

Stacy opened the door, and he walked through. "She's a lucky girl, you know. I may have tried to joke around, but it's clear that you love her. Even now, as you said her name...well, I wish someone would say my name like that."

He nodded, not sure what to say. Then he cleared his throat. "Yes, I hope you find that. I really do. And thanks again for the interview. And those song titles were pretty funny. I can't wait to share them with friends back home. They'll get a kick out of them."

Back home. Just a few more days and he'd be back home.

Chapter Four

SATURDAY, JUNE 24, WEST KOOTENAI, MONTANA

Marianna's body bounced with the motion of the truck driving over the potholes as Annie pulled into the Sommers' driveway. Through the passenger window, she saw the front door of the log home swinging open even before the truck had come to a complete stop. Three rambunctious boys rushed out as if they'd been waiting at the window. Boys who were looking more like men all the time.

The drive home had been filled with mostly small talk. Marianna's heart ached, longing for the easy conversation she usually had with Mem. More than anything, Marianna wanted a chance to slip away and go to the beaver pond. She could help Mem put away the groceries and then head out.

She needed time to pray and to think. Maybe she could even start a list of things that mattered most concerning their wedding. Then she and Ben could talk over those things and decide together.

Only a few more days, and he'll be home. She needed his steadfastness. Her heart always seemed more settled with Ben near.

"Boys, help with the groceries," Mem called as they circled around Annie's truck, eyeing the food boxes with excitement to see what had been purchased. While down in Kalispell, Mem had taken advantage of bulk shopping. However, Marianna knew with the way the active boys had been eating, the food would go quicker than Mem thought.

"All of it?" Josiah asked, mouth agape.

"*Ja*. We already dropped off Annie's things at the store, so the rest of what's back there is ours."

Sunshine warmed the top of Marianna's head, and the shimmering leaves of the aspen trees welcomed her as if waving a greeting. The promise to herself of time alone at the pond put a new hop to her step as she moved to the back of the truck to help with the groceries. Marianna grabbed a gallon of milk and a large bag of rice. The quicker they could unload, the sooner she could head to the pond.

"I can carry more than you!" Charlie called out.

"No way!" Josiah shouted, grabbing a large package of paper towels.

David chuckled. “Oh, ja, you are strong, aren’t you, Joe?”

When Marianna had left to go to Indiana earlier in the spring, her brothers had all been shorter than her, but recently they’d stretched out. Thirteen-year-old David was taller than her, and nine-year-old Charlie was getting close to her height.

Five-year-old Josiah lugged a bag of rice to the house. In the doorway, four-year-old Ellie, with blonde hair and hazel eyes, waited with a barking Trapper at her side. The dog faithfully ran after Ellie until he saw that Marianna was home. Then his speed picked up, and he jumped as he raced to her, scattering pine needles.

The dog couldn’t hold back his excitement as he bounded before Marianna and danced at her feet. She laughed at his antics, wishing she had a free hand to pat his head. “Good boy, Trapper, good boy.”

Trapper leaped and spun until he heard Ellie’s call and noticed the stick in her hand. Ellie giggled as she circled the aspen, waving the stick, with Trapper closely following.

Marianna took a deep breath of air that smelled like pine, dust, and meadow grass from the field across the street, and she considered the home she’d soon be sharing with Ben. She liked the idea of settling in Montana and filling their home with children just as Mem and Dat had done. *But first comes the wedding. Once we get through that, our life can begin.*

As Marianna approached the front door, Dat

emerged with seven-month-old Joy sitting on his shoulder. Joy giggled as she reached a tiny hand in Mem's direction as they exited.

Putting down the paper towels inside the door, Josiah took the milk and rice from Marianna's hands, so she made her way back to the truck.

Mem was still talking to Annie, who stood by the truck. "And wouldn't you like to come in? I prepared sandwich fixings in the refrigerator to make things easy for tonight's dinner."

"That's mighty kind of you, but Ike invited Edgar and me over for some elk burgers he was grilling up."

Marianna clapped her hands together. "Edgar's back in town? The store hasn't been the same without him." She thought of the older man, a regular fixture in Annie's store. While most people retired at Edgar Miller's age, he always said working at the store kept him young and gave him a new purpose after losing his wife years ago.

"Yup, I told him I'm gonna put a time limit on it the next time he visits his sister. He'll be back at work Monday morning." Annie sniffed the air. "And I'm so hungry I can almost smell those burgers from here, but thank you again for the invitation."

Marianna turned and offered Annie a quick hug. "Thank you for taking me to the bridal shop." A smile tipped her lips. "It really feels real now, knowing I have a gown." She chuckled. "Nothing else done, but at least I know what I'm wearing."

"It'll all work out. Everyone around these parts will

wanna help. You know how much we love you and Ben. Let's talk tomorrow, all right? I have more ideas for you. I thought we could have the wedding in the beautiful field behind the Kraft and Grocery, where the Amish Auction is held every year. Can you imagine how lovely that would be with the mountains in the background?"

"Ja, of course, that's one idea." Marianna stepped back and waved as Annie climbed into the truck, but an unsettled feeling came over her. *Would* there be a lot of help? Even though the Amish communities in Rexford and West Kootenai were more relaxed than many, most families still stuck to the Ordnung. They no doubt would stop associating with Marianna's parents for such a "worldly" wedding for their daughter. Maybe they wouldn't need much space for the wedding—at least not the large, beautiful field that Annie spoke of.

Marianna wondered what else would change. Could she still serve date pudding? Would the table with handmade server gifts be replaced with fancy flower centerpieces? One thing she would insist on was a traditional Amish sit-down dinner rather than a catered meal. Then again, would there be enough women to help with that? All her friends, aunts, and cousins had always had the same daydreams as she had. She'd never dreamed about a white dress, yet here she was.

For all of her life, she had worked to obey the Ordnung above all. When had things changed? When her friendships had grown with people like Annie and Ben, who loved God with all their hearts yet didn't follow the Amish rules. When she began reading the Bible herself and saw that the laws she'd learned from childhood and lived by were nowhere to be found within God's Word. She'd started thinking of the words to the hymns she'd sung in German and understood what they meant. And now she was wearing a satin gown at her wedding, no less.

Marianna grabbed the last bag of groceries and followed the others into the house. Nineteen-year-old Eve Peachy sat just inside the front door, peeling potatoes at the kitchen table. Eve's red hair was perfectly combed and tucked under her kapp. She smiled as Mem entered, and then her smile faded when she noticed Marianna.

"Hello, Eve." Marianna consciously touched her hair where she usually wore her kapp. Her hair was down, falling over her shoulders.

Eve blinked twice and eyed the potato in her hand as if it were the most exciting thing in the world. Then she turned to Marianna's mem. "I hope you had a *gut* day. Joy is such a happy *boppli*. She did fine, but was happy to see her dat when he just got home not thirty minutes ago."

If Mem noticed that Eve didn't respond to Marianna's greeting, she said nothing. "Thank you for watching the baby. It made our shopping easier. But you needn't worry about dinner. I had sandwich things prepared in the fridge."

"Ja, *vell*, my mother doesn't believe sandwiches are gut enough for dinner. I have a chicken roasting, and I can finish peeling these potatoes. The water's already prepared to boil them."

Marianna moved to the sink and washed her hands, then held a clean hand to Eve. "I can do that."

Instead of placing the potato into her hand, Eve set it on the cutting board that sat on the table. Then she stood. "I also made some vanilla pudding. Ellie helped me. It's in the fridge." She moved around Marianna as if she wasn't even there. "But since you're here, I might as well get home and help Mem. She is giving Deborah Shelter a break and has Kenzie tonight as Jenny works at the Kraft and Grocery. That girl is all energy. She gets Evelyn Shelter into more situations." Eve chuckled. "Just a few days ago, they wasted a dozen eggs seeing if they could get one over the Shelters' barn."

"Oh, tell me they didn't." Mem's chuckle was forced. She removed some bills from her purse and pressed them into Eve's hand. "I'm sure your mother will appreciate your help, and thank you for dinner. I'm much obliged."

It wasn't until Eve had left that Marianna realized the boys sat on the stairs and had watched the whole interaction. Even Ellie sat with them quietly. Marianna settled into the kitchen chair in front of the potatoes, acting as if none of it bothered her despite the boulder that grew in the pit of her stomach.

All thoughts of going to the pond were gone. She needed to stay here. Had to help get dinner on the table. She felt two inches tall, and thoughts of going to the pond to write down plans for her Englisch wedding now brought a sour taste to her mouth. *If Eve treats me as such, is this what I have to look forward to from the whole community?*

"Did you see that, Mari?" Josiah pulled his hat from his head and rested it on his knee. "Every time you said something to Eve, she acted like she didn't even hear you."

Marianna picked up Eve's discarded potato and continued with the peeling. "Ja, I saw."

"Is it because you're not wearing a kapp?" Charlie asked.

"And because she's marrying Ben," David informed his brother.

Charlie jutted out his chin. "But Levi married Naomi, and people didn't act like that."

David poked his elbow into Charlie's ribs. "That's because Ben's not Amish, and Naomi is."

Charlie rubbed his forehead as if still not understanding. "But Naomi had a boppli before they were married. And I know marriage is supposed to come first. Everyone knows."

"Ja, but Levi and Naomi joined the church and married then." Frustration rose in David's voice as if he did not understand how his younger brother could be so dense. "Having a boppli doesn't matter as long as Naomi stayed Amish, married Amish."

"Boys..." Mem's voice was pinched.

Marianna looked at Mem's pale face. An ache filled

Marianna as she thought again of how her marriage to Ben impacted her family. No parent should have to deal with so much—to have all their Amish friends and neighbors again talking about them, judging them, just as they had when Marianna's brother Levi had first left the Amish.

This time, their talk centered around her.

Her brothers knew the conversation was over with that one word from Mem. Without much comment, they shuffled outside to do the afternoon chores with Ellie in tow.

Mem placed Joy in her high chair and handed her a teething cookie. Then Mem crossed her arms over her chest and looked to Dat, who was stacking canned foods in their pantry. "My guess is that news of Marianna without a kapp, scarf, or anything over her hair will be all over the community by noon tomorrow and as far away as Pennsylvania by Sunday next."

"And what does it matter?" her father said, lining up the cans of tuna next to the jars of pickles they'd canned last fall. "By next week, they'll have another person to talk about."

"What does it matter? We came to Montana because of Levi leaving. And then we stayed here among the liberal Amish with your brother Ike." She sighed. "I always thought it would be Ike who'd be first to marry an Englischer. But now Marianna's marriage... They'll have us driving cars and stringing electric wires in our home by Christmas."

Marianna paused her peeling, wishing she could sink into the wooden floorboards.

"And who says we won't be?" Dat straightened his shoulders. "We need to decide, Ruth. Now that we're reading God's Word and discovering our salvation is not based on Amish ways, why do we still live as such? Marianna's the only one brave enough to decide that what matters more is one's heart rather than one's dress."

Mem settled into the chair next to Marianna and placed her hand on her forehead. "But it's not as if everything can change overnight, can it?"

Dat cleared his throat. "Maybe not overnight, but the wedding's in just three months." He glanced at Marianna and smiled. "It'll take much prayer and thought about what's really important—to Marianna and Ben as they stand before God—and to us. Not to our neighbors, Ruth, but to us."

Chapter Five

SUNDAY, JUNE 25, WEST KOOTENAI, MONTANA

The sun hadn't yet peeked over the mountains when Ike rose and slipped on his boots. He'd had a hard time sleeping last night. The funny thing was that Ike could sleep through a thunderstorm while clinging to a mountain hillside, yet what kept him awake was planning how he'd get through another day without confessing his love to Annie.

Marianna, his niece, had done what he had not been brave enough to do. She'd decided that love was more important than being Amish. Love for God. Love for Ben. And now Ike had to go to Annie's house like he did every morning and pretend he didn't want the same for him and Annie—to be married. He'd always believed he was brave, but every moment spent with Annie reminded him that he wasn't.

Ike winced as he ran his hand down his clean-shaven face. He'd never expected to be over forty and a bachelor. He didn't want to spend another forty—or even four—years this way. Yet while Ben and Marianna had both finally admitted their love for each other, Annie only considered him a good friend and nothing more.

He dressed quickly and slipped out the door, closing it quietly. It made no sense, really. He lived alone, and no one from the bachelor cabins across the road would be awake to hear him leave.

It was just a ten-minute walk to the small ranch down the road—situated just behind Kootenai Kraft and Grocery—and the light of the breaking dawn was enough to walk by. But even if there hadn't been enough light, he could have found the way for the number of times he'd tromped down this early morning path.

Pink rays of sunlight stretched over the mountain as Ike approached Annie's place. He spotted movement in the chicken coop and sauntered in that direction. Weathered wood framing and chicken wire made up the rectangular structure. The door between the coop and the yard had already been opened, and a dozen chickens shuffled outside. Some chickens immediately moved to the grass growing along the edges, plucking at whatever bugs they could find. Ike opened the door and, with quiet steps, stepped into the coop lit by electric light. Annie's damp blonde hair was unbraided this morning, giving her a youthful appearance. Tingles raced up his arms at the sight of her.

Annie smiled up at him and pointed to her basket. "The ladies have done well this morning. Hope you're extra hungry."

Ike presented a simple nod. "When haven't I been extra hungry?" With a forced smile and a longing to give Annie a good morning kiss, he moved to the plastic watering tub, carried it toward the chicken wire, and tossed the dirty water onto the grass outside the coop. Whistling as if he didn't have a care in the world, Ike went to the spigot mounted outside the enclosure and rinsed out the tub before filling it again.

Annie sidled up to him. "You know, I've seen catalogs with some large, automatic watering systems that you just hook up to a hose. I've been thinking about carrying some in the store and maybe getting one myself."

"Humph." Ike waved a hand, wishing he could share his heart instead of this small talk. "You know how dirty the chickens get the water. Bet those are hard to clean. And sure, the chickens would have a continuous water supply, but would they want to drink from that muck?"

He set the tub back in its place and watched as two of the chickens immediately walked over for a drink. "Besides, what would you need me for if you did that?" He pressed his lips together, shocked that he'd let that last part slip out.

Annie crossed her arms over her chest and eyed him. "You mean you like getting up early every morning to change the chicken water and help me muck the stalls?"

Ike shrugged. "Wouldn't be here if I didn't." His heartbeat quickened, and he couldn't help but smile. Really smile.

"Oh, and it has nothing to do with my pancakes or scrambled eggs?" She winked at him.

"I didn't say there was only one reason I came." He chuckled. "And speaking of mucking, I'll handle it today, with it being Sunday and all. I know you have things to do before you head to church."

"Like change out of my muck boots to church boots?" One of the chickens stepped forward and pecked at her boot as if proving Annie's point.

"If you call your cowboy boots your church boots, then yes. Now, git."

Annie nodded her thanks as she headed into the house, and for a moment, Ike wondered what it would be like if he didn't have to walk to her place every morning. If this could be their place, if they could do life together. But as soon as the thought entered his mind, he shook it away. He was an Amishman, and she was an Englischer. Things were much more complicated for them than for Ben and Marianna. Impossible really.

After the mucking, Ike left his boots on the porch and washed up at Annie's back porch sink before heading inside. The aroma of bacon and eggs greeted him, along with the smell of coffee.

As he entered, Annie was just setting down two plates, and Ike took his spot. *His spot.* With a familiarity that came with time, Annie sat and placed her hand in his, and they bowed their heads to pray.

"Dear Lord, we thank Thee for this day, this food, and friendship's beauty. Amen," Ike prayed.

Friendship. The word lingered on Ike's mind. Annie was his dearest friend, and he hoped she understood that.

"Amen," Annie said and then rose and went to the food being kept warm on the stove.

"So, where is the church today?" she asked. "Martins', isn't it?"

"Ja. Which means that it'll be an extra-long sermon. Jonathan Martin loves the sound of his own voice, I do believe."

Annie served up Ike's plate and then hers. She settled into her chair. "I wish you'd try my church sometime. Summit Community Church is growing in membership. I believe we had forty there last Sunday."

Ike nodded, but they both knew it wouldn't happen. Ike was a pillar in the Amish community and a mentor to all the bachelors. Young men moved to Montana every spring to hunt in the fall. So many looked to him to live the good and proper way. Sure, he'd sought out adventure in Montana first—and he didn't mind working with the Englisch one bit—but when it came to the rules of the church, he stuck to them as well as any man. Still, he had to admit he liked the idea of going to the church that many of his friends attended and being able to have Annie sitting by his side during the service.

"Does Ben help with the music?" Ike asked, picking up a slice of bacon.

"When he's in town. According to Marianna, he should be home sometime this week. You'd be proud of her, still coming when he's not there."

"And she knows what to do?"

Annie chuckled. "It's not hard. There aren't as many rules of order as in an Amish service. A welcome from the pastor, we sing three or four songs, followed by a sermon." Annie reached over and patted Ike's hand.

Tingles shot up his arm, and he told himself to breathe. Just breathe.

"Don't you worry, okay? Marianna sits with me when Ben's not there, and she seems to follow along just fine."

"That's gut." Ike took a bite of his eggs. What else could he say? And though he wished he could linger and they could talk more, they each had to go their separate ways.

After clearing his plate, Ike moved to the door. He had enough time to put on his church clothes and walk over to the Martins' place. There was no use getting out the horse and hooking up the buggy for just himself. Especially when the weather was perfect for a walk.

Ike had just reached the door when Annie's voice called to him. "Oh, Ike, wait, I almost forgot. Give me a minute." She hurried in the direction of her room and returned a few minutes later.

Ike's eyes widened to see that she carried a denim jacket. "What's that?"

"I've been going through my father's things. They've just been piled up in boxes in the spare room. I gave Edgar a lot of his shirts, but then I came across this. Dad only wore it a few times. I got it for him for Christmas a few months before he...passed." She handed the jacket to Ike. "Looks about your size."

Ike didn't miss the glimmer of tears that rimmed Annie's eyes. She was as independent and tough as they came. Still, he saw the same tender emotions when she talked about her father. He'd passed away over ten years before Ike had come to West Kootenai. "Are you sure?"

"Yes. Does no good just sitting in a box." She granted him a soft smile. "Besides, it would make me happy to see it put to good use—to see you wearing it."

Ike took the jacket and slipped it on. Even though it had belonged to Annie's father, it smelled of the cedar and spruce candles she liked to burn. It fit him perfectly. "Thank you, Annie. I'll put it to good use."

"I know you will. Now get." She shooed him away. "I don't want to hear any of the gossips at the store later saying that Ike Sommer showed up late to church today. You know you can't get away with anything without me knowing."

Ike couldn't help but feel a lightness to his steps as he hurried home. Annie had given him her father's coat. That had to mean something. At least, it meant something to him.

Chapter Six

MONDAY, JUNE 26, WEST KOOTENAI, MONTANA

The aroma of fresh-baked cinnamon rolls greeted Marianna. It caused her stomach to rumble as she approached the front doors of Kootenai Kraft and Grocery. Even though Marianna didn't have to work today, she was eager to get to the store to see Edgar. She'd left Montana just before Christmas and stayed in Indiana until spring. Then when she returned, Edgar had left just a few days before, visiting his sister in New Mexico. From December to June was six long months—too long to not see a dear friend. Out of all the people in West Kootenai, Marianna could count on Edgar to be excited about her engagement. As childish as it was, she would feel better to know there were people on her side—those who'd celebrate her relationship with Ben and the wedding to come.

Yesterday she'd enjoyed the church service with Annie, and then she and Mem had gone through the items in Marianna's hope chest, making a list of things she still needed when she had her own home—their home. Soon she'd be living in Ben's cabin with electricity and a phone. She was still trying to wrap her thoughts around that. When she'd been hemming towels and embroidering pillowcases as a teenager, she had pictured herself living in an Amish home. Not an Englisch one.

Part of her wondered what Ben would think of her handmade things, but then she pushed those worries from her mind. Ben knew who he was marrying. He never seemed bothered by her simple ways. Out of all the fancy places, he'd chosen to live in Montana. And out of all the fancy women he could have had, he'd chosen her.

From the gravel parking lot filled with buggies and vehicles, Kootenai Kraft and Grocery appeared busy. This time in the early morning, she knew some people shopped and others enjoyed breakfast. As she stepped inside, a logger wearing dirty jeans, a flannel shirt, and heavy boots headed toward the door, with a breakfast bag in one hand and a to-go cup of coffee in the other. Marianna held the door open for him.

"Good day, isn't it?" she called out.

A smile filled his face, and he responded with one

quick nod. "If I was any better, I'd be twins. Thank you kindly, little lady."

Edgar's head popped up behind the counter, just inside the store door. His gray hair was combed back neatly, and he wore his familiar plaid shirt rolled up at the sleeves and overalls. He held a stack of paper sacks in his hands, no doubt trying to organize his domain behind the counter. "Is that my Marianna?" He set the bags down and walked around the counter to her with open arms. "You're back, young lady. Things weren't the same without you."

Marianna quickly stepped into his embrace and smiled as his trim gray beard scratched her cheek. Edgar smelled of smoke from his wood-burning cookstove and the bacon he'd no doubt cooked on it this morning.

She kissed his cheek quickly and then stepped back out of his hug. "Ja, well, I can say the same about you. I've been here for months, and where have you been?"

"Enjoying the hot springs near my sister's house, overeating, and getting into trouble. You know one can get up to no good in a place called Truth or Consequences—and yes, that's the real name of the town where my sister lives. The truth is there were mostly snowbirds around the Rio Grande. And the consequence is that I gained twenty pounds sitting around. I'm glad to be up here around young folks again and get back to work. I just hope you're staying around this time."

"I'm home, for good." A sweet peace settled her soul saying that word.

"And I hear there are some congratulations in order."

"Ja." Marianna's smile broadened. "I'll be Mrs. Ben Stone soon. Can you believe it?"

Laughter tumbled from Edgar's mouth. "Believe it? I saw that coming from the first time the two of you met." Edgar smoothed his gray beard with one hand. "You know, sparks aren't a good thing living in the middle of a forest—especially during this dry season." He let out a low whistle. "Yet the two of you, that kind of spark is the real deal, and you know I'll be in the front row cheering the day Ben takes you as his bride." Edgar scratched the side of his head. "That is, if you'll have me."

"Have you?" Marianna reached out and touched his arm. "Have you at my wedding? You're at the top of the list. And Annie is a bridesmaid, of course. She took me down to Kalispell on Saturday so we could look at wedding dresses. I'm not sure what I would do without the two of you."

The door behind Marianna opened, and Edgar greeted the customer before returning to his spot behind the counter. "Well, it sounds like the perfect excuse to buy a new flannel shirt. I've needed one, and a wedding is as good an excuse as any."

"Ja, I was thinking the same thing," a voice from the office just down the hall rang out. "I might need to buy a new flannel shirt for this occasion." Marianna recognized Uncle Ike's voice before she saw him. With a grin, he walked out of Annie's office with a beaming Annie following close behind. Marianna had known from the first day when she'd arrived in West Kootenai that her uncle and Annie cared for each other, yet she knew it would be hard to get them both to admit it.

Marianna tilted her head and glanced from Annie to Ike. "The two of you look like you're up to no good. Anything you're hiding from me?" She narrowed her gaze and lifted one eyebrow. "Maybe about Ben's house?" *Our house soon.*

Ike approached the front counter and leaned against it. Annie did the same.

"Just on the phone with Ben, as a matter of fact," Ike answered. "Needed to ask him about the windows for the addition. Wanted to try to get those in before he gets home in a few days."

Annie gasped, shook her head, and then elbowed Ike. They acted like friends, but Marianna could see even Annie wished it could be more as she stood close to him, looking up at him with respect and attraction.

Ike grabbed his rib cage where her elbow had grazed him, and let out a moan as if she'd done real damage, but his eyes sparkled.

Annie cast him a side glance. "Ike Sommer. I believe you were specifically told this was supposed to be a surprise."

His shoulders flinched in a shrug. "The windows are a surprise too? How many surprises are there?"

Annie's finger went to her lips, and she shushed him.

Ike waved his hands in the air. "Oh bother, I'd better stop yapping my jaw before I get in more trouble." Uncle Ike pushed his hands into his jeans pockets and shrugged. "It's not as if Marianna doesn't know about the work on the house."

Goosebumps rose on her arms at the thought of seeing what Ben was doing to create a beautiful home for their first days together. Yet, at the same time, a dull ache in her chest wished that Ike could be doing the same for Annie. Did he think about it, wish for it? She had no doubt he did.

Marianna reached over and patted his arm. She caught a whiff of his shaving soap and thought of his old-fashioned cup and brush that he always kept on his bathroom shelf. "No worries, Uncle. I can be prepared to act amazed. It makes me happy that Ben wants to surprise me, and that's good enough."

Even though Ben had only been gone a few weeks, warmth filled her body knowing he'd soon be home. When she saw him and he pulled her into his embrace, she'd know that all was right in the world again.

"Windows sound very promising," Marianna commented to Annie. "Ben hasn't let me see the addition yet, and I've resisted the urge to hike up there and take a peek myself." Even though she was excited to see the addition Ben was adding, it also brought a pinch of pain. She'd waited a year to see the cabin Aaron had built for her only to realize he wasn't the one who held her heart.

"Maybe after you finish Marianna's place, you can do some work around here. I haven't done much on the store since I bought it over a decade ago."

"Only a decade?" Marianna narrowed her gaze on her friend. "That's hard to believe. It seems as if this store is your second home."

"Well—" Annie started.

"Now it is, but for many years the Bob Marshall Wilderness was home to her," Ike interrupted. "Being up there working for an outfitter, I understand why Annie spent every summer in those mountains since she was fifteen. Every time I go up, I learn to appreciate the wilderness more and more. If one ever doubts there is a God, all he has to do is to get up in those mountains. Ridge after ridge as far as you can see and air so clean you're certain it hasn't been polluted since God first spoke this world into existence." Uncle Ike did a happy jig and turned in a slow circle, breathing in through his nose and blowing out his breath with a smile.

Laughter spilled from Marianna, who was surprised by her uncle's antics, although she shouldn't be. Ike had never fit into the Amish mold. He was a little too outspoken and a lot too bold. Uncle Ike was the one who'd moved to Montana first and urged her family to come.

"You better be careful, Ike. Word will get out in

The Budget that you've been dancing at the general store." Annie joined Marianna's laughter.

Ike guffawed, grinned, and then moved to the dining room area, no doubt in search of a cup of coffee, a newspaper, and a bit of peace before he headed off to work at Ben's place.

"I promise you I haven't told Ben anything about your dress." Annie's brows lifted. "Or how absolutely stunning you looked in it." She winked. "Have you thought more about my suggestion? We can fix up the meadow, all pretty like. You can even use my cabin for getting ready."

Marianna's smile faded. *How will I ever be able to make a decision about all of this?*

She rubbed her brow, feeling a headache come on. "I knew that once you helped me with that dress your mind would be busy with wanting to tackle all the details." She tried to keep her tone light even as unease rolled through her like a mounting thundercloud. "It's something I need to talk to Ben about. We haven't decided..."

Soon, it would be their time to plan and dream. Once they were together, hopefully, they wouldn't be separated like that again for a while. And after all the wedding planning, they could look forward to the rest of their lives.

Yet it was getting to the "rest of their lives" that caused the churning in her stomach. As much as she couldn't wait to marry Ben, the details kept her up at night. All she'd known growing up were Amish weddings. And she knew that in Ben's world, things were done differently. Buying that beautiful satin dress was proof of that.

Annie glanced at her watch, and Marianna knew she was estimating how much time she had before she needed to head to the kitchen and start prepping for the lunch rush. "Listen, I wanted to show you a rustic design for an arch for the altar I found online. Do you have time to sit a spell? I'll get us both some coffee and a cinnamon roll." Annie's face glowed with excitement as if she was the one getting married.

Marianna's shoulders stiffened. Her heartbeat picked up. "How can I refuse that?"

Everything within her told her to run, to head to the pond where she could think and decide what she really wanted. Instead, she followed Annie to a corner table. As soon as they sat, Annie set a printed picture of an arch before Marianna. "What do you think? Just this at the altar with the view of the mountains behind?"

Marianna lifted the printout and studied the wooden arch with ladder sides and a wide top reminiscent of an arbor. A lush display of flowers in blues, yellows, and purples wrapped around the sides and top. Ribbons and lace hung down too. Marianna scooted, pressing her back against the hard wooden chair. She placed the printout on the center of the table.

Annie leaned closer, eagerness in her gaze. "Don't you like it?" She slid the paper closer to Marianna.

"It's...fancy," Marianna managed to say, covering

the paper with her hand. Hesitant breaths mingled with her words.

"It's not too fancy, not really." Then a knowing came into Annie's eyes. "Oh, I understand. I suppose Amish weddings..."

"Are simple. There's not so much fuss." Marianna sighed. "I'm already worried that some of our family and friends won't come. Then some will be so focused on my satin dress they won't think of anything else."

Annie patted her hand.

"It's something I need to think about. Talk to Ben about—how fancy we want things to be." Marianna pulled her hand back from Annie's touch.

"Yes, of course. It's just that I haven't had much chance to plan a wedding. All my closest friends have no thoughts of ever getting married." Annie's gaze moved across the room. Following her gaze, Marianna saw that Annie was looking at Ike. He sat at one of the tables, reading *The Budget*.

"Uncle Ike is a self-proclaimed bachelor, I know." Marianna wrinkled her nose, thankful to get the conversation off herself. "I just hope that someday he'll open his heart." She studied Annie's face, hoping for a reaction. Yet while Annie was quick to encourage others to share their hearts, it was as if she had a ten-foot brick wall around hers. "I once overheard Dat say that Uncle Ike was scared of love. Scared of family."

Annie opened her mouth as if she was going to protest. But something about Marianna's comment must have made her change her mind. Annie pinched her chin and leaned forward. "Did your dat—or anyone—ever say why Ike was scared of...family?"

Another memory came to the surface. Marianna thought about the accident so long ago, which had robbed Mem and Dat of two daughters and caused her to be born early. Maybe Ike carried the same burdens she did concerning their loss. As if no matter what one did—how good or right they tried to live—they could not make up for that painful night.

"I remember my Aunt Ida talking once." Marianna studied the wood grain on the table as she answered. "She said Uncle Ike was the first on the scene of the buggy accident—the one where my two sisters died. He was also coming home from the ice-cream social that night."

Annie gasped. "If he was at the accident...do you think he saw the girls?"

Marianna lowered her gaze to her coffee. "Yes, I believe he did. I—I can't imagine."

Taking another sip of her coffee, Annie sat back in the wooden chair. "It's amazing what we do to protect ourselves, you know. Putting up walls around our hearts to keep away hurt while also missing out on love." Annie folded the printout. "Or being afraid of making any choice for fear of what others will say."

Like fear of choosing a simple arch because it's too fancy? Fear of wearing the satin dress I fell in love with?

Marianna blew out her cheeks. "I see your point.

And I will talk to Ben about our wedding being in the meadow and about that fancy arch." She wrapped her hands around her coffee cup. "But I don't think my uncle and I are the only ones who have put up walls around our hearts. I see a special sparkle in your eyes as we talk about my wedding, and it makes me wonder if you ever thought of getting married."

Annie's jaw dropped, and if Marianna wasn't mistaken, she noticed a flash of emotion in Annie's gaze, something similar to longing. Longing for a time past or hope for a time still to come, Marianna wasn't sure which.

Annie glanced at her watch again. "Yes, we can talk about these things all day, but the lunch rush should be coming soon, and I need to make sure everything's ready in the kitchen." Annie rose without looking at her coffee or cinnamon roll. Yet her eyes moved toward Ike, who just happened to glance up at Annie as she passed. His cheeks lifted in a tender smile.

Marianna picked up the piece of paper and studied it. The arch was beautiful. The flowers were her favorite colors—did Annie know? She closed her eyes and pictured the arch and the mountains framed behind it. She thought of the aroma of the flowers. How wonderful they'd smell with her standing under them in that white satin dress.

Mostly she thought about Ben. About how he'd been waiting for her after she'd returned from Indiana. How he'd asked if he could pray for her, and then after praying, asked if she would be his wife.

A smile curved up her lips, thinking of the way he tenderly loved her. Considering how she trusted him with her heart and with this strange journey they were on—merging two worlds into one. Just a few more days, and he'd be back. Then they wouldn't have to part again.

Chapter Seven

MONDAY, JUNE 26, WEST KOOTENAI, MONTANA

The lunch rush came, and Marianna retrieved a sack for the cinnamon rolls after realizing neither she nor Annie had taken a bite. At least the boys would enjoy them, she mused as she walked home. The air smelled sweet, like spring, even though it was summer. Winter had taken its time to depart, and she guessed that spring would stick around a bit to ensure it got its rightful time.

She had to work tomorrow, so this afternoon would be her one chance to list what really mattered for her wedding. In Amish weddings, the couple sat in chairs at the front while the minister gave a long sermon. Annie had told her that Englisch weddings were much shorter. Their minister focused on the couple and their love for each other rather than a sermon about marriage. Englisch weddings also had love songs instead of hymns. Would Ben want to sing? She smiled at the thought and clasped her hands in front of her.

Think of the good. Think of what I'll gain...not all I'm losing. Ben's love is worth it.

Marianna's feet stirred up dirt with each step, yet she chose to fix her gaze not on the road but on the landscape around her. Just a few miles from Canada, their isolated community didn't have many businesses, but that mattered little compared to the charm. With it being situated in the lovely, forested corner of northwest Montana—between the Purcell and Salish Mountains—Marianna couldn't imagine a prettier place. *Look for the beauty. Remember to focus on that. Ben loves me, and I love him.*

The thought was no sooner in her mind than Marianna's steps stopped short. Up ahead, their yard was filled with buggies. Had Mem mentioned the company?

Then she remembered Ellie's comment about the sewing circle. Was that why Mem had insisted that Marianna head to the store to visit Edgar after breakfast? Was she so ashamed of her daughter, who was due to marry an Englischer, that she wanted to make sure Marianna wasn't home when her friends were around?

She hoped that wasn't the case and smiled as she entered the front door. Marianna stepped into the open kitchen and living room, taking in the aroma of cinnamon and apples and the chatter of women sitting around a sewing frame in the living room. Upon her entrance, every woman in the room grew silent, unmoving—like mannequins in Englisch stores. Then, straightening her shoulders, Mem dared to meet Marianna's gaze.

"Well, you're home early." Mem's smile grew stiff as she pushed her sewing project to the side. "I thought you'd be at the store for a few hours catching up with Edgar and the rest."

Marianna shut the door behind her and crossed her arms over her chest, unsure of what to do or say. "It was getting busy. I didn't need to take their time. It was wonderful seeing Edgar, though." She tried to keep her tone light, but her mind returned to Eve Peachy and the way Eve had shunned her. Marianna scanned the room and saw that Eve wasn't there, but would these women do the same?

Today Marianna wore her hair in the tight, neat bun she usually wore under her kapp. Her dress was conservative, too, with sleeves past the elbows and a hem past the knees. But it was not an Amish dress, and she wore no head covering. Those things, she knew, mattered most.

Drawing in a breath, Marianna scanned the women again. Some returned to their sewing, and others attempted to look in any direction except toward her. She moved to the empty chair, joining the sewing circle. Then she waited. Would anyone comment? Would they ignore her or leave?

Pretending it didn't matter, Marianna reached

down into her mother's sewing basket for a needle and thread. She threaded a needle with white thread to join the others. She heard the scraping of chair legs on the wooden floor, then the soft huff from a heavyset woman rising to her feet. Anna Martin, the elder's wife, strode toward the kitchen with her head held high.

Knotting the thread, Marianna studied the patterned fabric encased in the sewing frame. With a square in the middle, strips of fabric had been placed in a sequence around the sides of the square, varying the values between light and dark. As her eyes focused, a soft gasp escaped her lips. She recognized the material. Strips of calico with pink flowers, dark blue strips, and more squares in patterns of pink and blue. This fabric was from her childhood dresses, which Joanna and Marilyn had worn before her—treasured dresses cut into uniform strips and placed in a log cabin pattern.

Then it hit her why the women were so quiet. Her mouth opened slightly and her eyes darted up. "Is this for me?"

A sly smile filled her mother's face. "Ja, there was a reason I wanted you to keep away. We've managed four gatherings without you being any the wiser. I suppose our luck is up."

Marianna touched her hair, which was missing her kapp. "But why?"

"Things aren't as strict as back east, but some of the women still didn't feel comfortable working on a wedding quilt," one of their Amish neighbors, Deborah Shelter, said plainly. "It was your mother's idea to work on a memory quilt instead. Few found fault with that."

Marianna fixed her eyes on her mother's solemn gaze. "And you wanted it to be a surprise?"

Mem nodded.

"But, Mem, these are the girls' dresses." Marianna smoothed her fingers over the fabric once again.

Mem's lower lip quivered as she looked to her lap.

Marianna didn't know how her mother continued each day, trying to move forward when so much was tied to her past.

Mem cut up those dresses to make a quilt for me? Warmth swelled in Marianna's chest, and tears filled her eyes.

"They were your dresses too. As much as I loved my daughters who were lost, I also love the daughter sitting before me." Mem jutted out her chin. "And as I told the others, I've already had two daughters lost. I will not lose another. I do believe the Amish way of life is still best, but I've also learned that there are others who so greatly love God too. And I see that in Ben. I will not shun my first daughter to marry because she chooses to love God differently. I know many won't agree with that, but I will not go through this loss again."

A sniffle sounded next to her, and Marianna looked over to see tears rimming the eyes of Mara Milner, one of their neighbors who'd lost her husband within the last year. Mara cleared her throat. "The older one gets, the more one realizes how fragile life is." She wiped a tear and turned to Marianna. "There's enough loss without us having to shun those who are truly seeking God's way, and I see that in you."

Marianna's eyes moved around the faces of the circle, and she noted slight nods. The only one not within the circle was Brother Jonathan's wife, Anna. She stood in the kitchen preparing herself a cup of coffee as if nothing else mattered. And as Marianna took in the faces of her neighbors and friends, she knew all had faced at least one significant loss in their lives. Could anyone get through this life unscathed?

She was starting to think it wasn't possible. And somehow, their pain had made them more open to seeking small joys wherever they could and more closed to turning their backs on those they loved, even though that's what their rules demanded.

Mem released a sigh and then wiped a stray tear and returned to her sewing. All the women joined her. Marianna did, too, making a line of tiny straight stitches. They worked in an uncomfortable silence with Anna Martin looking on, glaring over her coffee cup as she sipped.

"Do you know of places for family to stay in September?" Mem dared to ask the women, breaking the silence. "Abe's sister Ida is coming to visit. Our place is full because my sister Betsy is coming along with her kinder."

"Coming to the wedding?" Anna Martin's eyes shot up. Her voice rose in volume. "All this way to see

Marianna marry an Englischer? What will the folks back in Indiana say? I imagine someone's due to mention it in *The Budget*, and then word will be out for good."

"They were coming for a visit before these new plans. It's already been expected for a year—before we had any idea about the wedding," Mem insisted.

"Ja, and who are you to talk, Anna?" Deborah Shelter jutted out her chin. "You're the one who suggested working on a quilt for Marianna."

Anna waved a hand as if batting down her words. "But that's when I believed she was marrying that Amish young man. Wasn't that less than a year ago? Seems like things changed so quickly, and we all know what the Good Book says—'Feet make haste to run to evil.'"

Hairs rose on the back of Marianna's neck as they spoke about her as if she wasn't there.

"I know Marianna. I trust her," Deborah Shelter commented. "She's been a good friend to my Sarah. Surely there is a reason she broke things off."

Anna stood in the kitchen and folded her arms over her ample chest. "Ja, even if that were true, to marry an Englischer—one who plays music and performs on television, of all things."

Just as Marianna was about to rise and leave the room, a soft voice chimed in. "I know of a place for your family, Ruth. Mara Milner is planning to rent out the *dawdi* house for extra income, aren't you, Mara?"

Marianna recognized the voice of sweet Lovina

Graber. She was a bit older than Marianna and walked with a noticeable limp. Yet her heart was as kind and honest as anyone in West Kootenai. Marianna smiled at how the woman so casually attempted to change the conversation back to the visitors and away from Marianna's choice of husband.

Mara's forehead wrinkled as she looked at Lovina. "Ja, well, that is the hope. With my husband's death and Reuben being the only boy..." Mara pursed her lips. "Well, he's a busy young man these days. It's on Reuben's list of things to finish. He's been trying to do a lot of getting things fixed up. The problem is two more things break before one is fixed. Yet..." She paused as if deciding what to say. "Maybe if we know a date in September, I can help him some and even ask my daughter Penny to help too."

"The date is the last weekend in September. And if you'll excuse me." Marianna stood. She couldn't continue to sit there as they spoke about her instead of speaking to her. It was similar to how Eve Peachy had refused to talk to her a couple days prior.

They were working on a quilt for her, but would they genuinely accept her marriage to Ben? She pressed her fingers to her forehead, feeling an ache come on and imagining what would happen when her family from Indiana came. Aunt Ida was never one to keep her opinion to herself. More than that, Aunt Ida was a scribe for *The Budget*. As Anna Martin suggested, Marianna's wedding would make the paper, and Aunt Ida wouldn't hold anything back.

Needing someone to talk to, Marianna found her way to the back shed, where a phone had been installed before they'd moved into the place. The shed exuded a musty, dusty smell. When her family had first moved in, Marianna had been horrified about the phone. But now? She liked the idea that she could reach out to Ben even when he was gone.

She found the paper with Ben's number on it tacked to the wall. She picked up the phone and dialed the number. Then with a smile, she held her breath as the phone rang.

He answered on the second ring. "Marianna, is everything all right?" His words came out in a rush. "Are you okay?"

"Yes, Ben, I was just missing you."

He blew out a breath and then took in another one. "Oh, good. I'm glad to hear that. I was worried when I saw the number come up."

"Are you saying I only call when there's a problem?" She tried to keep her voice light, yet tears sprang to her eyes as she thought about the women around the sewing circle and Annie wanting to help with wedding plans. Worries about the satin dress, visiting family, and being shunned by Eve Peachy crowded her thoughts. She blinked back her tears, refusing to allow them to escape. Refusing to worry Ben.

He chuckled. "Well, yes. That's pretty much the only time you call."

"I'm fine." Her voice quivered a little. "I'm just missing you."

"I'll be home in a couple of days." His voice sounded hurried, and Marianna heard other male voices talking in the background.

"Did I interrupt something?"

"Actually, yes. Roy flew down, and we're here with a concert promoter. We're trying to set some dates for the fall...and into next year."

"Dates?"

"For concerts. After September, of course."

"You're going back on the ro-road?" Her words caught, and she attempted to swallow down the emotion. She pressed a hand to her throat. *He's leaving again just as our life is getting started? And I'll be alone in the cabin—Ben's cabin without him. This doesn't sound like much of a marriage.*

"I told them that I didn't want to be gone long. I'll be a newlywed. Unless you came with me. Wouldn't that be nice?" His voice sounded hopeful. "But I told them I'll ask my wife. And yeah, I love the sound of that—my wife."

Marianna could hear the smile in his voice, and she pictured the tiny dimple on his chin and the bright blue of his eyes. She didn't know what to say. If she had thought of it, it would have been evident that Ben would have to go back on the road sometime. That was how he made an income, especially after his songs had become so popular. But she certainly hadn't entertained the idea of going on the road with him.

No, I'm not going to do that. That's not in the plan —has never been in the plan. She rubbed her brow as her headache grew in intensity. Marianna sucked in a long breath, telling herself to hold it together. To not cry on the phone. "Ben, I—"

"But listen, can I call you back?" Ben interrupted. "Roy is catching a flight back tonight, and we need to nail this down."

"Ja. I mean, yes, of course."

"Wonderful. See you soon, Marianna...and I love you."

"I love you too—" she said, but the phone call hung up before the words were out. She held the receiver in her hand until it buzzed, then hung it up.

A chill ran down her spine. Loneliness descended on her. She loved Ben, she really did, but with each passing day, more questions filled her mind. Was she really ready for this? Prepared to be Mrs. Ben Stone?

Chapter Eight

TUESDAY, JUNE 27, WEST KOOTENAI, MONTANA

Marianna entered Dat's barn to check whether it would be big enough to hold a wedding reception in the large, open area. But as soon as she stepped inside, she knew that it wasn't. There wasn't enough room for even ten tables, let alone an open area for guests to mingle or space for food service. The barn seemed empty without her father. He was working up the road with Uncle Ike at Ben's house. Soon her house. The scents of hay and animals, the moist warmth inside—even warmer than the morning air—brought on a sense of familiarity and peace. How many mornings had she spent in the barn with her father? Too many to count.

She thought back to the gray silo and tall silver

windmill peeking over their red barn's sloping roof back in Indiana. She'd always planned on getting married in that barn. Many of their neighbors cleaned out their barns and set up tables and chairs inside for the wedding and reception after.

In their old community, there had been a wedding wagon that could be moved from place to place and set up as an extra kitchen with six propane gas stoves. There'd also been sinks with hot and cold running water, cookware, dishes, and everything one would need. Family and friends would come together to cook for three hundred guests. Of course, in Montana, Marianna couldn't imagine three hundred guests, even with their Englisch friends included. Unless Ben had other Englisch friends he wished to invite. Marianna hadn't thought of that.

Seeing a five-gallon bucket turned over near one of the stalls, Marianna sat on it, just as she had when she was little. She thought of Ben's place, so different than this. So Englisch. Marrying Ben meant raising her children differently than she'd been raised.

Trust Me. God's still, small voice stirred within Marianna, surprising her. She sat up straighter, scuffing the toe of her tennis shoe on the concrete. She was used to talking to God and hearing His soft voice gently stirring within when she sat at the pond. Marianna also felt His precious presence when she sat with her open Bible in her bedroom. But was God here too? Could He speak to her heart in other places?

Trust Me, He had said. Did that mean for her to

trust God with Ben? With their lives together? To trust God in this new journey of marriage that would cause each of them to lay down so much of their lives to come together in unity?

Marianna plucked up a piece of straw and twirled it between her fingers. She smiled, remembering Ben's strong hug as they had parted. Marianna had seen a glimmer of tears in his eyes. She remembered his kiss. It would take trust for the days to come. That was certain.

The footsteps coming across the gravel driveway caused Marianna to sit up straighter. Mem traipsed toward her with Joy on her hip. Four-year-old Ellie trailed behind, carrying a small basket in her hand, pausing every now and then to pick up an interesting pine cone or rock.

Mem must have seen Marianna enter the barn, because she strode in with purpose. It was clear she had something on her mind. Yesterday her focus had been on the memory quilt. What could it be today? Something about the wedding, Marianna was certain.

"I know you told me you wanted time to think things through—of where you want the wedding yet—but I was thinking of asking Reuben Milner to build us a large picnic table in the yard. With so many family visiting, I imagine we will need more places to sit."

"Ja, well, that's a gut idea."

"Do you think I should have him make two tables?"

"For more seating?" Marianna cocked an eyebrow.

"If we need more seating, we can ask to use the church wagon." Marianna thought of the large trailer filled with benches that went from place to place, bringing seating for every church service or gathering. "Then we'll have plenty of places to sit..."

Marianna's voice trailed off as she saw the pinched expression on Mem's face. It was then she remembered that this would not be an Amish wedding. And indeed, the elders would not make an exception for one who chose to leave the Amish. "Let me guess. We can't use the church benches?"

"*Ne*. They're only for Amish weddings."

Marianna's mouth went as dry as the hay scattered across the barn floor. Her breaths drew in slowly. *This is really happening.*

Over the last few months, as she'd taken steps away from the Amish lifestyle, she'd considered it like Ellie with her basket of pine cones and rocks. She almost pictured herself dropping old traditions and habits, leaving a trail behind her like debris upon the path. Yet if that were so, she'd still feel her complete self.

Instead of stripping away, this was more like death. The Amishwoman she once was no longer existed. A numbness came over her at that thought. No wonder she was having difficulty making sense of this new path. She didn't understand this new version of herself. How could she ever feel right or wrong about any decision when she had no idea what choice this different Marianna should make? And she wasn't the only one trying to figure it out. Those closest to her struggled too.

Marianna thought of Mem's words just yesterday. *I've already had two daughters lost. I will not lose another.* Yet wasn't this what had already happened? It was as if there were three headstones back in Indiana. Two daughters were lost in a buggy accident, and one to the Englischers' ways. Ne, that wasn't right. Another lost to...relinquishment to God and His ways, not those of her ancestors. But did that make the death to herself and her ways any less painful? She guessed not.

"Of course I cannot use the church wagon. I am no longer Amish. What was I thinking?"

Marianna's eyes fixed on Ellie as she lifted a handful of gravel from just outside the barn door and let it slowly slip through her fingers. Was that how Mem felt, like everything she'd lived her whole life for—all their Amish ways—were slowly slipping away?

It caused an ache inside Marianna too. A pain for how she'd always imagined things being. She'd always planned for an Amish wedding. She'd always expected things to be done a certain way, just as they'd always been done. Yet how could she explain the emptiness—this death—to others, especially since these should be the happiest days of her life as she prepared to marry the man she loved?

"Ja, if you need a picnic table for the yard, then it might be gut to put in an order with Reuben Milner." Marianna kicked at a small tuft of hay with the toe of her shoe. "But maybe you should wait to order two tables. Ben and I still have to talk about where we're going to have the wedding." The answer didn't seem sufficient, and she noted the confusion in Mem's eyes even as she bounced Joy on her hip.

"Are you saying you might not have it here? But I just assumed..." Mem shifted Joy to her other hip. "Back in Indiana we'd always talked about the barn. This is different, but we can still make it work." Disbelief, a struggle to cope, up and down emotions. Marianna noted the denial of this death in Mem's gaze.

Marianna stood and brushed the straw off her skirt. "But this isn't Indiana, is it? This house is much smaller than the one back in Shipshewana. There's room for buggy parking but not enough parking for the vehicles of our Englisch friends."

Ellie had sat down inside the barn door and sorted her collection of pine cones, rocks, and sticks into piles. She seemed quiet—too quiet. And Marianna guessed she was listening. Even though they were speaking in Englisch, Marianna knew that Ellie could probably understand most of what they were saying. Unlike the preschoolers in Indiana, who spent almost all of their early years around Amish alone, Ellie had just as many Englisch friends as she had Amish ones. Also, most of their neighbors in this area were Englisch, giving Ellie an advantage in learning the language and the Pennsylvania Dutch she spoke at home.

Joy began to fuss, and Mem turned her face outward. Joy's eyes were round and gray, the same color as

Marianna's, but her hair was dark brown, opposite of Ellie's blonde hair and at least three shades darker than Marianna's light brown. Seeing Marianna, Joy stretched out her hands and kicked her feet. Marianna stepped forward and took Joy from Mem's hands, attempting to ignore the pained look on her mother's face. The feeling of Joy in her arms settled her somehow. Her baby-fresh aroma mixed with the barn scents, smelling like home, like family.

Yes, Marianna reminded herself. Some things were changing, yet so many others were the same. She still had her parents, brothers and sisters, and even most of her Amish friends. Not many young women who chose to leave the Amish could say the same. And this was only possible because they lived in Montana, she knew. Back in Indiana, she would have been shunned. The ministers and the elders would have demanded it. Just like her brother Levi had been shunned until he'd chosen to be baptized into the church and marry Naomi. Two years ago when he'd first left, Marianna would never have believed their roles would be reversed. Never. Yet here she was.

Joy giggled as she reached up and placed her fingers on Marianna's lips. Marianna pretended to nibble on them, which was their favorite game, and Joy laughed again.

Mem worriedly nibbled her lower lip and crossed her arms over her chest. Her kapp strings fluttered softly in the breeze that blew in through the doorway.

"Do you think Ben will invite many Englisch friends? What of his family? Are they coming?"

"I'm not sure, Mem. We still need to talk about it. But he is Englisch, you know." Marianna reached up to twist her kapp string around her finger—a habit since childhood—but she remembered it wasn't there and brushed her hand over Joy's smooth, fine hair instead.

Mem nodded. "Ja, of course."

The clomping of a horse's hoofs coming down the gravel roadway caused Marianna to look out the doorway. Then the jingle of the tack and traces on a buggy. Walking to the barn door, she smiled to see Uncle Ike driving the buggy up the road. Instinctively, she shifted Joy and waved a welcome. Then a new thought hit her. Once married, she'd be listening to the sound of Ben's truck engine and not the jingle of tack and traces. Her shoulders drooped with a sigh, realizing that. Ike slowed the buggy and waved.

After parking the buggy, Ike hurried over to the barn. Seeing him, Ellie quickly picked up all her treasures and put them back into the basket and set it to the side. Then she rushed to Uncle Ike, and he swung her up to sit on his left shoulder in one smooth motion, just as he'd used to do with Marianna when she was a child.

"Sack potato!" Ellie shouted with glee, and then Uncle Ike put her down to the ground again with a squeal. It took a few seconds for Ellie to catch her balance, then she hurried over to the basket to again dump out her things.

"Did you need something, Ike, for Ben's house?" Mem asked.

"Well, if I did, I wouldn't mention it." Ike winked at Marianna. "Got in trouble enough yesterday for ruining a surprise." He pulled a handkerchief from his front jeans pocket and wiped his brow. "I actually came by to see if I could borrow your phone. Annie sent a note with our lunch saying someone called about needing an outfitter for a trip they'd like to take into the Bob Marshall at the end of July. They want me to call them back."

Mem tipped her head and made eye contact with Ike as she stepped closer to her brother-in-law. "Have you led a trip before? That wilderness isn't a friendly place. I hear stories all the time."

"I've been assisting for five years. I could do a fair job. It's Annie who recommended me to one of her friends. So, can I use your phone?"

"Ja, of course," Marianna answered, wondering why Mem was being so quiet. Mem eyed Ike with curiosity, her eyes filled with questions. Did Mem find it interesting how Ike and Annie seemed to depend on each other more and more as the days passed? Did Mem worry that Ike would soon leave the Amish in the name of love?

Ike hurried to their phone shed, and Marianna turned her conversation back to the wedding. "When Ben gets home, we'll talk about all these things concerning the wedding. Don't worry, Mem. I'll talk to him about the location. Maybe we can find a way to work it out?"

Mem's face brightened. "Really? Oh, thank you. There will be so many different things with this wedding. Having some familiar things around will ease my soul." She placed a hand over her heart. "And maybe if it's here, your aunts will be more inclined to attend. You know how they can be, especially Aunt Ida," Mem said with a windy sigh.

Marianna wanted to remind her mother that she'd only said she'd try to find a way to work it out. It wasn't a guarantee. But the color that had returned to Mem's cheeks brought Marianna pause. She would talk to Ben. They would make a decision together, and if Mem wasn't going to get her wishes in the end, at least she could think for a while that her wishes were a possibility.

Chapter Nine

TUESDAY, JUNE 27, WEST KOOTENAI, MONTANA

Ben couldn't help himself. He'd been gone for weeks and missed Marianna like crazy. He stood on the dirt road outside her family's house. It was a new moon, which wasn't visible in the night sky. Instead, the stars sparkled like fistfuls of diamonds tossed on a black velvet fabric.

Shifting from side to side and kicking up dirt and gravel from the road, Ben contemplated if he should sneak to her window just to see her beautiful face, even for ten minutes. The house looked quiet, and he guessed that the rest of her family had already fallen asleep. But didn't she say she often stayed up to read or write in her journal? Seeing the joy on her face was worth the risk when she realized he'd come home a day early.

He slowly walked toward the house by the light from his cell phone, realizing for the first time how loud walking on pine cones could be. Ben strained to see if there was any sign of lantern or candlelight—evidence that she was awake. Hopefully, Trapper wouldn't hear him and bark, waking everyone up.

Step by step, he made his way to the side of the house toward her downstairs bedroom window. He felt like a teenager again, parking his truck down the road to sneak into his girlfriend's house. Yet this wasn't just a girlfriend. This was his fiancée, soon to be his wife. His smile widened even as he hunched down under the window. He was about to reach his hand to tap on the window, but his cell phone chimed its familiar tune. Ben jumped and stood erect. He'd forgotten to put his phone on silent, and at the moment, the chiming sounded as loud as a shotgun going off in the night.

Ben quickly shut off the ringing and stood as still as possible.

"Marianna." His voice was just louder than a whisper, but even through the closed curtains he could see no light was on. She must be fast asleep. Trapper too. He tapped the window as softly as he could. No response.

He considered tapping louder, but Ben knew that would wake Trapper. He'd just have to content himself with seeing Marianna's beautiful face tonight in his dreams instead of in person. Sighing, he slowly crept back the way he had come.

Once on the road, Ben quickened his pace. He also wondered what Roy wanted. He rarely called this late. Instead of calling, Ben texted Roy back.

BEN

Did you call?

ROY

Get home?

Ben glanced at the Sommers' cabin one last time as he crested the hill toward his truck.

BEN

Yes. Dodged a few deer but made it.

ROY

Bad news.

BEN

What?

ROY

Confirmed Stacy's story.

BEN

Serious?

ROY

Lotsa reporters have plans to be in Montana the last week of September.

BEN

Please no.

ROY

Elope? Televise it?

Ben read the last line twice, and worry gnawed at his gut. Those couldn't be their only options. Even though he was looking forward to marrying Marianna, he'd been procrastinating about talking to her concerning wedding plans. After all, she only knew Amish weddings. Ben had attended one before. He cringed at the thought of the guests sitting on long, backless benches, with him and Marianna sitting on chairs at the front of the room, listening to a preacher yammer.

Reading the last text a third time, Ben blew out a frustrated breath, and heat flushed through his body. How could he tell her that whatever plans they made would be overrun by paparazzi?

Over the last few months, Marianna had faced more changes than many women did over a decade. Changing how she dressed. Not wearing a kapp. Attending a new church. Even though she'd been raised to love God, His Word was new to her too. When Ben sat down with her and they read the Bible together, every belief had to be weighed and examined to determine what was God's truth and what was Amish tradition.

Would the same contemplation be needed for their wedding too? Would she want to stick to Amish traditions to honor her family? Well, except for the dress. For some reason, Marianna had wanted to at least try on English wedding dresses. He hadn't heard yet if she'd chosen one. And now he hated thinking that the paparazzi would invade their wedding. They'd see the whole thing as a spectacle instead of the beautiful union of two people willing to go against the norms of their societies for the sake of love.

ROY

Let me know how I can help.
Signing off.

BEN

I'll figure it out. Thanks.

He needed to find an answer, yet he knew he couldn't tell her about the paparazzi. She'd called him on the phone, and he'd heard the worries in her voice. His guess was trying on English wedding dresses had been hard. Were people around the community giving her a hard time too? The last thing Marianna needed was another heavy burden to pile on top of the rest.

Sticking his phone in his pocket, Ben climbed into his truck and headed for home. As he drove, he remembered something his grandmother had told him during one of her anniversary celebrations. *I was told a growing moon and a flowing tide are lucky times to marry.* Ben wished planning a wedding would be as clear cut for him. His grandmother hadn't had the paparazzi to worry about.

As he drove up to his cabin, noting the new construction, Ben worried the impact would go beyond him and Marianna. Would the media leave them alone after the wedding? Or would their pursuit continue? Folks in this area lived here because they were independent and liked it that way. How would they feel knowing a camera could be put in their face at any time? Would more tourists come, knowing they could have the chance to spot Ben Stone and his Amish bride?

What am I getting Marianna into? And this whole community too.

He parked his truck and jumped from the vehicle, then grabbed his suitcase from the back. Someone had left the porch light on. His guess was Ike. It was just something his friend would do.

Walking inside, Ben flipped on the living room light and sucked in a breath as he viewed the new addition. Abe and Ike had been busy. Before the expansion, the living room, small dining area, and kitchen had filled one boxy room. While he'd been gone, the back room had been knocked out, and a wall of tall windows had been framed, allowing for a large dining room.

His plan was to purchase a long dining table from Montana Log Works. Six chairs would line one side and two long benches the other—perfect for filling up with as many brothers and sisters, nieces and nephews as would fit. And maybe in the upcoming years, children of their own. He liked the thought of that.

The addition ran the whole length of the house. Down a new hall beyond the kitchen was their new bedroom suite, complete with a rock fireplace. Next to that was a small additional room that Ben hoped could be used as a nursery in upcoming years. His heart swelled as he thought about Marianna's reaction. And to think soon this would be her life too. A life they could enjoy together.

Blue plastic covered the hole where a new roof would soon be added, doing little to block out the cold night air, but that didn't dampen Ben's spirits. He smiled, thinking how much extra loving care Abe had put into this addition since it was for his daughter.

After walking appreciatively around the new construction, Ben yawned and reminded himself that the sooner he went to sleep, the sooner he could wake up and see Marianna. He had just shut the door behind him and locked it when his cell phone buzzed again.

Ben pulled his cell phone from his pocket. *Honestly, Roy, aren't you going to get some sleep tonight?*

But as he looked down, it wasn't Roy's name on the screen. Sucking in labored breaths, he took two quick steps to the living room recliner and sank in.

Jason. He recognized the name and the number.

Yet he knew it wasn't his friend on the other end. Ben clicked the message icon to read the text.

JASON

Seven years ago in just a few days. It doesn't seem that long, does it? He would be 27. Probably married. I hear you're getting married. I have to admit I cried myself to sleep when I heard that. I don't understand how you can go on with life after you took my brother's. It's not fair that you get what my brother never got a chance to have.

Ben closed his eyes and thought of Hannah. Jason's younger sister had hung around them most days whenever they performed. Even though many siblings didn't get along, that hadn't been true of Hannah and Jason. Ben had thought she was cute and even considered asking her on a date, but Jason wouldn't allow it. *Dude, I know how you break hearts. I'm not going to let you do that to my sister.*

And after Jason's death, Hannah had kept her brother's cell phone and kept his number active. Then, Hannah would text Ben every year around the anniversary of Jason's death. She didn't want Ben to forget how much his actions hurt others. Not that he'd ever forget. Like the refrain of a song, the pain of Ben's mistake repeated in his mind and heart. The only thing that eased Ben's distress was that Jason had loved God, hadn't he?

Jason hadn't been perfect by a long shot. Still, whenever he'd started to get off the straight and narrow path, he'd returned to God again—until the broken path on earth had led him to eternity. Hopefully, eternity with God.

Two unread messages from Hannah remained, but with the heaviness on Ben's chest, he couldn't read them tonight.

"God, I wish I could know that he was in heaven with You." Ben whispered the words spilling out through trembling lips. "Since I can't go back and redeem my mistake, I wish there was just some way I could believe that Jason was in heaven, to smooth a balm over my heart."

At that moment, a melody filled Ben's mind, and with the melody came the words.

As you walked away, I welcomed him into My arms. My mercy over him is love.

Even more than the shock of the text message from Hannah, the impact of the words playing through his mind hit Ben's heart. The cell phone felt heavy in his pocket, as if it weighed as much as the stones around his fireplace. And he almost wanted to push the phrase from his mind. But it came again.

As you walked away, I welcomed him into My arms. My mercy over him is love.

Ben's eyes burned, and his throat grew thick and

dry. He shuffled into his dark room, but instead of turning on the light, he flung himself across the bed and the quilt Marianna had made for him. The quilt she'd given him last fall, even though she'd thought of marrying another at the time. The quilt had reminded him to pray for her. The quilt urged him not to give up hope and to believe God had a plan for him, even though his past choices had caused pain, darkness, and death.

As you walked away, I welcomed him into My arms. My mercy over him is love.

"But I'm getting married," he croaked into the darkness. His words did little to penetrate the silence of his cabin. Only the shuffling of the wind on the plastic over the addition alerted him that he was still breathing and hadn't slipped into the dark abyss of depression that he'd once known. Where life seemed to be happening around him but he wasn't a part of it.

I'm getting married, and Jason never had the chance. Ben pressed his eyes tight, knowing he couldn't tell Marianna about this either. He'd just have to do his best to figure out the pain and the paparazzi on his own.

Chapter Ten

WEDNESDAY, JUNE 28, WEST KOOTENAI, MONTANA

The sounds of boys playing filtered into the second-story window—Ellie's window—waking Marianna from a deep sleep. She rubbed her eyes and yawned, and then she sat up, noting the thin ribbons of light trying to creep around the edge of Ellie's blackout curtains. Dat had put them up when Ellie started rising with the sun. Dawn came early during Montana summers since they were so far north. Marianna rubbed her neck, feeling a crick, and then reached over and opened the curtain with a tug, allowing light to spill in.

Last night Ellie had begged Marianna to read her stories before bed. Marianna had fallen asleep in the upstairs bedroom, curled next to her little sister's side.

She tried to slide out of the bed, hoping not to wake Ellie, and noticed that Trapper was curled up on the rug in the middle of the room.

Marianna leaned over and petted her dog. "You didn't plan on a sleepover, did you?" She chuckled. "Me either, and I'm too big to fit well in Ellie's bed. Especially with Ellie in it." Still, it didn't matter. Nothing could sink her mood. Ben would be home today. Ben.

With a smile, she moved to the window to peer down at her brothers chopping wood, feeding the animals, and mucking the stalls loudly with lots of gusto. They deserved this life—to be boys who could be loud and boisterous without the neighbors raising an eyebrow or presenting an opinion on how well they went about their work.

If ever a place was created for boys, it was Montana. The creeks and beaver ponds, fishing, building forts, climbing trees. More than that, the privacy—not living according to the judgments of the community every single minute.

As she watched, Josiah rushed up to the porch, carrying a stick. He darted behind one of the porch posts. Then he lifted it up like a bow and pretended to pull back a string.

Josiah shot an invisible arrow toward Charlie, who ran with the slightest limp due to the severe burns he'd received the previous year. Charlie feigned being hit and then stumbled back into the barn where his chores still awaited.

Ellie still snored softly as Marianna slid on her robe and then hurried downstairs. She hadn't planned on sleeping in—slacking on helping Mem prepare breakfast. She wanted to make sure that she could help her mother as much as possible before moving out in a few months.

When she got downstairs, she saw that the boys had already eaten. Mem was sitting in a living room chair, nursing Joy beside the hearth where a small fire burned. Even though it was June, the morning was nippy enough to need warmth.

Dat sat alone at the table that still had remnants of the morning's breakfast. Small gobs of oatmeal clung to the sides of one of Mem's large crockery bowls. A jar of honey and a bowl of raisins sat next to the bowl. Splatters of honey covered the table. It was clear where the boys had sat, eaten, and then carried off their bowls to the sink when they were through.

Dat glanced up as she entered the room. His Bible was open in front of him on the table. Marianna had come to expect and appreciate the peace on his face.

She delivered a sheepish smile. "Morning."

"Good mornin'. I suppose those blackout curtains we put in Ellie's room worked for you too."

She nodded and shrugged. "Ja, believe so. I can't remember the last time I slept in like that."

"Looks like you needed it."

"Ja, well, I told Annie I'd come in and work for lunch and dinner today. It was nice sleeping in. And..."

Marianna raised up on her tiptoes. "And Ben should be home tonight."

"Then take the rest of the morning for yourself." Mem placed Joy on her shoulder to burp her. Joy with her plump legs and round, unblinking eyes. Joy reminded them to slow down and enjoy the morning instead of hurrying through the day.

Mem smiled at the babbling baby and then looked again at Marianna. "Dat and Ike are waiting for some supplies to come in before they head up to their worksite." She looked at Dat. "You can help me clean up the dishes this morning, can't you, Abe?"

Dat grimaced and scratched his cheek, and Marianna saw the silent conversation pass between their gazes.

You would have never asked me such a thing in Indiana, his gaze seemed to tell her.

And this is not Indiana that you brought me to, remember? her wide-eyed glance and peaked eyebrows responded.

Their playfulness brought a lightness to Marianna's soul. "If that's the case, I think I'll walk down to the pond. There's so much going on. I just need time to think."

Mem's bright eyes fixed on Marianna. Compassion filled her face. "Go to the pond. You have a lot to think about, pray about."

Marianna didn't have to be told twice. She dressed quickly and headed to her favorite spot, not far behind her parents' home.

The large pool of water glimmered in the morning light. A curved dome of sticks and branches, mud and stones, formed a beaver dam that sat near the center of the oval of water. Floating lily pads and water lilies polka-dotted the water. Stripes of tall grass swayed around the water's edge. Marianna walked through the wildflowers and knee-high weeds toward her favorite fallen log that made the perfect bench. The smell of rotten eggs grew as she neared the pond. It wasn't enough to keep her away, but she wrinkled her nose.

As she sat, Marianna wrapped her arms around herself, trying to hold down her excitement. Ben would be home tonight. Last night she had dreamed that he had been singing outside their cabin. In her dream, he had believed the cabin was all right for her but not for him. That he had to stay outside. Of all things to dream.

She bowed her head to pray, and the sound of footsteps caused the hair on the back of her neck to stand. Had one of her brothers followed her? No. The sound was too heavy to be one of the boys.

Her eyes shot open, and she was almost afraid to turn. She knew bears were out, foraging with gusto after spring had come so late and everything had taken longer to grow and bloom. If she didn't turn and acknowledge the bear, would it rumble right past her? Goosebumps rose on Marianna's arms.

Then with the crunching of footsteps came a soft whistle. Her heart leaped as she recognized the tune.

Marianna's heart doubled its beat, and she stood and turned. Her hand flew to her mouth. "Ben?"

She took two steps toward him, and Ben made up the space between them. A happy cry escaped Marianna's lips as Ben lifted her and swung her around in a slow circle.

"Oh, Marianna, I'm so glad to be home. I missed you. I can't tell you how much."

Tears filled Marianna's eyes as all the emotions she'd been damming up threatened to break through. She attempted to speak—to tell him how much she loved him and was so thankful to see him—but the softest sniffle broke through.

Ben pulled his head back slightly. Surprise registered in his blue eyes. "Oh, sweetheart. Is everything all right?" He lowered her to the ground. Ben leaned down to kiss her, and it wasn't a simple kiss. Their lips touched, and then the kiss deepened, fuller, firmer. Emotions within her caused warmth to move outward from the center of her chest, and Marianna relaxed in his hold. Her arms wrapped around him. Her fingers entwined at the base of his neck.

His lips were tender as he lingered, then he drew away by small degrees, as if he were afraid she'd slip away.

As soon as his lips pulled back, he lifted his chin and tugged her body tight against him, as if attempting to protect her from whatever worries and fears she'd faced while he'd been away.

Marianna allowed herself to be pulled in, nestling

against his chest. She lost herself in the scent of the skin of his neck, the warmth of his body, the sound of his breath, and the whispered laughter that escaped from his lips. "I'm sorry. I should have let you answer that question." His husky voice was filled with desire. His breath was warm on her ear.

They'd shared many kisses before but never like that. Was it his time away that made the longing deeper? Perhaps, but from the way Ben still held her tight, there seemed to be more. She pressed her lips together, preparing to ask, but he beat her to it.

"So, let me try this again. Is everything okay?" He kissed her above the temple with those words.

She pulled back slightly, peering up at him. "I missed you something terrible." She hoped he wouldn't think she didn't appreciate his work or how he cared for her. "It's just that now that I know we're going to be married, it's so hard not to have you here. I love being with you, Ben. I love time with you. I love seeing your smile. Things don't seem right when you're away."

One of his hands reached up, his fingers brushing across her cheek. Ben bent his head down so their foreheads touched. "I know what you mean. Every day I thought of you. I thought of being back here. I thought of our wedding day. Time can't go quick enough."

His words were genuine, filled with hope and joy. Yet Marianna saw something different in his gaze.

There was a lost look there and an uncertainty she didn't expect.

"I'm fine, especially now that you're here. But what about you?" She stepped back even more to get a clearer look at his face. Her shoes stepped on dry pine needles and pine cones, and a breeze blew through the trees, bringing a sweet smell and pushing away the musky aroma of the pond. "Is there something going on?" Marianna bit her lip, and she hesitated. "It seems like something's wrong. Is everything okay?"

Ben's lips parted slightly. He took a step back and brushed his hair from his face. "It's just a different world out there, you know? Going from place to place, sharing my music. I like that part. But then there's the whole promotion aspect. On the one hand, I like that people care and want to know more about me and my life. On the other hand, I wish I could just come back to Montana and escape their interest. You know what I mean?" He grimaced as if there was more to say but he was holding back.

Marianna nodded even though she didn't know exactly what he meant. Although she had listened to him play in a smaller venue, she'd never attended one of his larger concerts. It seemed more straightforward to know Ben for who he was here, in Montana, with her.

He stood there silent, looking at the pond. Something was heavy on his thoughts. *At the right time, he'll tell me.* Ben was always good about expressing what was going on in his mind and heart.

Without a word, Marianne entwined her fingers in his and pulled gently, leading him to the log. She sat, and he sat next to her. She scooted a few inches closer and rested her head against his shoulder.

Ten minutes passed. Then fifteen. He seemed to be lost in his thoughts. It didn't matter. What mattered was they were finally together.

When Marianna remembered that she was supposed to work at the store for Annie, waitressing for the lunch crowd, she lifted her head to look at Ben.

"There's so much about the wedding I want to talk about. My mother has a lot of ideas. Annie has even more." A nervous laugh escaped her lips. "And I want to tell you about dress shopping too, although I don't want to give too much away. There will be family visiting from Indiana. My mother says my aunt Ida is coming. She keeps her eyes peeled on all the Amish in Shipshewana, and I wonder how she will handle Montana and the fact I'm not marrying an Amishman.

"Mom's closest sister, Betsy, is coming too with her children. I just can't imagine what they will think when they see these mountains. And after running around in these woods, I'm certain my cousins won't want to go home." Marianna's voice trailed off, and even though Ben appeared to be listening, she could tell his mind was still in another place. She forced herself to broaden her smile. "But that's not something we need to talk about right now. Perhaps since I have to work, you should try to get some rest. I can't even imagine how hard it is with all your travel."

"The travel's not too bad. You don't need to worry about me." Yet with his words, Ben's brow furrowed.

"If it's not the travel, did I do something wrong? Maybe I shouldn't have called the other day. I'm sorry to have interrupted your meeting."

Ben's hands reached for hers. He grasped them and rubbed his fingertips along the back of her hands. "No, Marianna. It's not that. I'm so sorry if I seem lost in my thoughts. I'm here if you want someone to listen."

She glanced down at his watch, noting the time. "I do have to go in and work for Annie today. Things are always busier during the beautiful Montana summer days. Maybe we can talk later? Unless you want to tell me now." Silence followed then, and she could tell from the look on Ben's face he did have something to say.

Ben cleared his throat. "Jason's been on my mind a lot." Just saying the name caused Ben's face to fall.

"Your friend who...died?"

Sadness turned down his lips, and her heart ached, knowing how many years Ben had lived with this burden.

"He was a year younger than me, which would have made him twenty-seven. He'd most likely be married by now. Maybe even have a baby on the way."

"And thoughts about our wedding make you think of him?" She struggled to understand.

"I suppose, although it might not make sense." Ben shrugged. "It's just that he'll never get one, you know?"

It had been Jason's death that had led Ben to leave behind his band and music to come to Montana. He'd come to hide, but God found him here—or at least that's what Ben had always told her. They'd found each other here too. But were they taking things too fast? Was that also part of Ben's regrets?

"There's something else I wanted to talk to you about. Well, actually, more than one thing, but we'll start with one."

More than one thing? Lots of problems surrounding their wedding, their marriage? If she was counting on anyone to see this wedding as a blessing and not a problem, it was Ben.

Yet if even the man she was going to marry had worries, maybe it was a sign that things weren't as happy or joyful as she'd imagined. *Perhaps I'm the only one who's been disillusioned all along.*

Marianna winced, and her toes tapped on the ground.

"I'm bringing this up because it's something timely. There was a voicemail on my phone when I finally checked my messages this morning."

"Ja, go ahead."

"I assume we're going to be married by the pastor of my church?" His voice lifted in a question.

"Ja. An Amish minister would have no part in a marriage like ours." She bit down on her bottom lip.

"Pastor Phil left a message and wants to meet with us." Ben released her hands and rubbed the back of his neck as if to ease a kink.

"Is there a problem?"

"Lots of couples go through something called premarital counseling. He doesn't do that, but he does want to talk to us and hear our ideas about marriage."

Marianna's knees trembled again, and weight grew in the pit of her stomach. "Will he tell us if he thinks we shouldn't get married?"

"I don't think it's anything like that. More like expectations about the future—where we will live, our ideas on children, our faith."

Marianna pressed her fingertips to her temples, feeling an ache come on. "I didn't know there was such a thing as this. Everyone had the same idea of marriage in the community I grew up in. Of the husband's role and the wife's. Having all the children the Lord gifted them with. Being part of the same community and church. Our churches consisted of the families who lived closest to us. There was nothing to discuss."

"And outside the Amish, there are many types of churches and styles. There are lots of choices of where to live, of the number of kids. And about careers—specifically what our lives will look like concerning my career." Ben kept his voice gentle. Still, the tension building within Marianna strained around her shoulders and chest like a cinch pulled tight inch by inch.

"There are so many things to think about." Her words released in a whisper. "So many choices. I didn't realize how much comfort one can get in understanding one's exact role and tasks at any moment."

Ben rubbed the back of his neck. "It's hard, I know."

Overhead, a birdsong filled the air, but other than the sweet song, the woods suddenly seemed like a dark and cold place.

"I've been thinking about our wedding, too, and I feel pulled in different directions. Mem wants one thing, and Annie has ideas for something else. Neither is unrealistic or outrageous. But the more I think about disappointing either of them, the more I believe that we can just skip so much of the fuss. Let's just do something simple. It's our wedding, and the most important thing is that we'll be committing our lives to each other, right?" She presented what she hoped was a reassuring smile.

"Simple?" He rubbed his brow and released a heavy sigh. "If you're marrying me, there might not be anything simple about it."

Ben's face fell, and panic clawed at Marianna's chest. Something was going on. Ben was always the one who shared his thoughts and feelings. But here he was, holding back.

The pounding of her heart propelled Marianna to her feet. She turned to face him, even as it took every ounce of control to hold back her tears. "Of course, if you still want to get married?"

"Of course I want to get married, but we can discuss it later. It's just that tomorrow is the anniversary of Jason's death." Ben rubbed his eyes and then his brow. "I didn't mean to ruin our time together, but I just can't talk about this now." His chin quivered, and his voice cracked.

"Tomorrow is the anniversary of Jason's death?" Pain scratched the back of her throat to see the empty look in his gaze. Dark circles ringed his eyes too. "Oh, I'm so sorry. I didn't realize." Taking a step closer, Marianna took his hand and squeezed.

He wiped his eyes with the back of his free hand. "It doesn't seem right, does it, that I've found an amazing woman who loves me, and I'm getting married. I'm sure it hurts his family knowing that."

"You know God has forgiven you, right? And while it's hard to forgive yourself, you can't keep looking back. Like I read in *The Budget* once, 'Regrets over yesterday and the fear of tomorrow are twin thieves that rob us of the moment.' We're finally together, Ben. We have this moment together. We need to trust God and not let regrets or fear—"

"But what if I'm about to mess everything up again?" he interrupted, pulling his hand from hers. "Every reporter and podcaster wanted to know about the wedding. What if they don't let it drop? People in these parts want their privacy. And surely you wouldn't want someone following you around with cameras on you."

"Of course I don't. I hate the thought of that. I'm proud of you. I really am." She shivered. "But you know that world, well, it's not for me."

"Don't you understand, Mari? Accepting me is accepting that world. My music is a way I care for my fans. And the concerts… I was just hoping—"

"You're not thinking I should travel with you? I—I can't do that."

Pain flashed through Ben's eyes, and then he quickly looked away. She took a step back, and he turned his back to her.

"You know, maybe this is a wake-up call." Ben's voice was low, flat. "You have a lot of worries about the wedding. And I have a lot of worries about *after* the wedding. Maybe I'm not letting future fears rob us. Maybe I'm just being realistic. I feel called to make music and share it, yet if you're not even willing to think about coming on the road with me…maybe we should just put things on hold until we can figure this all out."

Maybe we should just put things on hold? He'd just come home, and for the past few weeks, all she'd been able to think about was them being together. It was hard to suck in a breath. This wasn't the homecoming she'd expected.

Ben turned slowly, and his eyes focused on hers. Sadness filled his gaze. "I'm sorry. Before I saw you today, I wanted to shake off these regrets and worries. But, if I'm going to be truthful, that date on the calendar haunts me." He opened his mouth as if he wanted to tell her more and then closed it again.

She crossed her arms over her chest, pulling them in close. If she stayed around any longer, she'd be late. Surely Annie would understand, but would sticking around do any good? Or would it just make things worse?

Ben reached for her hands, and she placed hers into his. With a sweet tenderness, Ben pulled her hands to his lips, softly kissing the back of her fingers. She waited for him to comfort her worries and tell her everything would be okay. Instead, he nodded in the direction of her parents' house. "I parked my truck at your house. I'd be happy to give you a ride to work."

"Yes, of course. Thank you." What else could she say?

Chapter Eleven

WEDNESDAY, JUNE 28, WEST KOOTENAI, MONTANA

Marianna tied on her apron in Annie's office. She took a deep breath, willing her nerves to calm. *Please let Annie be busy, real busy.* She didn't know if she could put up with her friend's large smile and bubbly attitude today. Or any more wedding ideas.

I can't believe this is happening. Is our wedding really on hold? I'm not soon going to be Mrs. Ben Stone?

Yet when Annie emerged from the kitchen, Marianna had just made it to the dining room area of Kootenai Kraft and Grocery. Annie's smile was as welcoming as the two slices of apple pie she carried. Marianna didn't want to feel welcomed. She didn't want to feel a part of this community. All she wanted was to escape to her place near the pond *alone*. To have time to think and to pray.

Annie's long blonde ponytail rested across the front of her shoulder. "I have to run to Kalispell tomorrow. There was a message on my phone that the alterations are done on your dress. If you'd like, I can take you down for the final fitting."

"Final fitting? So soon? It's only been four days. The shop owner said it could take up to three weeks. And we don't even know where we'll have the wedding yet." Or if they were going to have a wedding at all. She swallowed down her emotions and tried to hide her trembling hands.

Annie spun, facing Marianna. "Whoa, I didn't mean to stress you out. I simply thought that you'd be happy to know it's done. You know, mark something off your list and not worry about getting to Kalispell at a different time."

"Yes, of course. That makes sense." Marianna reached up to fiddle with her kapp string before she remembered that she wasn't wearing a kapp—and wouldn't ever wear a kapp again.

Annie's eyes searched Marianna's face, and her forehead scrunched up in worry. "Hold on. Stay right here. Let me deliver this pie." She motioned to the nearest booth against the wall, and Marianna obediently sat there.

Wonderful aromas drifted from the kitchen. It smelled like brewing coffee and cinnamon rolls. How often had Marianna worked in that kitchen and wondered whether to stay in Montana or return to Indiana? About whether to dare to open her heart to Ben or to stay with the safe bet of Aaron. Yet after what she'd learned about Aaron, she'd discovered he wasn't the safe bet. Not only had he proven unfaithful to her, but he'd also fathered a child with Naomi and tried to act as if nothing had happened. No thanks to Aaron, baby Samuel had a wonderful father in her brother Levi.

After delivering the pie and checking on the other customers, Annie slid onto the wooden bench across from Marianna. "I have to ask, is everything okay?"

Marianna traced the woodgrain pattern on the table with her finger. "Oh, Annie. How do I know I'm doing the right thing? What if I'm making the wrong decision? What if I'm missing something...and I will end up hurt again?"

"Missing something? Is there something I should know? Has Ben done something to hurt you?"

"No, not Ben. Aaron."

"Aaron? Why are you thinking of Aaron? And what does he have to do with Ben?"

"Everything, don't you see?" Marianna reached for a paper napkin, folded it, and unfolded it again. "I thought I knew Aaron, really knew him. I was ready to give him my heart only to discover that I didn't know him."

"But Ben is not Aaron."

"Yes, but what if I'm missing something? This is a lifelong decision."

Annie nodded, yet questions still filled her gaze. "But you already made the decision to leave the Amish, yes? Or did you leave for Ben?"

"I left because I realized that God did not require me to be Amish to have a relationship with Him. In fact, I discovered He has more in store for us than we imagine."

"So, things will work out either with Ben or without Ben?"

Heat ringed Marianna's neck, and she felt it hard to breathe. "Ja, but I don't want to imagine life without Ben." The words rushed out. "I'm just scared that he doesn't feel the same."

Annie opened her mouth but closed it again. She rose, poured two cups of coffee, and returned with them, yet neither took a sip. Instead, Marianna wrapped her hands around her mug, letting the warmth seep in.

"I know people talk about getting cold feet, but I never thought it would happen to me. And then there's my mother and her friends. No one knows how to act or what to say, but Mem has ideas too. I know my mem has been waiting for years to have a daughter married..." Marianna let her voice trail off.

"It sounds like you don't feel in control of your wedding. No wonder the worries have started to build. Have you talked to Ben about it?"

"A little, but that's another problem. Something is going on. I'm not sure what. Maybe Ben's having second thoughts? Maybe we should wait? Maybe I should tell Mem not to have the announcement of our wedding published."

"It sounds like you have some thinking to do. And praying."

"Yes. And after work, I know just where to go." Marianna took a sip of her coffee and bounced her knee. She needed to go back to the beaver pond. To think. To pray.

"I'll only need you for lunch today, if you don't mind. Jenny asked if I could give her more hours. Kenzie will start school in the fall, and Jenny needs to save up for school clothes."

Jenny was one of Marianna's coworkers and a single mom to a beautiful little girl. "Thank you, Annie, for the way you care for all of us."

Annie pointed at her. "You're done at two o'clock, but if you go to the pond, don't forget the bear spray."

Marianna nodded. "Bears and fires in the summer." She chuckled. "Just a few dangerous things in these parts."

"Although, we might have fires sooner this year than most. We didn't get as much snowpack this summer. It's dry out there. They're predicting things could be bad."

"Let's hope not. Summer in Montana is my favorite." She rose and gave Annie a hug. "Thank you for listening. It helps to get everything out instead of letting my worries circulate in my head."

The lunch crowd was steady, and Marianna served plate after plate of the lunch special of a chicken salad sandwich with homemade potato salad and a slice of apple pie. Of course, every local also had to ask about how the wedding details were coming. She smiled and told each person that the planning would begin in earnest now that Ben was back home. She only hoped she was telling the truth.

When her shift was over, Marianna tucked Annie's bear spray into her satchel and headed again to the beaver pond—the place she felt closest to God.

The dirt road to her house had been sprinkled with gravel to keep down the dust, and Marianna's tennis shoes crunched on the rocks as she walked. Then near her parents' house, the small pathway opened up. This morning the path to the pond had seemed bright with promise. But now, the ache of her conversation with Ben grew with each step.

When Marianna made it to the log she'd sat on with Ben just hours before, her body seemed to wilt. "Oh Lord, help. What am I going to do?"

~

Wednesday, June 28, Kalispell, Montana

Less than twenty-four hours after getting home, Ben found himself leaving again. After dropping Marianna at work, he couldn't imagine returning to his cabin and sitting alone with his thoughts. He'd told Marianna that he needed time to think. And he'd found himself driving past the turnoff to his house and making his way down the winding road toward Kalispell. Before he knew it, he arrived at Roy's door.

Thankfully, his manager was at home. And now that Ben sat there, he knew why he was here. He needed Roy's advice. Roy had discovered him when his band played at coffeehouses and cafés. And when Ben had escaped to Montana, Roy had not only found him but built a retreat for himself in the area. Roy had picked out the songs that became Ben's hits. Roy had a way of knowing what mattered and what didn't and how to pull Ben up from the muck. Ben needed that now.

He settled into his favorite spot on Roy's leather couch in his media room. The room smelled of wood polish and the orchids from the fresh-cut bouquet on the table next to him. Soft music played over the sound system. Tall windows looked out onto a manicured lawn and the Rockies beyond. Every room of Roy's house was designed to be a place of retreat from his busy Los Angeles lifestyle. Still, at this moment, Ben felt anything but peaceful.

The click of Roy's leather shoes sounded as he crossed the polished wood floor. He handed Ben a soda and settled into the high-backed upholstered chair across from Ben. Roy's eyes fixed on him—a cue for Ben to spill his guts.

Ben squeezed his eyes shut and then opened them again. "I need your help."

"My help?"

"For the wedding." Yet even as Ben said the words, they sounded flat. He should have been excited that he was getting married soon. Yet why should he get to marry the woman of his dreams—someone kind, pure, and loving—when his best friend would never get that chance?

He also had to figure out what to do with the reporters planning to invade West Kootenai the weekend of their wedding. It wasn't a big place. Even outsiders could quickly figure out where the wedding was. In the meantime, he couldn't let the worries and the ache keep him from following through with the best decision he could ever make.

"We need to figure out what to do about these reporters."

Roy leaned forward. "Is that what's really bothering you?"

Ben rubbed his brow. "Why don't we start with that?"

"Yeah, leave it to you to find the one woman to marry who doesn't want everything popularity and fame dole out."

"Which is exactly why I want to marry her." He ran his hand through his hair, wishing away the ache in his heart and hoping Roy wouldn't pick up on it.

"What do you need help with?"

Ben sat up straighter as he eyed the view of Roy's expansive backyard and the view beyond. "Maybe we could have the wedding here. Your property is large enough. It's fenced, and you have a gated entry. We could hire security. And rent some large tents for your backyard to keep anyone who tries to get a drone or a plane overhead from getting any good shots."

Roy held his finger up to his lips. "There's only one problem. Everyone Marianna invites will be coming by horse and buggy. It's at least a day's buggy ride from the mountains. Not to mention I don't really have stables around here."

"Or they'd hire a driver." Ben chuckled. "I still have to talk to Marianna about it, but I think we'd like to keep it small. Just her and me, our families, and a few close friends." His stomach knotted, knowing he wasn't sharing the whole truth, especially the fact he'd told Marianna that he wanted to put the wedding on hold.

"And still, you know how large Amish families are, correct?"

"We'll limit it to just immediate family and hire drivers to bring them down the mountain. I'm sure Marianna will agree it'll be better than trying to keep the media away from any location we choose in West Kootenai."

"Yes, of course, but I don't think it will happen like that."

"What do you mean?"

"First, a woman's idea of a small wedding differs from a man's. And second, she has a mother—an Amish mother—who I assure you will have a say about who's invited." He swept his hand around the room. "And I don't think this is really the Amish style."

Ben nodded. "But you'll think about it?"

"I don't need to think about it. If that's what the two of you decide...it's yours." Roy leaned forward, resting his hands on his knees as he studied Ben. "Just promise me one thing—you won't bring it up until you give her a chance to think things through. Take it from someone who's learned the hard way. Men like to sweep in and find solutions when women just want someone to talk to. Give her a chance to think about what she really wants. Then, if she doesn't have an answer in a few weeks, ask her to consider my place. By then, Marianna will have had a chance to consider what matters. And you will have too."

~

Thursday, June 29, West Kootenai, Montana

Ike blew out as he eyed the finished roof joists on Ben's cabin. Well, finished for now. He knew that Ben and Marianna would probably have a few babies within a few years, and then they'd want to add on. The roofers would be up next week, which meant his work here was done. Ike liked how the place had turned out—perfect for a newly married couple. Something he'd like to replicate someday if things ever changed and he left behind his old bachelor cabin.

The front door opened up to a living room and kitchen area. The open cabinets were custom-made by

Ben, and the wood floors had been planed by the Log Works near the Kraft and Grocery. The floor-to-ceiling windows in the living room, which were a surprise for Marianna, were a new addition. They provided the perfect view of a small meadow, pine trees, and the peaks of the mountaintops. The second surprise was the river rock fireplace with the pine mantel that Abe had lovingly worked on, as only a father would for his daughter.

Ike sidled up to his brother and pulled his hat from his head, wiping his brow as they studied the finished mantel. "It turned out nice, didn't it? You did a great job."

Abe grinned. "You're my brother—you have to say that."

"Ja, well, I'm Amish. I can't lie."

"Can't?"

"Won't."

Ben approached and handed them each a glass jar with iced tea. Ike took a long drink and eyed his friend. Ben was usually happy-go-lucky. Ben looked on the bright side of life, but not lately. Ever since he'd gotten home from his most recent trip, it was clear that something was wrong.

Come to think of it, Abe had mentioned that Marianna was distant and aloof too. Ike just hoped these two young folks weren't going to do something foolish like call off their wedding because planning a wedding—or their lives—wasn't as easy as they'd expected.

If Ike could go back in time, he'd tell himself one

thing: Don't be so concerned about the picture looking different than he'd hoped, because love was worth it. He'd made those mistakes, and now he found himself still a bachelor when almost everyone his age was married with a dozen kids.

Ben went to the kitchen, returned with his own glass of iced tea, and settled down into one of his living room chairs. He was quiet, too quiet, and Ike didn't like it one bit. But what could he say that Ben would listen to? What advice could he give?

Instead of trying to figure that out, Ike smiled at his brother again. "I am serious, Abe. You did a beautiful job on this house. It will be hard to move on to another."

Abe shook his head, and his eyes sparkled with mischief that Ike had known since childhood. "Oh, we're not doing another house. Not right away. We're taking a break for a while. I'd like you to take Ben and me to Bob Marshall. Maybe for a week. Will next week work?"

The Bob Marshall? Over a million acres of wilderness, and Abe talked as if he were asking for a buggy ride down to Lake Koocanusa.

"We're just going up to Bob and leaving everyone behind?" Ike pointed to Ben. "What do you think of this idea?"

"Well, I just got home..." Ben's voice trailed off. But did Ike see hope in Ben's eyes? Maybe he liked the idea of getting away and having space to think. "More than that, is it safe?"

"Safe? I've worked for an outfitter every summer for the last five years. I've learned all the ropes." Ike smirked. "Or at least most of them."

"That makes me feel better," Ben said.

"So, what's the point of this, Abe?" Ike asked. "You're a man of responsibilities."

Abe stroked his beard. "Would you believe me if I told you God was calling us to the wilderness?"

Ben set his iced tea on the side table and crossed his arms over his chest. "Calling you?"

"Calling us." Abe nodded as if agreeing with himself. "Sometimes the only way we can hear God's voice, to get our answer, is to get away from all the other noise."

"And what's the question?" Ike dared to ask.

"The question is whether the two of you will let go of that pain from the past and open up your hearts to God's love for you."

The sun streaming in through the tall windows was warming the place. The way it flowed around Abe, framing him in a golden glow, it was almost as if God was giving His approval.

Ben unbuttoned his shirt sleeves and rolled them to his elbows. "I know God loves me. That's the one thing I do know."

"Ne, I'm not talking about the love God has for you, but the love He has given through the women He's put into your lives." Abe spoke slowly and gently.

Ike fiddled with the top button of his shirt as if suddenly finding it hard to breathe. "I know you're not talking about me. My heart is like a secondhand store. Nothing but cast-off expectations and discarded hope." It was easy for his brother to say such things, married for nearly thirty years. Yet a glimmer of hope warmed Ike's chest. A hope he hadn't dared to allow in lately.

"That's what you say, but I think God has other ideas, if you're willing to listen."

Ike nodded once, and Abe chuckled. Then Abe lifted his face to the wood-paneled ceiling. "Lord, You'll have to be the One to do the talking here. I doubt I can get through my brother's thick skull that learning to love a good woman is worth it."

Ike couldn't help but chuckle at that. But come to think of it, it wasn't a bad idea to head out to the Bob Marshall for a week or so.

Then there was Ben. Ike glanced in his direction. As much as he appreciated the young man and had even chosen Ben over Aaron for his niece, something made Ike question this union. Ben loved God and Marianna, but something was holding Ben back like a beaver dam blocking a wide, expansive river. Although Ben continued to take steps forward to his marriage with Marianna, there was hesitation in his gaze.

Abe must have realized it too.

"I was reading in my Bible this morning," Abe said, "and I just knew this is what we are supposed to do. I read in Mark's book, 'Come away by yourselves to a desolate place and rest a while.' So, what do you think?"

When Ben didn't give a response, Abe turned to Ike. "When I was still back in Indiana, you wrote to me many times about your adventures in the wilderness. I pictured the beauty and the solitude. With none of the world's distractions, we'll have space to listen to God's still, small voice. We'll have time to talk, really talk, and pray."

Excitement stirred within Ike over his brother's words. "You know, I've always wanted to go into the Bob on a shorter trip without a trail of packhorses following behind." Ike reached over and grasped Ben's shoulder. "And I'd say this one needs a bit of adventure before he ties the knot." He chuckled. "As our mem used to say, 'Marriage may be made in heaven, but man is responsible for the upkeep.' Not that it's a problem, but it's work. I can see that even from a distance. Ja, I say we do it. Let's go."

Chapter Twelve

Friday, June 30, West Kootenai, Montana

On most dirt roads in West Kootenai, one typically found a house or two every mile. Yet when one drove past the Kraft and Grocery, they soon found themselves in bachelor territory, with Ike's cabin to the left of the road and the bachelor cabins on the right.

Ben chuckled, thinking how guys were in dorm rooms or the Montana woods. Instead of gathering for frat parties, the bachelors around West Kootenai spent their evenings digging holes to erect log beams to practice axe throwing, or skinning the latest critters they'd caught.

This afternoon it seemed at least a half dozen young bachelors had crossed the dirt road, curious about what Ike was up to. Ben guessed it wasn't every day that someone they knew was planning a pack trip into the Bob Marshall. And after looking at the weather reports, they'd decided to leave the next day, on Saturday morning. That would give them three days of travel into the wilderness, a day to stay in the mountains, and three days back before storms swept down from Canada.

Yesterday Ben had stopped by to see Marianna and tell her about their trip, but his future father-in-law had done most of the talking. Marianna hadn't seemed too disappointed that he'd be leaving again after just getting back. Instead, she'd seemed lost in her thoughts, and he'd promised to stop by again today after he helped her uncle pack things up in preparation for their trip.

Ben knew things were getting serious when he arrived at Ike's place to find two large canvases rolled up and piles of supplies off to the side. He parked his truck and climbed out, then walked to the tall double barn doors.

Ike's place couldn't be more opposite than the bachelor cabins across the road. While random animal pelts were nailed on the log walls of the bachelor cabins, the exterior walls of Ike's cabin and barn were pristine.

"Ike around?" he asked the group of young men around the barn.

One of them pointed to the barn.

"He just went inside to grab a few more things," another of the guys, with black hair, called out.

Their buddy, who looked a few inches shorter and twenty pounds heavier, adjusted his hat over his red hair and eyed Ben. "And how did you luck out being the one who gets to go on this trip?"

Ben knew his ripped skinny jeans and fitted black T-shirt looked out of place among the Amish. "I suppose it's because I'm going to marry the daughter of the one who planned the trip." He didn't always dress this way up in West Kootenai, but he hadn't done much laundry with all the travel. This was what he'd found in his closet.

The redhead tucked his thumbs behind his suspenders. "So, does your fiancée have any sisters?"

"Oh, yes." Ben smiled brightly. "Ellie and Joy."

"Really?" His jaw dropped.

Ben reached over and patted his shoulder. "Yes, and they are four years old and going on one. It'll be a long wait."

The man's shoulders slumped, and the other bachelors chuckled. Stepping inside Ike's barn, Ben noted the smell of fresh hay. Hooks lined the interior walls, and on them hung Ike's tack. The bridles, leads, and halters had been cleaned, oiled, and looked as good as new. Other equipment, such as ropes, pitchforks, and brooms, each had their place. Even though Ike always seemed easygoing, Ben could tell he took pride in owning his things. He'd be in good hands. Going deep into the Bob Marshall wasn't for city boys like him—unless he picked the right friends to ride with.

Ben found Ike near the back of the barn, taking down lengths of rope. “Can I help?”

Ike handed Ben a coil of rope and took one himself. “Sure. You might as well know how everything’s best done too. In case somethin’ happens to me and you need to tie up the load on the mule. We’ll take the pack mule for supplies and take turns riding the horse.”

Ben didn’t mean to suck in a breath. “If something happens to you? I don’t like the sound of that.”

“Yeah, well, most trips go off without a hitch, but it’s always good to be prepared.”

Ben followed Ike outside and watched, noting how Ike was using this time to teach all the bachelors how to pack a load for the mule.

“The idea is to pack everything we need without putting too much weight on the mule.” Ike eyed the pile as if doing weight calculations in his mind. Ike’s horse, a beautiful Tennessee walker, whinnied from the corral as if he was getting excited about the adventure they’d be going on. The mule stood next to the horse, eyeing everyone with curiosity.

Another truck parked next to Ben’s, and he wasn’t surprised by who else showed up to watch Ike pack. Annie strode up and eyed one of the canvas tarps—manties. Ike spread the two manties flat and then arranged the gear along the diagonal of each one. The piles next to the manties had sleeping bags, clothes, food, cooking gear, and grain for the horse and mule, among other things.

"The items lying directly on the manties are against the mule. That's why I start with something soft like a tent or sleeping pad," Ike explained.

Ben, Annie, and the bachelors stood next to the corral and watched as Ike packed the two manties, folded them, tied them up, and weighed them. Amazingly, they were within four pounds of each other. Ben knew it must have taken a lot of trial and error over time to figure that out.

Annie smiled like a proud parent when he'd finished. "You did a mighty fine job, Ike. It seems you've been taught well."

"That's the easy part." He stood, blew out a breath, and placed a fist on each of his hips.

Ben replayed the steps in his mind. "Really, why?"

"The harder part is attaching everything to the pack mule once you get up the trailhead. You'll kill the mule if you don't fix the loads and the ropes. Each pack mule has 160 feet of rope on it. There's the manty rope, sling rope, and lead rope. One rope knotted up wrong can cause a load to shift and take the mule down a ravine."

The horse and the mule watched from the corral. Ben reached up and patted the top of the mule's head. He had the urge to stroke her long ears, but he refrained.

"So, do you know where you're going?" Annie asked.

"The Scapegoat Wilderness."

Annie eyed Ike. Then she turned to Ben and let her

gaze sweep over the bachelors. "I'm going to run to the store. I'll be right back."

She returned a little later with hot dogs and buns and gave them to the bachelors, who eagerly started a fire in the fire pit. The aroma caused Ben's stomach to churn. It seemed like the perfect afternoon with the laughter of the guys and the abundance of hot dogs. Yet even as he finished his third hot dog, Ben knew he needed to head out soon. He'd promised Marianna he'd stop by. And for the first time since he'd met her, he worried about where their conversation would go. Wondered if Marianna would have questions he couldn't answer about their wedding. If she had finally figured out that marrying him would bring too many challenges that she didn't want to face.

Yet, instead of leaving, Ben squatted by the fire next to Ike. "One horse for three people?" He chuckled. "Ike, it looks like you're walking."

The laughter of the others joined in.

Ike shook his head. "We'll take turns. It's a beautiful country either way. I promise you, you won't mind the walk."

When the hot dogs were finished, a group of the bachelors moved across the dirt road and returned with a hand-cranked ice cream machine. Ben's stomach fluttered with excitement as if he was a little kid again. He'd always loved watching ice cream being made, and he and his cousins would take turns turning the crank over and over at his grandparents' house. The young men seemed proud as they set up the ice cream churn on a stump in Ike's yard and added the ingredients.

"A little treat before you head off into the wilderness," the red-headed bachelor said, bringing Ben a small bowl. "Can't get this up there in the Bob Marshall."

"I don't know what you're talking about." Ike smirked. "If you can pack it on a mule, it can go up. I've been on a trip once when an ice-cream churn just like this was taken up to the Danaher Valley."

"I can beat that." Annie strode toward the fire and sat on a stump next to Ike. "I have a friend who hauled a piano up there. I never thought it possible until I saw how carefully he loaded the mule." She chuckled. "That's the thing about us old outfitters. If you think something can't be done, it's almost a dare."

"I was counting on that." Ike leaned over as if he wanted to give Annie a side hug but then straightened just before his arm wrapped around her shoulder. "I saw some items in the back of your truck. And I feel you headed out for more than hot dogs." He winked. "What did I forget?"

"You got what you need, I suppose. You know enough to get up there and back without much trouble." She smiled. "I've actually come to help Ben. This is his first time in the mountains, and I want him to be prepared." She shrugged. "Or maybe it's because I know he'll listen to me." She stood and eyed Ben as if testing to see if he would let her boss him around, and then she motioned to her truck.

"Of course I'll listen to you, Annie." He rose and followed her. "I've learned over the years that I need to listen when you talk."

Ike was right about Annie having a few things in the back of her truck. There was a backpack, some type of waist pack, and at least two dozen other items.

She picked up a small bag that looked as if it had something rolled inside. "I'm sending you my wickiup. It's a tarp that's rubberized on one side. It only weighs a couple of pounds, but I don't leave home without it. If something happens to your tent, you can set it up for a covering." She held up the bundle so he could see it better. "There are rings on this bag, which can be used to tie it to the saddle or your backpack."

"I just assumed we'd sleep under the stars."

Annie leveled a gaze at him. "This isn't camping in your backyard, Ben. We're talking about real wilderness, unlike many places in the US. The Bob is beautiful, but it's no picnic. It's big and wild, and honestly, there's no place I'd rather be."

Ben furrowed his brow. "That's surprising. You seem so content at the store."

"I love my store. I love the people, but it's an all-day, everyday thing. I don't regret moving up this way and setting down roots." She released a heavy sigh. "I just wish..." Annie shook her head. "Let's not get distracted. We're here to get you set up for your big adventure."

Annie watched as Ike loaded his many packs in the back of the truck with the trailer he'd borrowed for

Ben to drive tomorrow, and then she turned to Ben. "Do you have a backpack?"

"A small one. Just something I picked up from the sporting goods store."

"How about a waist pack?"

"Can't say I do."

Annie pointed at the packs in the bed of her truck. "That's what I thought, and that's why I brought these. I can't in good conscience send you out without being prepared."

She had him try on the large hiking backpack, adjusting it to his frame. And then she started adding items, explaining what each was for.

By the time Annie was done, the backpack bulged. "I seem to remember this." He chuckled. "The same thing happened when my mom packed me up to go to my first Boy Scout camp." He cast a crooked grin. "I think we forgot to pack the Pop-Tarts."

Annie didn't seem quite as amused. "No, we only packed things to keep you alive. You'll have to pack your own Pop-Tarts next time."

Then she started on his waist pack next. "Pretty much everything needs to stay in this bag for protection." She held up a large, clear Ziploc bag. "Everything needs to be kept dry, especially you. Getting wet means hypothermia. Be careful crossing rivers and creeks."

Annie added items to the Ziploc bag: a map, mittens, and a stocking cap. A small notepad and pencil.

"What's that for?" He pointed to the pad and pencil.

"It's great to have along to keep track of things you forgot. Or things you would like to have brought. That way, you can reflect on it for the next trip."

"And..."

Annie shrugged. "And you can guess. If you're in trouble, you can leave notes for someone who might be looking for you."

"Or write a song?" Ben started to hum.

"Yes, I suppose there's always that."

"Is there room for my cell phone in there?" he teased.

"You think there's cell service in those parts? Half of Montana doesn't have service, especially not the wilderness areas." Annie eyed him. "If you take it, you might be able to find a signal from a high peak, but I don't have a solar charger. Then again, I wouldn't bother. It'll probably be impossible to reach a peak if something happens."

"If something happens? You're the second person who's said that."

She eyed his ripped skinny jeans and fitted T-shirt. "You may be a rock star, but this is the wilderness, Ben. So much can go wrong, but at least you won't be unprepared. I saw Marianna in her dress, and I have to make sure you make it back so she can wear it." Annie nodded. "Yes, you're not gonna wanna miss that."

Chapter Thirteen

FRIDAY, JUNE 30, WEST KOOTENAI, MONTANA

All it took was Annie's mention of Marianna and her dress to snap Ben back to reality. He loved her, and more than anything, Ben wanted to see her walking down the aisle in the wedding dress she'd picked out.

As soon as Annie finished loading his waist pack, Ben said goodbye to Ike and to Abe, who'd just shown up. Then he headed out with promises to meet them bright and early in the morning and to make sure he did laundry before then so he didn't look like a rock star in ripped skinny jeans up on the trail.

Ben parked his truck in the driveway of the Sommers' home. Before he even got out, Marianna exited the door with a tentative look. As he approached, Marianna tried to hide her laughter as she noticed what he wore. "Well, Dat told me you were supposed to be packing over at Ike's, but it seems you perhaps were putting on a concert?"

He glanced down at his skinny jeans. "Don't tell me you don't like how my legs look in these?"

She pointed to the rips in the knees. "And don't tell me that you bought them that way. They look like they need some serious mending."

Ben took the front porch steps two at a time. Her smile and laughter made him forget what they'd been arguing about.

"There. It was worth wearing these jeans to see that smile." Ben swept Marianna into his arms. "I can't explain it, Mari, but from that first fifteen minutes of meeting you, I wanted to know you better. How you bossed that train attendant and nearly climbed into the train compartment for your missing box was amazing. And then how you cared for your young brothers and sister with such tenderness—you were beautiful, unlike any woman I'd met."

"Ja, well, I'm surprised you also didn't notice my anger for Dat bringing us to Montana. Although, it's hard to stay mad when one's gazing upon such beauty as the mountains and becoming curious about the handsome Englisch driver."

Ben stood straighter. "So you thought I was handsome—even from that first day?"

"I'd be lying to say I didn't." She leaned into him, resting her cheek on his chest with his arms wrapped around her.

"You know, holding you, I'm suddenly wondering why I agreed with your dat to go up into the Bob Marshall with him and Ike."

"Well, Dat's determined it's for a reason, and you know that says a lot. After years of never even reading a Bible for himself, Dat believes that God has a purpose."

"That's good, then, but I'm still going to miss you."

He tucked a finger under her chin, tilted up her face, and placed a soft kiss on her lips. "Just that I know you'll be waiting. That's all that matters." His voice was soft and husky.

They moved to the porch swing and sat side by side. Ben thought about telling her what Stacy Cannon had said—that the media were already planning to come to West Kootenai to invade their privacy and photograph their wedding. Still, he didn't want to ruin this moment. He'd talk to Marianna about it after he got back. Tonight he simply wanted to enjoy this beautiful woman by his side. Talk of the wedding could wait.

"You know, Ben, what we have is beautiful. Some people never get this. Sometimes I wonder why God chose me to have such a blessing. Just when I thought I was giving up everything by coming to Montana, God gave me you."

Marianna's words were like a gut punch. Ben sucked in a breath as the pain coursed through him.

He knew she meant well, but her words were exactly what he'd been trying to keep out of his mind.

Some people never got this.

Again, Jason's face came into his memories. Jason had always been the one to do everything right, until Ben had thought it would be funny to have some fun with him, to get him drunk... and then left him to die.

Beside him, Marianna kicked her legs to make the swing rock, and he suddenly felt horrible again. The words from Hannah's text replayed in his thoughts. *I don't understand how you can go on with life after you took my brother's. It's not fair that you get what my brother never got a chance to have.*

And Ben knew Hannah was right.

~

Friday, June 30, West Kootenai, Montana

The warm June day cooled quickly as the afternoon slipped into evening, but Marianna didn't want to go in. Not when she had Ben by her side. Not when she felt at peace with him again.

Part of her couldn't believe this was really happening. Ben loved her, and she'd dared to open her heart to him. They were to be married soon. The loving was easy. It was figuring out all the days to come that were harder, starting with the wedding.

"I know we made a date for September, but all the

opinions and talk about our wedding hurt my head." She pressed her fingertips to her temples. "Some days I think we should simply stand before a minister—you and me—yet I know doing that would hurt my mother's heart."

Marianna placed her cheek on his shoulder and continued to kick her feet to propel the swing, expecting Ben to chime in and say that sooner was better for him. Ben's playfulness was something she especially loved about him. But instead, he sat there silent, looking ahead as if she'd never spoken.

After a few uncomfortable minutes, Marianna lifted her cheek from his shoulder.

Ben shuffled his feet and turned to her frowning. "Listen, I think we need to take time and think about this. We don't have to stick to that date in September. You are right. We should choose another day."

Tension moved to Marianna's neck like a vise grip clamped down her hairline. "That's not what I said, Ben. You're putting words into my mouth."

"I'm trying to listen and understand what you really need." His voice lowered, and he released a frustrated sigh. "You grew up with weddings one way, and honestly, I still don't get what's important and what's not. But I do think we need to pick a different date. Why don't we both take some time and think about what matters, and then we can talk about it. I'd rather not talk about it anymore tonight, though. I was just enjoying our time together. I'm leaving for a week, remember?"

Marianna nodded, but deep down, she wondered

if it was an excuse. An uneasy feeling came over her. Had she done something wrong? Ben had been acting different since he'd returned from his last concert tour. Something had changed—he'd changed—and she couldn't figure out why.

"Ben." She spoke his name softly and waited. His head was lowered, and he fiddled with his hands, clenching and unclenching his fists as if he was trying to find relief from the tension she felt radiating off him.

"Ben," she repeated.

Finally, he looked up. His gaze was sad as he focused on hers.

"I need time to figure things out," he said. "I don't think you know what you're getting yourself into, Marianna. The wedding is just one thing. But these clothes, the concerts, my fans...there's this whole other part of me you don't know. There are other things..." His voice trailed off as if he were changing his mind about what he wanted to say. He sighed. "You've already had to make so many changes, and I think these details about the wedding are just the tip of the iceberg."

"What do you mean?"

"What I wanted most—to be known and to have my music hit the charts—is still part of me. Part of what I do. As much as I want us to enjoy a private life up here, it's not going to happen. And I'm not sure you're ready for all of it."

"All of what? Ben, you're not making any sense."

Marianna's mouth grew dry. She held her breath, expecting his frown to smooth and his tone to soften. She waited for him to explain that they'd face any challenges *together*.

Instead, he rose. "My life—the whole other part of me—well, I don't think you're ready for that. For you to accept that part of me, it'll bring too many changes...hurt too many people. And maybe all the burdens and regrets I carry around with me will also. I just need time to think."

Ben turned his back to her, tucking his hands into his jeans pockets. And as she looked at him—in his edgy musician clothes—suddenly Marianna was unsure if she knew him anymore. From the time she'd met Ben, Marianna had been drawn to him and he to her. Yet it was the Montana Ben she knew, not the rocker Ben. And while she still loved him, an invisible wall had been erected between them.

Marianna rose, too, and brushed the back of her skirt. "I suppose there's nothing else to talk about, then. I hope you have a safe trip. I believe my father is right—you do need time to get away and think."

Then, with determined steps, Marianna moved across the front porch and slipped inside the front door of her house. She paused at the door and listened, waiting to hear Ben's footsteps leaving the porch.

But deep down she hoped, more than anything, that he'd softly knock on the door and ask for one more kiss. Tell her that things would work out. Say that he'd made a mistake. Marianna wanted Ben to wrap her up in his arms and say that no matter what conflicts arose, he still wanted to marry her, but that didn't happen. Instead, she heard his footsteps and then the roar of the truck engine as he left.

How could things have changed so quickly? Something was going on with Ben. Marianna just wished she knew what. Hopefully he would find his answers in the mountains.

Because if he didn't, Marianna wasn't sure if this relationship would survive.

Chapter Fourteen

SATURDAY, JULY 1, WEST KOOTENAI, MONTANA

People thought about going into the Bob Marshall Wilderness to relax and connect with nature. Still, there was nothing relaxing about riding a horse over narrow mountain trails with sheer, gray slate cliffs that fell to deep ravines five hundred feet below.

As Ike awoke and the first rays of light stretched over the mountains, he wondered if heading into the wild as a guide was a good idea, especially with his brother and Ben. The Bob Marshall Wilderness was made up of more than 1.5 million acres, and if anyone spent time around outfitters, they'd hear a thing or two about what could go wrong.

He'd gone as a helper for five summers, but this

was the first time leading a group, even if it was just two men. Out of all the places he could take them, something inside said that Scapegoat was best. If one wanted a view, the vast stretch of the Chinese Wall was hard to beat. The bare summit stretched as far as the eye could see and never got old. And on the way up, wildflowers clinging to the tundra hillsides would distract from any discomfort.

After dressing and packing the rest of his things, Ike got the horse trailer ready. Abe was already walking toward the horse with the halter behind his back as Ike neared the corral. He now knew that having an older brother like Abe had been a blessing. Abe always rolled up his sleeves and got to work first. He was used to shouldering the responsibility.

As Ike watched, Abe reached Shadow and patted his neck, sliding a friendly hand toward his chest. Then in one smooth, graceful motion, Abe looped the lead rope around Shadow's neck and guided him to the horse trailer. Ike loaded Shadow in. They had just finished loading Flint, his mule, when Ben arrived carrying his backpack and waist pack with all the things that Annie had insisted he take.

The ride down to Ovando from West Kootenai took four hours, and Ben did a fine job driving the truck with the trailer. He'd learned the skill while driving for the Amish and others over the last four years.

Ben had been quiet during the drive, and Ike guessed he had a lot on his mind. He supposed that

Ben getting married in a few months could have that effect.

They'd left so early. The breakfast crowd was going as they grabbed a second breakfast of a cinnamon roll and hot coffee at the Stray Bullet restaurant in Ovando before heading up to the North Fork trail.

Ben followed the signs to the trailhead, and upon their arrival, Ike swung the door open just as the truck came to a stop. Since summer hadn't had the chance to warm up the mountains and not all the trails were yet cleared of snow, Ike wasn't surprised that there were no other vehicles in the parking lot.

Ike got out and smiled at Abe as he stretched. "This is it, brother. If God told you we must head into the wilderness, I can't imagine one finer than this."

Abe climbed from his center position in the truck seat and gazed up at the peaks, delivering a low whistle.

Ike chuckled. "That impresses you, does it? Just wait until we get started."

With expert efficiency, Abe didn't take long to saddle the horse. Then with Ben's help, Ike loaded their supplies onto the mule. This was it. They were headed into the wilderness for the adventure of a lifetime.

~

Saturday, July 1, West Kootenai, Montana

Marianna's mind was still on her conversation with Ben as she approached the Kootenai Kraft and Grocery. Today she worked the lunch and dinner shift and was thankful for something to occupy her mind. She'd asked Annie if there were any extra shifts she could pick up this week. The thought of sitting at home replaying her conversations with Ben over and over held no appeal.

The air was windy today, and looking at the dark clouds on the horizon, Marianna wondered if it would rain. If it did, Annie would insist on giving her a ride home. She was always thoughtful like that. But what about the guys in the wilderness? They were hours south, but what would happen if a storm came upon them while they were out in the elements? Marianna didn't want to think about that.

Her eyes were fixed on the first step just outside the store when a voice she didn't recognize called out her name. "Marianna!"

A woman stood there with a camera in hand. She wore a crisp white blouse, capris, and heels. Heels in the West Kootenai? *She's not from around here, that's for sure.*

The woman lifted her camera and snapped a photo. Next to her stood a man with a professional video camera.

"Wha-what are you doing?" Marianna stuttered, taking a step back.

The woman lowered her camera and stepped forward, extending her hand. "I'm so sorry to startle you.

I'm an entertainment reporter and just wanted to talk to you for a few minutes."

Marianna's brow furrowed in confusion. She reached out her hand and shook the woman's, not knowing what else to do.

"An entertainment reporter? Are you looking for Ben?" Marianna asked. "And why are you taking my photo?"

"I actually came to talk to you." She swept her light-brown hair back from her shoulder and offered a dazzling smile. "I thought we could talk about your engagement. I'm Linsey Ledbetter, by the way." She pulled a business card from her pocket and handed it to Marianna.

Marianna studied the small rectangle of thick paper with fine lettering and gold embossing. Linsey Ledbetter, *Entertainment Weekly*, Los Angeles. "You're here to talk to me about our engagement? You came all this way?"

Linsey chuckled. "It's not every day that a rock star gets married to an Amish girl."

Marianna touched her hair where her kapp used to sit. "I think you misunderstand." Her hair was pinned up in a soft bun at the base of her neck.

"Former Amish, of course. And that's the interesting part." Linsey waved a hand, motioning the cameraman closer. "I'm curious about this relationship. Ben fell in love with you when you were still Amish, and you decided to leave your faith for him."

Marianna held up her hand to the cameraman to

block his view of her, but she knew it did little good with the way he sidestepped. "I have not left my faith. Things are different than people imagine. Ben and I have something no one can understand...but I don't need to explain it to you. And please, would you stop filming me?"

Linsey plastered on a smile and motioned to her cameraman. "Yes, of course. You just needed to ask." Then she pointed toward the video camera. "I got just what I needed. I think *People* will be interested in this clip, and then maybe other tabloids will follow."

Then, as she gently set her camera into its case that hung around her neck, the woman's laughter filled the air. "And you know what, Bryson?" Linsey said to the man with her. "I think ole Ben's more intelligent than we think. What news isn't going to pick up the story of a music star marrying an Amish girl? Talk about good promotion." Linsey grinned at the cameraman. "We better get going if we want to make it back to Kalispell to catch our flight. Do you want to drive, or should I?"

The cameraman tossed her the keys. "It's your turn to try to dodge the free-range cattle."

Marianna didn't know what to think as she watched Linsey pull out of the parking lot. Had that just happened? And what did she mean by people being interested? What people? She could understand some were interested in Ben, but they weren't married yet.

Marianna walked into the Kraft and Grocery without knowing what else to do. As long as she'd lived in Montana, she'd grown to count on the familiar rhythm of daily life—working and spending time with friends and neighbors. She wasn't used to strangers, or reporters, showing up just to take a few photos and videos of her. First, Ben acting aloof, and then this. Was this the type of life she was getting into? Could live with?

Just inside the door, Marianna felt weariness and wondered if she was coming down with something. Or perhaps it was her overwhelmed thoughts sapping away every ounce of energy she had.

"Marianna, is everything all right?" Edgar dropped the loaf of bread he'd been scanning at the checkout. "I'll be right back," Edgar rumbled to the customer. Then he rushed around the counter to her. Marianna felt her knees softening and leaned into Edgar's open arms as he approached.

"Annie!" Edgar called. "Something's wrong. It's Marianna."

Edgar led her toward the restaurant area, guiding her to the first open chair. Marianna willingly sat.

Annie hurriedly approached and placed a hand on Marianna's forehead. "You look pale. Are you all right? A woman came in a few minutes ago looking for you. Did something happen?"

"Something happened, but I don't know what. Ben is acting strange, and he postponed our wedding. Then that woman. They were recording me...the reporter seemed nice, and they left when I told them I didn't want to talk."

Annie breathed out a sigh of relief. "At least they left." Annie glanced at Edgar, and a knowing look passed between them. "I was afraid of that."

Marianna looked from one to the other. "Afraid of what?"

"The reporters showing up. Everyone's interested in this engagement. I can't imagine..."

Pressing her hands to the table, Marianna stood. "What?"

"Reporters don't report the news anymore. They make it. The most innocent images or comments can be...changed. I can't imagine what story they will come up with now."

Edgar took the chair across from Marianna. "I think you need to tell Ben what happened—"

"I would, but he just left to go into the Bob Marshall for a week." She shrugged. "Oh, Annie...I thought when I returned from Indiana that I'd have no more questions. I made my choices and had joy in my growing relationship with God and Ben. Still, now everything seems even more confusing than before."

"I wish I could say I didn't expect this, but it takes a lot of shifting and compromises to merge two lives into one."

"Is that why you never got married, Annie?"

Annie opened her mouth as if she was going to say something but then closed it again. "I made wrong choices, that is for certain. Sometimes I wish things would have turned out differently, but if they had, I wouldn't be where I am or who I am."

Marianna sat again. "I just wish things were easier."

"They might not get easier anytime soon, but I will pray that they won't always be as hard." Annie winked.

"Thank you, Annie. I can use those prayers."

"The problem is God never promised quick fixes when it comes to answering our prayers," Edgar added as he headed back to the front counter.

And even though Marianna didn't like that answer, she couldn't disagree. She just hoped that the wall between her and Ben would be broken down—even if it meant doing so brick by brick.

Chapter Fifteen

SATURDAY, JULY 1, SCAPEGOAT WILDERNESS, MONTANA

There was a lot of time to think as one journeyed up the trail to their first destination. And Ben had a lot to think about. Even though it was the beginning of July, the air was nippy. Snow clung to the tallest peaks and down in the shadowed areas of the valleys that didn't see direct sunlight.

Ike rode on his horse, Shadow, first to see how he handled being in the mountains again. He also checked ahead for signs of fallen trees or other obstacles blocking the trail. The pack mule, Flint, followed next with her heavy load. Abe followed next, then Ben.

The burden of the wedding to come and the responsibilities of being a husband, and perhaps someday a father, weighed on his heart just like the pack weighed on his back. Yet as the day went on, Ben felt the thoughts turning away from all the worries he hadn't been able to leave behind. Instead, he took in the beauty—the swaths of trees that extended in every direction. The mountain grasses that swayed in the field. The birds and small critters scampering about.

The wilderness reflected God's beauty no matter what happened in the valleys below. It reminded Ben of the Creator who knew and saw all—even three guys dotting the long mountain trails.

They crossed a wide river that wasn't too deep, and on the other side, they worked to set up camp for the night, even though it wasn't quite dinnertime.

"I'd rather enjoy the beauty and get our socks and boots dried out by the fire," Ike commented. "It's no fun to walk in wet boots."

"Annie said that getting wet means hypothermia," Ben added as he helped Ike unpack the mule while Abe led Shadow to pasture and set out a picket line.

"Well, she's right, which is why we're stopping. The temps will dip up here in the mountains. You might fall asleep in summer but wake up thinking it's winter. That's why I'd rather take the time to set up camp right than go a little farther up the trail today."

"Is there a destination we're headed to?" Ben asked, untying the manty rope just like Ike had shown him.

"There are lots of places to head to. Each trail takes you someplace beautiful. We'll just play it by ear and see where we end up. But no, there's not a Holiday Inn or a chalet that we're heading for, but that would be nice, wouldn't it?"

Once Shadow had been tied to the picket line, Abe headed back in their direction.

"Isn't he going to tie Flint up too?" Ben asked, pointing to Abe.

"Nope, that ole mule ain't going nowhere. The mules always stay with the horses, whether we have one horse or ten. Flint will follow wherever Shadow leads, so we need to ensure Shadow stays tied up."

It took them over an hour to set up camp, but it was worth all the work when they were done. Ike and Abe shared a two-person tent, and Ben had a one-person pop-up.

"You know why we set things up thata way?" Abe asked, pointing to Ben's small tent.

"Because brothers like to cuddle?" Ben said with a chuckle.

"Actually, we know if there are any wild animals out there, they always start with the small appetizers first before they head for the main course." Ike laughed.

"Gee, thanks. Good to know I'm good for something." Ben slumped back against a log and watched as Ike and Abe set to work making dinner of the elk steaks they had carried in their cold packs. There were also beans from a can and apple hand pies that Annie had made as a surprise, which Ike had managed to tuck away in his backpack without getting too crushed.

After dinner, with a full belly, a warm fire, and a sky full of stars overhead, Ben sucked in a large breath through his nose. The cold mountain air stung his nostrils, but his soul felt more alive than it had in months. Sitting here, he realized how being on the road had narrowed his perspective. With traveling from place to place singing, it got easy to focus on the crowds, the sales numbers, and plans for which song to record next.

Yet being here, none of those things mattered. Looking at the starry sky reminded Ben that the universe was created by a God who loved him immensely. A God who, like Hannah, knew how much he'd messed up. Yet instead of pointing a finger of blame and shame like Hannah had in that text, God welcomed Ben with open arms. Grace. That was something he'd forgotten about down in the valley. God's unending, undeserving grace.

Ben started to hum as the fire crackled beside him, and then he felt the song release with his breath into the night.

Amazing grace, how sweet the sound
That saved a wretch like me!
I once was lost, but now am found,
Was blind, but now I see.

The other two men perked up, and Ben knew they were paying attention to the words.

'Twas grace that taught my heart to
fear,
And grace, my fears relieved;
How precious did that grace appear
The hour I first believed!

Ben continued the song, picturing it exiting his lungs and rising and drifting away with the calm wind into the night. When the song ended, there was only silence. A silence like he'd never known.

Finally, Ike cleared his throat. Ben glanced over and noted the older bachelor wiping the tears on his cheeks with the back of his hand. "And just think, I went to Montana for adventure, and I found—we all found—so much more in the process."

Abe lowered his head, tracing a circle in the ground with the end of a stick. "Thinking about growing up, our dat was the most diligent Amishman we knew. Yet, to think of all he missed within the pages of the Bible...it's as if he dug for gold his whole life thinking the digging was the point, not knowing that the treasure was just waiting for him within the pages of God's Word."

"Reminds me of a legend one of the outfitters used to tell guests," Ike began. "Over in the Bitterroot Wilderness, there's the legend of Arthur Woods." He paused for effect. "Arthur Woods was a prospector in the 1920s who panned about seventy pounds of gold dust from a remote area south of the Lost Trail in the Bitterroots. On his way down from the mountain, he told his friend Bill Ward, sheriff of nearby Darby, that he would return to stake a claim in spring. Woods then traveled to Butte to spend the winter with his sister. He died soon after, never making it back to his mother lode. For years after, Sheriff Ward and Woods's sister searched, as have many others, but no one has ever found Woods's lost bonanza, as it came to be called. Arthur's grandson continued to search, even up to the 1960s, which is not too long ago when you think of it."

"Do you know what I think about that? They had all these mountains and most likely didn't appreciate it in search of the gold," Abe said.

"Makes me think about all I've taken for granted, who I've taken for granted." Ike sighed heavily and closed his eyes.

Ben thought about that too. He'd taken Marianna for granted lately, hadn't he? Just six months ago, she'd been determined to be baptized into the church and marry a good Amishman. She'd changed her mind and chosen a close walk with God instead. Chosen him.

Lord, I know I've been a fool, Ben prayed along with the sound of the fire crackling. *I know I've mistreated Marianna's heart too. Even though I'm not there, would You help her remember my love for her? Forgive me for being a stubborn-headed mule. Instead, allow me to walk the path You've given me with love for those You've brought into my life, starting with Marianna.*

Chapter Sixteen

Sunday, July 2, West Kootenai, Montana

With slow steps, Marianna made her way through the front door of Summit Community Church. The new church building had been built when she'd been in Indiana, and the interior was still unfinished. Pieces of carpet of various colors had been laid down on the plywood floors. The sound system consisted of a few microphones and speakers hung from chains from the ceiling—not that Marianna minded. She was still getting used to the instruments and the faster-paced songs. Her favorites were the hymns.

She'd barely reached the sanctuary area when Millie Arnold greeted her with a hug. Millie's red lips smiled, and wrinkles extended around her mouth, splaying like cracks in weathered paint. A rancher's wife all her married life, her face was as weathered as a leather saddlebag. She was the first to connect with anyone who came into the church. Millie was a greeting committee of one and did a fine job.

Millie pulled back from the hug and eyed Marianna approvingly. "Look at you. I love how you did your hair, and is that a new dress?"

Marianna touched the loose bun she'd twisted at the base of her neck. "I'm still not used to my hair down. Changing my clothes has been easier than changing my hair, especially when I find dresses this comfortable." She glanced down at the dress. It was long, nearly to the floor, and a purple-gray color that wasn't too bold. She liked the capped sleeves and how they hung loosely, not too tight. "Jenny picked up a few things for me at a yard sale down in Eureka. I think I'm still finding my style, but I do love this one."

"Good for you." Millie patted her arm. "I love how God created each of us unique. Did you know I grew up in Seattle and my first job was dressing mannequins in a store? Can you imagine? I never felt I fit in until I joined a friend on a trip to Montana to visit her aunt and uncle. My friend didn't like the ranch or the hard work, but I'd never felt more myself than I did that summer. Didn't take me long to move here for good."

"I understand what you're saying. When I got off at the train station in Whitefish, I was angry I had to leave my whole life. But it didn't take long before Montana started to feel like home."

"That's good, real good. And I know Ben likes it here too. It'll be good to know that wherever the two of you travel, you'll always have Montana to come back to."

"Travel? But—" Marianna's words were interrupted by chords on a keyboard, a sign to the members that church would be starting soon and it was time for everyone to take their seats.

With a quick wave to Millie, Marianna hurried to the third row on the left. She scooted in to sit next to Annie. Edgar sat on the other side of Annie. Pastor Kellen rose to give the announcement, but Marianna had difficulty focusing on his words.

Travel? Millie had assumed that Marianna would be traveling with Ben when he went on the road with his music. They hadn't really talked about the possibility...well, except for her outright refusal a few days ago.

"You're not thinking I should travel with you? I—I can't do that."

Marianna winced even as the rest of the congregation stood and started singing. Anguish grew like a deep ache in Marianna's heart. Perhaps it had been wrong of her to refuse to even consider traveling with him. To at least talk about it with Ben. After all, she loved the Ben she knew and spent time with in Montana—but shouldn't she also take time to know all of Ben?

The singing continued, but it wasn't until Pastor Kellen told them they could be seated that Marianna realized she hadn't even been paying attention to any of the words.

Holding her Bible on her lap, she attempted to focus on the pastor's sermon. These sermons differed from those she'd heard her whole life growing up in the Amish church.

The pastor told them to open their Bibles to Acts, chapter nine. Pastor Kellen shared Saul's conversion story and the dramatic event on the road to Damascus. The encounter was the first step to Paul becoming an important evangelist of the early church and writing most of the New Testament books.

"Saul usually gets all the attention, but we can't forget how God used Ananias. Ananias didn't travel the world like Saul, later named Paul, did. God didn't ask him to do that. God asked him to reach out to one person.

"This wasn't just an ordinary person who God asked Ananias to reach out to. It was an enemy. Saul was a murderer of all those who followed Jesus. How would you like it if God asked you to reach out to someone you considered an enemy?"

Edgar cleared his throat on the other side of Annie, causing Marianna to smile.

"You and I may never be asked to change the world," Pastor Kellen continued. "But you and I will be asked, from time to time, to change the world for one person. And maybe it's the last person you want to help.

"When the Lord gave Ananias his assignment,

Ananias had time to ask one question of the Lord. 'Lord, I have heard many reports about this man and all the harm he has done to Your saints in Jerusalem. And he has come here with authority from the chief priests to arrest all who call on Your name. Are You sure this is the man You want me to go see?'

"And the Lord responded with one instruction—'Go!'

"When God gives you an assignment, you always have the choice to say yes or no. What about you? Has God brought someone into your mind who you might consider an enemy? Maybe today, you can pray that God will show you how you can pray for that person. Maybe He will even use you to reach out to them—to him or her."

Marianna ran her fingers over the edges of her Bible. She bowed her head to pray, but even then, she wondered if this sermon applied to her. Instead of like many Amish sermons that told the congregation exactly what to do, Pastor Kellen had asked each person to search their hearts—whatever that meant.

Music played as those in the congregation bowed in silent prayers. *Lord, if there is anything that applies to me. If there is anyone—*

At that moment, a face popped into Marianna's mind. The beautiful reporter that had stopped her at the store. Who had taken her photo. Marianna folded her hands and squeezed her eyes tighter. Yes, she'd considered the interaction with the woman an inconvenience. But surely she wasn't an enemy, was she?

Marianna had Linsey's business card with her name and number. The thought of reaching out to the woman caused Marianna's heartbeat to quicken, and she felt her throat grow tight.

What would Marianna do if she reached out to her? What would she even say? She thought about Ananias again.

This is different... But was it?

Marianna sucked in a breath and released it with a prayer. *Lord, at the right time I will reach out to Linsey if I know what You're asking me to do.*

There. She'd prayed what she felt she should. *But still,* she questioned, *does God speak to people in the same way today as He did then?* Maybe someday she would find out, but today she was content to stand and sing the closing song as church was dismissed. She felt a sense of peace, knowing that today she was willing to do all God asked her to do.

Chapter Seventeen

MONDAY, JULY 3, WEST KOOTENAI, MONTANA

An early morning knock on the door caught Marianna by surprise. She glanced around their living area. Dirty dishes were stacked on the kitchen table. Clumps of dirt, which the boys had carried in this morning on their shoes, littered the floor. Mem and the children had walked down to the Carashes' house to borrow an ice chest for their afternoon picnic on the lake. Maybe she should pretend she wasn't home. Then she remembered that she wasn't in Indiana anymore. No one in the West Kootenai expected their home to be perfect.

Marianna hurried to the door. She opened it and was surprised to find Jenny there. Jenny swept her blonde hair from her forehead, tucking it behind her ear. "I'm sorry to bother you."

"Oh, it's really no problem at all. Come in. It's sort of messy." She stepped back and welcomed Jenny inside.

Jenny entered, looked around, and laughed.

Marianna glanced around. "Is something funny?"

"If you think this is messy, I don't want you to see my place." She scanned the room and immediately moved to the table and sat. "Oh, those biscuits look good. Do you mind if I have one?"

"Not at all. Let me get you a clean knife."

"Nah, I'll just use one of these." Jenny placed a biscuit on a napkin. Then she grabbed one of the butter knives from the plate, smeared butter on the biscuit, and then jam. Jenny took a big bite and rolled her eyes. "Wow, these are so good. We must talk to Annie about putting your biscuits on the menu."

"Ja, I'd need to talk to Ben about that. I'm not sure if I'll be working much after our wedding."

"Oh, yes, of course. I should have thought of that. That's actually why I came." She picked up another biscuit and put butter and jam on that one too. But before she took a bite, she pulled out her phone.

"So, I have to admit that I like to read entertainment websites. I find them interesting."

Marianna sat next to her and decided to have another biscuit herself. "I don't really know what that means."

"Oh, on the internet, you can see photos and read stories about actors and musicians." Jenny typed something into her phone, then handed the phone to Marianna.

Glancing down, Marianna gasped. She was staring at a photo of herself from Saturday. There also was a photo of Ben onstage in his torn skinny jeans and a fitted T-shirt.

The Two Lives of Ben Stone, the caption read.

> *"Ben and I have something no one can understand," says his fiancée, Marianna Sommer. But maybe his innocent fiancée is truly the one who doesn't understand Ben Stone. Stone is among the hottest new artists, and his fan following is growing online. Yet his choice of wife is someone with no social media presence who doesn't even own a phone or computer. What a perfect setup for Ben to hide his life on the road from a housewife who will be awaiting his return with a hot meal and a warm bed.*

Marianna scanned the rest of the article, and her cheeks reddened. According to the report, Ben led a double life as a modern musician and a subdued Montana hermit. The article claimed that Ben's life on the road might not be as innocent as he made it seem and that he had perhaps fooled everyone in the West Kootenai, especially Marianna. The worst part was that, since Ben wasn't available for comment, the reporter believed he was attempting to hide now that the truth was exposed.

Never mind that he's in the Bob Marshall and unable to be reached.

"What am I going to do?" Marianna covered her mouth with her hand. Her heartbeat pounded, and her jaw tightened. So this was what Annie meant by reporters making news instead of simply reporting news these days. For someone to catch her off guard like that and then take her words and twist them was just wrong. Linsey Ledbetter had definitely put Ben in a bad light and made Marianna look like a fool.

Jenny's lip pouted out, and she shrugged. "I suppose there isn't much you can do. This photo isn't just on this site. It's on many."

"And what do the others say?"

Jenny took the phone back. "I'm not sure that you really want to know."

"What do you mean?"

"They all have a different spin, like Wild Ben finally finding wife material or you escaping a cult. None of them are even close to the truth."

Marianna nodded. "It makes no sense that they would talk about us like that when they really don't know us." She stood and moved to the window, looking outside yet not seeing anything as she tried to make sense of what Jenny was telling her.

"I got used to this some in Shipshewana. People liked to come to see the Amish. They'd take lots of photos and pretend they weren't. Some of the bold ones would ask questions. But I never thought about what they did with the photos afterward."

"They probably just shared them with friends or on Facebook," Jenny guessed.

Marianna agreed. She had heard of Facebook before, but she'd never used it herself.

"I just can't believe that news about my wedding is big enough for someone to come all the way to Montana to find me and ask me a few questions."

"Well, it's not every day a rock star marries an Amish girl."

"Former Amish."

"Well, yes, but most people don't understand that. Even without your kapp, you look Amish enough."

"I do?" Marianna touched her hair that she had braided today. She wore no kapp. Her dress had a pattern. She wore a simple engagement band on her finger. There was nothing Amish about any of those things.

She felt her face getting hot and her shoulders tighten. Then Marianna thought of yesterday's sermon. Yes, Linsey Ledbetter was more than just an annoyance. After this, she indeed was an enemy.

Lord, what do I do?

Marianna tried to calm her tense nerves and think rationally. "If she had approached me respectfully, I would have sat down to talk to her," she finally said.

Jenny chuckled. "And I bet if she knew that, she'd be on a plane tomorrow."

"She'd come all the way up here again?"

"Guaranteed. And I have a feeling this isn't a one and done. More reporters or bloggers are going to find their way up here." Jenny shrugged. "Who knew purity could be so hot?"

Heat rose to Marianna's cheeks again, and she decided not to comment. She touched her engagement band, twisting it around her finger. "I still can't imagine coming all this way for that. It's something I need to talk to Ben about for certain."

"Yes, and he'll probably need to talk to his management. They might want to set up some media opportunities."

Marianna pressed her fingers to her forehead, only understanding half of what Jenny was telling her. An ache started to throb at her temples. "Ja, I will have to talk to Ben about all these things when he returns."

Jenny reached forward and picked up her third biscuit, slathering it with butter and jam. Then she wrapped it up in a napkin to take with her. "That's a good idea." Jenny rose and patted her stomach. "Well, I was going to buy something to eat at the store, but I'm stuffed now." She laughed. "Thank you so much."

Walking Jenny to the door, Marianna forced a smile despite the pricks of pain in her heart. "Thank you for coming. I do appreciate it. Even though I don't understand so much of this, I'm thankful that you do and that you cared enough to come by."

She followed Jenny to the front driveway where her small car was parked. As Jenny drove away, Marianna saw her mother strolling down the road toward the house with Joy on her hip. There was no sign of the other kids.

Marianna waited for her mem in the yard. "Where are the kids?"

"Dave and Susan are heading down to the lake. They said the kids could go with them for a while and play with Sally. Then they'll come back up around dinner time and pick the baby and me up for dinner and fireworks. Even though tomorrow's the holiday, their kids don't want to wait. And you, too, if you'd like it."

"I'm not sure..." Marianna rubbed her brow. "I don't really feel up to it."

Mem grabbed Marianna's arm. "Did something happen? Are you all right? Your face looks pale." Mem led Marianna into the house.

Inside, Marianna sat on the sofa and grabbed one of the embroidered cushions, hugging it to her chest. "I didn't tell you this, but a couple days ago, a reporter was there as I got to the store for work."

Mem placed Joy on her mat with toys and sat across from Marianna. "A reporter?"

"She reports on entertainment things and asked me about my wedding, about Ben."

"To think she'd come all the way for that." Mem clucked her tongue.

"Ja, well, today Jenny came by, and those photos are on the internet. All these made-up stories about Ben and me too."

"Oh, Marianna, I'm so sorry."

"I wish I could talk to Ben about it..." But even as Marianna said those words, she wondered if it would help. She hadn't been able to talk to him about so many things, and when she tried, it seemed to just push them apart.

Compassion filled Mem's face, and then she rose. Blowing a breath, Mem went to the pantry and pulled out a broom. She began sweeping up the piles of dirt on the floor as if attacking the dirt would somehow help her get control over Marianna's situation.

"I'm sorry to make you upset." Marianna shrugged.

"Ja, I am upset, but that's not going to help the matter, is it?" She paused with her broom. "And honestly, it's not going to help you to be upset if you want to know the truth."

"I know, we are supposed to forgive..." Marianna left out 'our enemies.' She didn't want to think about Pastor Kellen's sermon just yet. "But it is hard knowing that all these people think ill of Ben and me. That he's leading a double life. That he's acting one way to get me to marry him. Or worse, I'm a fool and don't understand who he really is."

Mem finished sweeping up the dirt and then returned the broom. With a heavy sigh, she sat back down across from Marianna. "Ja, well. As much as we don't like it, we can't really control how people think of us, can we?" Mom's voice was stern, which surprised Marianna.

"Ne, of course not. But it still hurts."

"It hurts, but sometimes we let it fester, making it hurt even more."

"What do you mean?"

Mem leaned forward on her chair and fixed her eyes on Joy and her toys as if the words to come were hard to get out. "For so long, Marianna, I spent my time burdened by the weight of everyone's opinion of me. I was that woman who nearly gave her heart to an Englischman at the expense of her family. I was that woman who lost her girls. Then I became the mother whose son left the Amish."

She glanced up at Marianna. Mem blinked back tears. "At first, I liked it in Montana because no one knew me. Then, as your dat and I have been reading the Bible more, I've realized that what others think matters not as much as what God thinks. Even our Lord Jesus was accused of being the prince of demons. Can you imagine? Heartache has hit our family, and I've made choices I'm not proud of. People may continue to talk, but it's God and me in the end. I hate to think of all the years I carried the burden of others' opinions. Just a waste of time and energy."

"Yes, but this goes beyond the Amish community. That photo of me was spread in magazines and online."

"And...still, do their opinions matter? People love Ben, and they love his music. They might find an interest in who he marries, but I guess they'll soon be chasing another story."

Mem moved over, closer to Marianna, and took her hand. "You have to let it go. You really do. Learn from me, daughter. Those burdens are too much to carry and get you nowhere." She gently touched Marianna's cheek and smiled. "I know who you are. I know who Ben is. God does too. Remember this. Think of what really matters."

Chapter Eighteen

MONDAY, JULY 3, SCAPEGOAT WILDERNESS, MONTANA

With the fire just a warm glow, Ben kicked off his boots and climbed into his sleeping bag. It was hard to imagine that folks were already setting off fireworks down in the valley for an early celebration of the Fourth of July. Up here in the mountains, everything was quiet, still—including Ben's heart.

Somehow, over the miles of trail, all the busy, hurried thoughts of the last few months had stilled to the steady rhythm of the horse's hooves. Ben had insisted on walking more than the other two, and his legs felt warm and tight after hiking up the trails and along ridges. Now, with nightfall, there was a change in the air—a danger with the darkness, as if the wild country around him had just been playing nice when the sun was out. But even in the dark, he felt more settled, freer.

They couldn't have asked for a more beautiful moonlit night. The howl of a coyote carried down into the hill just beyond them, and then it swept up again, causing a second echo. It was peaceful here, and he wished he could show Marianna how the stars looked.

Ben let his eyes flutter closed, and as his breaths grew steady, he prayed for her. He prayed for himself also. Prayed for answers. He prayed for this peace to settle into the deepest parts of his soul. How could he celebrate in marriage while knowing his actions meant Jason would never have a bride? His soft breathing soon matched his prayers. Out with worry, in with peace. Out...

A man's scream split through the dark night. Ben bolted upright. He gasped for breath as he tried to remember where he was.

"Ben? You all right?" Abe called from somewhere in the darkness.

Ben turned his face in the direction of Abe's voice. "Who was that? Did you hear that man scream?"

"Ben, it was you," Ike called from within his tent.

"Me? What do you mean? I just laid down."

Ike's voice was gruff. "Just laid down? It's the middle of the night. You've been sleeping for at least a few hours."

Ben ran his hand through his hair, causing it to

stand on end. Had he been dreaming? Of course he had. Over the last week, his dreams about Jason had come as regularly as Ike's morning visits to the Kraft and Grocery.

"I'm sorry. I didn't mean to wake you." Ben slipped back down into his sleeping bag.

The other men were silent for a while, then Ike cleared his throat. "Ben, who's Jason?"

Ben's throat felt tight, as if the scream had scratched its way out of his throat. He tried to clear it. "We can talk about it tomorrow. It's late."

There was a shuffling sound and the unzipping of the other tent's zipper. "Well, I'm awake now." The voice came from outside the tent. Ike must now be sitting next to the small, smoldering fire.

"Ja, me too," Abe softly called out from the other side of his brother.

Ben got out of his sleeping bag, slid on his fleece jacket, and joined them. He sat on one of the logs they'd set up as seats earlier in the evening. He lifted his eyes to the stars as if counting on them to give him courage.

Ben tried to find the words, realizing that although Jason was always a part of his thoughts, he didn't talk about him much. "Jason was my best friend since I was five. His house was two doors down from mine, and he stayed as many nights at my house growing up as he did his own. And vice versa." A sad smile lifted Ben's lips as the memories flooded in.

"If I was the daredevil, Jason was the peacemaker. I

got us into trouble, and Jason talked us out of the consequences. He played baseball because of me but mostly sat on the bench. I learned about music because of him, actually. His father was the band teacher, and I would never have signed up for any music class if it hadn't been for him. That, and Jason taught me how to play the guitar one sleepover at a time. Looking back, I'm not sure why his parents didn't tell us to quiet down more than they did."

"So I suppose that learnin' helped you become the singer and musician you are?" Ike's voice rose with the question.

"No doubt. While Jason went to Chapman University to get his music degree, I went on the road. I started singing at state fairs and barbecue joints. I didn't make much money and even took a job one summer in Montana for the Forest Service, clearing brush and cutting fire lines. That's how I grew to love the place."

"And then something happened to Jason." Ike's words were more a statement than a question.

"You can say that again." Emotion rumbled in Ben's chest like shale rock sliding down a ridge. Ben found himself slipping into it, being carried away.

"After that summer, I hit it big. A bigwig music manager who had a summer house in Montana heard me at an open mic event at a city park. Before I knew it, I was on big stages, and according to *People* magazine, I was the next John Mayer, except with a mix of rock and country vibe. The country thing took me by surprise, but I leaned into it. Pretty soon, I was living the dream, and when I made it home one weekend, I wanted Jason to celebrate with me."

A cold wind blew, and Ben tucked his hands deeper into the pockets of his fleece jacket. A shiver ran down his spine. He sucked in a cold breath as the memories found him, even on this mountain.

Every hour of that day was forever stuck in Ben's mind, and scenes clicked through like still images captured in time. The dinner out and the girls they'd picked up, trying to impress. Drinks sitting on an outcropping overlooking the beach. Jason declining drinks...until he hadn't anymore. Then taking a taxi home. Ben struggling to get Jason into his parents' house.

Jason's parents had been out of town at their class reunion. Otherwise, they'd most likely have awakened and immediately spotted how much trouble Jason was in.

"My friend wasn't one to drink, ever, and didn't have a tolerance for it. Add that to the fact that he'd always been smaller than me and was about forty pounds lighter. He was nearly unconscious when I dropped him off on the sofa, and I was too gone to notice if he was already blue or had clammy skin."

The words tumbled out now, escaping Ben's tight grip on them for years. "I didn't wake up until noon the next day, and by the time I found him in the same sitting-up position with his head tilted back that I'd left him in, he'd been dead for hours.

"I called 9-1-1, but his body was already cold and stiff. He was only twenty then, and I was a legal adult who'd provided him with the alcohol. Because of his death, I was fined and faced jail time. Then, instead of serving the full year, the judge let me out early and ordered me to write a letter every week to a minor who'd been caught drinking—something I've been doing since that time. Because of my name and newfound faith, the judge thought it would have more impact than just jail time alone."

"So, were you dreaming about him tonight? Is that why you called out his name?" Abe asked.

"I guess I was, but I don't remember what I was dreaming exactly. I've been thinking about him a lot, you know, how I'm the one getting married and planning a good future. And the fact that he isn't."

Abe shifted. "Have you talked to Marianna about all this?"

"Yes, some, but it scared me, you know? Jason's death isn't the only thing I have regrets about. And sometimes, especially in the last few weeks, I keep wondering if I'm just being selfish. If there's someone out there better for Marianna. Someone without all this pain and baggage they're carrying around like those heavy packs on Ike's mule."

Abe tugged on his beard as if considering it. "That could be the case. Maybe there's an Amishman who's never put a friend in danger, who followed the straight and narrow during his rumspringa and has stuck by every rule. Would that make you feel better?"

"Well, does he love God?" Ben asked.

Abe nodded. "Says he does."

"But a true relationship?"

Abe shrugged. "As you know, judging a man's heart is hard."

Ben blew out an exasperated breath. "Well, you know what I'm talking about. Someone better who's maybe not Amish."

"And could there be anyone out there who doesn't have what you call 'baggage'? Sometimes things happen to us. Other times we make mistakes. They're all burdens, and we can either try to give these things to the Lord, or we can keep carrying them."

Ike sat between the two, listening. And from the look on Ike's face, Ben wondered if he was taking it all in too.

"I've tried to give it to the Lord, but the memories are there. The regrets are there."

Ike pointed his finger into the air. "Which I believe is a good thing. Regrets remind us what not to do next time, don't you think?"

Ben folded his hands behind his head and lifted his face to the stars. "I wish things were just easier, you know? I love her so much I want to ensure she has the type of love and a husband she deserves."

"You know, if someone had told me a year ago that I would be trying to convince an Englischman—a singer and musician—that he's good enough to marry my daughter, I would have called that person a liar and a fool." Abe smiled. "As you know, I love my daughter more than one can imagine. Marianna was the balm to my soul and Ruth's soul after the loss of our daughters. I wouldn't tell you that God's hand was in this marriage unless I thought it was."

Ben's eyes welled up at Abe's reassurance. He needed to hear these words. He needed this conversation. Ben blew out his cheeks, willing himself not to start crying. The other two men were already dealing with being woken up from a deep sleep. They didn't need to deal with a blubbering fool too.

"With that being said, I think it's time for us to go back to sleep." Ike stretched out the last word for emphasis as he moved back to his tent. Abe nodded and did the same.

Around Ben, the wind swept down the mountain, carrying with it a soft hushing as if the mountains were shushing him back to sleep.

Instead of answering Ike, Ben also moved back to his tent and snuggled down deeper into his sleeping bag. His eyes fluttered closed, and he realized that some of the baggage might have lifted tonight. Talking with his friends had lightened his load and helped him to understand that maybe God did have a good plan for Marianna...one that he was part of too.

Chapter Nineteen

Tuesday, July 4, Scapegoat Wilderness, Montana

Ben would have thought it was the middle of winter, because the wind nipped his face as he peeked his head out of the sleeping bag in the morning. The air smelled of spruce, and a chilly breeze slid down from the snow-covered peaks above. Birds chattered in the trees, and he hummed along with them.

Glancing up, he saw the mountains had lost their peaks in the clouds, and it was hard to believe that they'd reach the closest one by the end of the day. Steep, narrow trails awaited them—or so Ike had warned. If the last three days were an easy ride, he couldn't imagine today. As Ben sat up, he felt every inch of the many miles they'd walked and ridden yesterday.

Looking around, he spotted Abe walking down toward the river with a fishing pole. Fish for breakfast? It didn't seem wrong to him. Ike followed after his brother, hands tucked into his pockets.

Ben quickly climbed from his sleeping bag, slid on his fleece jacket, and slipped his feet into his boots. Running his fingers through his hair, he whistled the tune to *The Andy Griffith Show*. At the same time, he tried to push down the ache in his chest. A pain that reminded Ben he couldn't even enjoy a getaway in the mountains without his past tagging along. Last night was proof of that.

At least he felt more peace about Abe's feelings about him marrying Marianna. More settled that Marianna's family approved, which he supposed was a miracle.

Ben walked in the direction of the other men, pushing those thoughts out of his mind for now. White, purple, and yellow wildflowers swayed in the grass near his feet. He couldn't help but think about all those poor souls who'd soon be stuck in Los Angeles traffic like he'd been most of his life. It amazed him that he was here of all places. He shuddered to think he could still be living that lifestyle, spending every moment trying to find success and be noticed.

Lush green foliage led into a wide rocky shore that lined both sides of the river. The water looked clear but a bit chalky at the same time.

"Is there something clouding that up?" Ben asked as he approached the river.

"It's the limestone the water runs over. Beautiful, isn't it?"

Morning light glimmered over the surface, sparkling like a million jewels. Ben gave a low whistle. "I've never seen anything like it."

Abe cast the first line into the gently flowing water.

Ben watched with curiosity. "Think you'll catch anything?"

"Oh, we'll have some trout, don't you worry," Ike said, answering for his brother. "You can't see them, but the cutthroat up in these parts take on the river's pale color."

Abe slowly turned his reel with his eyes fixed on his line.

"Today's gonna be a great day," Ike added. "Not too far ahead, we're going to be able to see the Chinese Wall—just a part of it, of course. It runs over fifty miles."

Abe sat hunkered down at the creek, looking up at the sky. "I've never seen a more beautiful sunrise."

Ben sat on a large rock not far from him.

Ike glanced to the sky and rubbed the shadow of a growing beard. "Ja, the sun hasn't risen yet since it's still behind the mountains."

Abe smiled. "But the golden rays...they do brighten the sky."

"And you better hurry and catch something so we can get going. It'll take the day to ride to where I'd like to sleep tonight." Ike's voice teased, and Ben wondered if he regretted heading into the mountains with two newbies, especially because they were now behind schedule. While he and Abe were both in good shape and could keep up, most of the work packing up the animals, tending to their needs, and setting up and putting away camp was up to Ike.

A wheezing cry filled the air. Then a warbling call—deep, full, and reverberating. The hairs on the back of Ben's neck rose. The noise came from the direction where the horse was picketed. "What's that? I sure hope it wasn't a grizzly."

Ike looked to Ben, eyes wide. "How fast can you run?"

"Are you serious?"

Ike posed as if he were ready to run back to their camp.

Abe waved his free hand. "Don't listen to Ike. It's the mule." Abe chuckled. "Quite the noise, isn't it?"

A bit of a grin twitched on Ike as he hunkered down to fill his water bottle from the creek. "Up in these parts, they call mules mountain canaries. But that would be a sad canary to sing like that."

Before long, breakfast was caught, and Abe and Ike cleaned and cooked the fish. They were delicious, but Ben couldn't get Marianna off his mind. Since they were continuing over the Continental Divide, it would be even longer until he saw her again.

"This isn't the journey we thought it would be, is

it, Abe?" Ben asked. "I thought we'd be turning back by now."

"It never is, just like life. We set our eyes on the peaks and don't realize what it takes to get there. And I'm talking about marriage especially."

Ben waited quietly. He guessed that sometime on this trip, Abe would want to talk more about the upcoming wedding to his daughter. And the marriage to follow. Getting approval was just step one.

"No marriage is easy, or so I've been told," Ben admitted. "But I guess ours will be especially hard when one person was raised Amish and the other anything but."

"For any marriage, it's tough. Each one has different challenges. To be honest, there were a few times when I was certain that Ruth and I wouldn't make it."

"But Amish don't believe in divorce," Ike piped in.

"That's true, but that doesn't mean it doesn't happen." Abe took in a deep breath. His forehead folded, and his eyes squinted as he eyed the rising sun. "Ja, I have known of divorce of an Amish couple once, but since they can never remarry, it usually deters most Amish. Still, I was certain that would happen to us for a time."

"After the death of your daughters?" Ben asked. "I've heard that a child's death can push couples apart as they each deal with their own pain." Ben tried to speak as reverently as possible.

"Ne, even long before that. Marianna most likely hasn't told you this, but not many years after we were married, an Englisch neighbor wooed my wife and won her heart for a time. That's when I was certain Ruth would leave me." Abe's voice broke, and he wiped at his nose. "A miracle happened, and she stayed by choice. She chose to deny her feelings for this other man. And that gave our love time to root again."

"And after the loss of the girls?" Ben picked up a dry pine cone and scraped his thumb over the pointed edges.

"After we lost our girls, Ruth and I lived like strangers for many years. We were married but were hurting so much that we had very little love. Looking back on both cases, I'm not sure how we made it, but I thank God daily that we have. I wouldn't trade my wife for all of Montana."

Ben set the pine cone on the forest floor. "Somehow, I always think that life will be easier than it is."

Abe tilted back his head, gazing up at the high-pointed peaks overhead. They rose sharp and jagged into the sky, dangerous and beautiful. "This world is a harsh, unforgiving place," he said no louder than a whisper.

Ben wasn't sure if the older man was talking about the mountain peaks or life. Probably both.

Chapter Twenty

TUESDAY, JULY 4, SCAPEGOAT WILDERNESS, MONTANA

On this fourth day on the trail, Ben knew what life was like at three miles an hour. It was the pace of a horse. It was the pace of one's thoughts too. Time to think about what really mattered. Time to remember that beauty was out there if one just took the time to get away and enjoy it.

The rocky landscape rose sharply on one side of the trail, which wasn't more than three feet wide. Not wide enough for two men to walk side by side. Barely wide enough for Shadow, it seemed.

On the other side, the cliff fell off in a severe drop toward the creek. Abe led the way on Shadow, followed by Flint, the pack mule's big ears flopping forward and back in sync with her feet. Right, left, right, left. One swinging up, and then the other, with each forward step. The wind blew against them as they walked, sweeping down the mountain trail like a cool breeze, ruffling their hair, chapping their cheeks.

Ben followed Flint, with Ike behind him. Just like yesterday, they'd taken turns riding Shadow. Ben told himself that he should ride less since he was almost twenty years younger than these men. But by the time his turn came around, his aching feet outvoted him. More than that, his pack shoulder straps and hip belt dug in, the weight of their contents pressing into his flesh and muscles. Were all the things he'd packed necessary? He hadn't used a quarter of what Annie insisted he take. The thought of enjoying the walk without the straps rubbing the skin under his shirt raw seemed like a dream. But he wouldn't complain.

Pine trees lined the creek below, and Ben wondered if up ahead they'd find a path leading down to it. He'd give anything to rest under the shade of a pine tree, even for a few minutes. A melody played in his mind, and words soon joined it.

Under the vast Montana sky, I discovered...

What? What had he discovered? Abe had told him they needed to go into the mountains to connect with God. While the idea was excellent, it wasn't as if Ben read a message in the clouds above, which looked like long swipes of white paint slashed across the sky.

Ben adjusted his heavy pack. His gaze moved from the sky to the unending expanse of mountains, and then he stopped as the mule just ahead of him stiffened and froze.

Something was in the path. Shadow's snort confirmed Ben's guess as the horse lifted its nose, smelling the air.

Flint spun and barreled forward in a split second, smashing Ben against the cliff. Before Ben could shout a warning, Flint knocked into Ike. Flipping Ike into the air, pack and all, the mule raced down the narrow trail back the way they'd come. With a rumbling, disbelieving shout, Ike skidded downward, his arms reaching, grasping, as if attempting to swim up the rocky cliffside.

No! Ben took two steps toward the steep hillside and sucked in a breath as Ike managed to grasp a stunted pine, clinging to it for dear life. Ben moved to assist Ike when Abe's shout split the air. Ben turned back to the trail.

Shadow leaped and skittered as Abe fumbled to pull his rifle from his scabbard. Then, as if in slow motion, the horse shot up the steep hill of rock and shale as if it believed it was a mountain goat instead of a Tennessee walker. Shadow's legs looked like they were on a treadmill, lunging and flinging shale to the trail and the cliff beyond.

Abe cried out again, attempting to jump from the saddle, but he wasn't fast enough. Shadow tumbled backward at nearly the same time as Abe's body hit the ground with a thump. Shadow's legs jerked skyward as his body slid in Abe's direction. Abe's rifle flew from his hand. He scrambled to move out of the way of the falling beast but failed. Shadow landed on Abe's leg with a loud thud and whinny. Abe's cry again split the air, and his face contorted in pain. Ben rushed forward just in time to see Abe's body go limp under the horse's weight.

With eyes wild and frantic, Shadow rolled back to his feet. Standing, the horse connected his back hoof with the rifle. A loud crunch sounded as the rifle stock broke in two. Then with another sweep of Shadow's hoof, it was kicked off the trail, skittering down the shale hillside, landing in the creek below. In an instant, Shadow raced in Ben's direction. Ben lunged for the rock cliff, clinging to it. The horse rushed by him, picking up steam.

A moan from the trail. Abe. Then, ahead, Ben spotted the problem. Two brown cubs ran down the path, away from them, frolicking and tackling each other like two puppies playing. One paused and rose to its feet to inspect the visitors on the trail. A trembling moved up Ben's arms at the sight of the bears.

If there were cubs, the mama grizzly had to be close—most likely around the bend just ahead. Everyone knew a mother protecting her cubs was the most dangerous of all animals. The curious cub dropped to all fours again and followed his twin.

Go, keep going, little cubs... At the sight of their retreat, Ben hustled to Abe's twisted body with quickened steps.

Abe was turned away, facing down the trail. His small pack was still strapped to his back.

Ben couldn't tell if Abe was awake or unconscious. Not that it mattered. The way Abe's leg twisted awkwardly to the side, Ben knew there was a break and a serious one.

Looking back, Ben spotted Ike crawling around up the slipping rocks. It appeared he wasn't seriously injured. Taking a deep breath, Ben darted the rest of the way to Marianna's father.

Ben sank onto the ground next to him, unsure what to do. How to help. His first aid training came to mind. *Assess the area.* A cliff, a rock wall, and cubs with a mother no doubt nearby...not good.

Check for consciousness.

"Abe, can you hear me?" Ben spoke clearly but not too loud in case the bear heard him. Abe's only response was a low moan, but at least he was breathing. Ben unstrapped Abe's pack and slipped it off his arms, pushing it to the side.

Evaluate injuries. Ben knew the leg was bad, but there also could be internal injuries. *Dear Lord, I need help here.*

"Ben..." Abe's voice croaked. His head turned, and his eyes flickered open. They attempted to focus on Ben's face. Abe's face was still twisted in a grimace of pain.

"I'm here." Ben kept his eyes focused on Abe. "You're going to be fine."

"Shadow..."

"He ran off, but listen, we need to take care of you." Though Ben tried to sound confident, he felt anything but. His eyes scanned Abe's body again, and he sucked in a breath at the blood seeping into the ground under Abe's lower pant leg. Ben knew he had to stabilize and elevate the leg and stop the bleeding. He reached up to undo the backpack's buckle across his chest, then paused when a rumbling on the trail caught his attention. The curious cubs had turned back in their direction, and the angry mother was right behind them.

Dear Lord, help! Ben instinctively started slowly crawling backward. Then his eyes fixed on Abe lying between him and the bears.

The mama grizzly rushed past her cubs, thundering toward Abe like a freight train. Two brown ears rose from the large skull. The silver tips glimmered at the ends of the tan pelt.

Sending up another prayer, Ben stood and jumped between Abe and the bear. He reached for the can of bear spray on his hip belt, then remembered he'd hooked it onto the saddle rather than his belt that morning.

"Ben, go. Run..." Abe's pained voice croaked behind him.

"No! I'm not leaving you." Ben rose higher, his hands balled to his sides. Then with the fervor of a boxing champ, he punched his fists toward the sky and stomped his foot. "Get out of here, bear! Get, get!"

Instead of backing off, the bear lunged, resting her weight on her front paws as if preparing to leap.

Ben stretched his arms out, reaching toward the sky, attempting to look as large as possible. Yet he could see from the rage in the mama grizzly's eyes it did little good. The bawling of her cubs behind her on the trail alerted Ben to what was coming next.

The mother grizzly charged with ears laid back, coming fast and low to the ground. Without hesitation, Ben turned his back to the bear, dropped to his knees, and covered Abe's body. Within a few seconds, the grizzly was on him. Her hot, rank breath blasted him as her teeth sank onto Ben's backpack, still strapped on him.

Ben felt his body lifting. Under the bear's power, he hung in the air as if he were a doll she was tossing around. Fear gripped his heart, but then another emotion too. A sense of protection. God was here with him, even now.

Abe reached his hands toward him. Ben's arms flailed as his body hit the ground with a thud, and then the bear grabbed up his backpack again, tossing him around. She snorted in his ear, and pain radiated in Ben's neck.

"Unclasp your pack!" It was Ike's voice. "Unclasp it and cover your face!"

Ben's fingers moved to the clasp, but it wouldn't budge. The tension of the bear's bite and hold made it impossible to unsnap it. "Lord, give me strength." He hit the ground again and felt the pack release from the bear's mouth. He quickly unclasped it just as the bear took another bite of the pack.

As the pack slipped from his arms, Ben tucked into a ball, covering his head. At that moment, he felt the blast of bear spray rush past him, carried by a strong wind directly into the bear's face. The wind...the wind that had been blowing against them now swept the other way.

As quickly as the grizzly had rushed toward him, Ben heard the rumble of her body—and the scratching of her claws on the trail—as she hurried away. He dared to take a breath. The scent of the bear spray was intense, causing him to cough, but he was alive. They were all alive.

Ben dared to turn and look at his pack—Annie's backpack. Pieces of blue fabric littered the ground, and all the supplies were strewn on the trail. Somehow it had held together enough to keep the bear from biting into him. Ben reached a hand to his neck, expecting to feel a wound, but there was none. Not a scratch. The twisting of muscles, as he'd been flung to and fro, brought him pain.

Taking a deep breath, Ben scrambled on hands and knees toward Abe.

Ike stood at his brother's head, can of bear spray in hand. "I didn't think it would work." Ike's jaw went slack. He shook his head in disbelief. "The can was hooked to my waist belt, and as I ran up, the wind was still blowing toward me. I knew it would do no good to spray it except to add some pepper seasoning to that grizzly's lunch. But right when the bear lifted you a second time—and then dropped you—the wind shifted, and I knew I had my chance."

"It's our first miracle," Ben muttered as he reached a hand toward Abe's twisted leg. "Now we need a second one. We have to stop the bleeding fast. We have to stabilize his leg."

Ike nodded understanding. "The bear may be gone for now, but we're not out of the woods yet."

Chapter Twenty-One

TUESDAY, JULY 4, SCAPEGOAT WILDERNESS, MONTANA

Ben supposed it was a blessing that Abe passed out as Ike and Ben worked to stop the bleeding from the gash on his lower leg. Ben cut away the bloody fabric around the wound with his pocket knife. Then Ike pulled a clean shirt from his backpack and ripped it into pieces. With the water bottle that hung on his backpack, Ike gently cleaned the wound and applied pressure. The gash didn't appear to go too deep. What bothered Ben most was how the leg twisted to the side, clearly broken.

That and the fact that the mama grizzly could return at any moment.

A fluttering sound caused Ben to jump. He looked up and noticed a flock of chickadees dropping down.

They settled on a patch of sparse grass down the hill on the trail in a flurry of wings. Above them, the sun shone in a big sky pocketed with clouds as white as the wool of a baby lamb. How could the day be so beautiful and horrifying?

Ike's face looked as pale as the clouds above as he kneeled at his brother's side. "This doesn't look good. We're so far in. How are we gonna get him down the mountain without the animals?" Ike moaned. "And the first aid kit was packed with the supplies." He appeared to be talking to himself as if he'd forgotten that Ben was there.

"I've got a first aid kit." Ben's heart pounded, and he glanced over his shoulder every few seconds, expecting the mama grizzly to return.

Ike's eyes were red. His lips were drawn into a thin line, and he wore a confused look on his face.

Ben quickly unzipped the waist pack. He pulled out the Ziploc bag of supplies. "From Annie."

Ike smiled at her name. "If we always listened to Annie, we'd be in much better shape, wouldn't we?"

Taking off his outer shirt, Ben laid it on the trail. Then he quickly dumped out the bag of supplies. Skin blister tape, a paracord, burn gel, sunscreen, a whistle, and a dozen other useful items.

Ben quickly grabbed the whistle and hung it from its lanyard around his neck. He grabbed the gauze pads and triple antibiotic ointment packets. Then he stuck the pain relief pills in his pocket, having no doubt they'd be needed as soon as Abe came to. Of course, how would a half dozen over-the-counter pain pills help when they were a four-day journey into the mountains?

After applying the ointment and the gauze, Ben leaned back so Ike would have room to secure the gauze with strips of cloth from his shirt. They looked at each other, knowing one small step was done. Yet getting Abe down the mountain would be the bigger problem.

Ben stood and patted his knife on his belt. "I'm gonna get some sapling branches to stabilize this leg."

Ike nodded and looked over his shoulder as if hoping the horse and mule would appear out of thin air, but there was no sign of them as far as they could see.

Finding a path to the river below and the lush, flat area surrounding it, Ben found two sticks to help them stabilize Abe's leg. He hurried back up to the trail, still scanning for the bears.

Abe moaned as they placed the sticks on either side of the leg.

"Should we try to straighten it?" Ben asked.

"No." The word shot from Ike's mouth. "We can nick an artery or cause nerve damage. As awkward as it is, we need to brace it just like that."

"So this has happened to you before?" Ben rubbed the base of his neck, still sore from where the grizzly had twisted and tossed him. *Thank You, Lord, it wasn't worse.* How could Ike have cared for him and Abe both?

"I've been around when something like this has happened." Ike swallowed down his emotion. "It didn't turn out well."

Ben nodded, knowing better than to ask more questions.

Once they stabilized Abe's leg with the sticks and the rest of the strips from Ike's shirt, Ike eyed Ben's pack again, pointing to the small tarp in its bag that Annie had insisted Ben take.

"We can take that wickiup tarp and tie it around two tree branches to make a stretcher."

Ben glanced toward Abe's leg and winced. "It's gonna hurt to move him."

"Ja, but we can't keep him on the trail. We need shade, water, some sense of protection."

"But won't it be more likely that animals will head to the creek?"

Ike didn't give Ben an answer. Instead, he looked again down the trail. "As soon as we get him in a better spot, I'll head back and see if I can find Shadow and Flint."

The sun was warm overhead, and Ben used the back of his hand to wipe the sweat from his brow. "Do you think you'll find them?"

Ike glanced over his shoulder again. And Ben could tell from his eyes that he didn't have much hope.

"I have to try," Ike finally commented. He took a step forward and limped. Then he took another step forward and limped again.

"Wait. You're hurt." Ben stood and paced toward

Ike. "You're not going be able to go anywhere on that ankle."

"I have to."

Ben squared his shoulders. "I can do it. I can look for the animals."

"But they don't know you. They won't come to you even if you find them. You're not going to be able to round them up, let alone bring them back."

"If they can be found," Ben added.

"Ja, if they can be found."

Ben found two more long branches, and together they used the tarp and extra rope from Abe's pack to make a stretcher. Even though they worked together, carrying Abe down the sloping hill to the level ground by the creek was a challenge. Somehow they made it, and then Ike pulled a hatchet from his pack, cut down fir boughs, and laid down the branches on the ground for them to transfer Abe onto.

"We'll string up this wickiup as a shelter over Abe. I saw Annie pack a space blanket in your bag. That and your sleeping bag and mat...we should be able to keep Abe warm."

"They're ripped up, but we'll make them work." Ben nodded.

"It's the best we can do." Ike rubbed his brow. "While I'm gone, why don't you gather up the things we left on the trail." Then Ike limped off, struggling up the hill to the trail.

Ben followed him. He placed everything salvageable in his outer shirt and tied it up. Then he put

Abe's pack on his back and carried the bundle to where Abe lay. Ike still wore his waist pack, but they didn't have much between the three of them. Ben knew that if the horse and the pack mule weren't found, they would be limited to these meager supplies on hand.

Settling down by Abe's side, Ben began to sort through their items. In addition to the things Annie had packed in Ben's backpack and waist pack, Abe had a large map of the Lolo National Forest. Ben opened it to see a trail marked with arrows. He guessed that Abe and Ike had planned the route to Scapegoat Mountain. And from the proximity to where they were and where Scapegoat Mountain filled the sky, he guessed they were near Cave Creek.

Within Abe's pack, Ben also found a flashlight, knife and knife sharpener, a water bottle with a purifier, a pitch stick for starting a fire, and other items.

Abe moaned again and moved his arms pressed against the ground as if trying to push himself into a sitting position.

"It's okay, Abe. Just rest. Everything's going to be all right." Abe settled down, and Ben prayed that Ike would make it back quickly. Preferably with the horse and mule. But even worse than knowing they'd run off was that Ben was here alone. What would he do if the bear returned or if Abe took a turn for the worse?

Ben made good use of his time by filling his and Abe's water bottles and gathering dry sticks and pine cones for a fire. The crunching of rocks caused Ben to sit straighter. It was a shuffling sound. Not the sound of a man walking. Had the cubs come back?

His eyes darted around. Ben looked behind him for the cause of the noise. His hands began to shake. He knew the mother wouldn't be far behind wherever the cubs were.

Weren't bears drawn to the scent of blood? He thought he'd heard somewhere that they were. Ben's hands tightened around the large stick he'd found, but what good was a stick against a bear? Still, better to fight and die trying.

The shuffling sound grew louder, and Ben fixed his eyes on the trail above. "Lord, help me to stay strong. Protect us..." Ben stood, and his knees grew weak.

The shuffling stopped. "Hey, Ben!" a voice called from overhead. "Can you come up here?"

Ben lifted his face and raised his hand to block the sun. There. On the trail, the form of a man was peering down.

"Ike? Is that you?"

"Who else is it going to be?"

Relief softened Ben's shoulders. "The bear?"

"Well, I'm not the bear. Can you come up? And bring that notebook and pencil if you can."

Of all the things.

Ben looked over at Abe, who moaned softly in a restless sleep. He grabbed the notepad and pencil from the pile of things he'd salvaged from his torn backpack and headed up the hill.

At the top of the hill, Ben found Ike sitting on a

boulder on the trail with a large square of cotton cloth spread in front of him. Ben didn't have to ask about the horse and mule. It was apparent they were long gone.

Ike folded the fabric in half to form a triangle shape. Then he began to roll the long end toward the point. As he reached the end, Ike folded the point inward and continued to roll.

When he finished and had a long snake-shaped piece of material, Ike turned to Ben. "This is where I need your help. We'll brace my ankle but keep my boot on."

Ben kneeled beside him. "Just tell me what I need to do."

Ike placed the middle of the fabric coil under the sole of his boot, crossed the fabric around the back, then brought both sides back up to the front. "Okay, I need you to take these two ends and pull them fairly tight. Then I need you to cross them, and while I put tension on the middle, I need you to loop them under the fabric on the sides of my boot."

Ben nodded and did what he was told. It was apparent that Ike was trying not to wince.

"Okay, now pull upward," Ike said between gritted teeth. "Ja, see how it's bracing my ankle all the way around? Gut, now do a square knot. Right over left, left over right. Ja, gut."

When Ben finished, Ike took the tag ends and tucked them in. Then he stood and nodded. "Ja, this is better. At least it'll help me make better time."

Ben stood too. "You're leaving now?" The tremors of his voice gave away his fear. "Are you sure you don't want to rest and start in the morning?"

"Abe doesn't have that type of time. Sleep is the least of my concerns right now. I need to get down that mountain as fast as I can."

"But you can't just walk through the night. That's a rough trail we just came up. And if you're tired..."

"I have two flashlights in my pack. I'll be smart, I promise. But if anything happens to Abe...I won't be able to live with myself if he ends up dying because I didn't realize how bad off things were and I wanted a full night's sleep."

Ike's words hit Ben like a hammer blow to the chest. "Like Jason."

"I didn't mean—"

Ben raised his arms as if in surrender. "I get it. I understand. You don't need to explain."

"I didn't mean to imply—"

"I'm not faulting you for your words. You're right. Hindsight is twenty-twenty. I'd give anything to go back now and change things. To call for help instead of heading to my bedroom and falling asleep. Everything could be different."

Ike adjusted the straps on his backpack. "I'll hurry, but I'll stay safe."

"How long do you think it'll take?"

"It took us over three days to get this far. And I'm afraid my ankle's going to slow me down." Worry filled Ike's eyes.

"I have our water bottles, shelter, the pitch stick, and matches for the fire."

"But food?"

Ben shrugged. "There was some jerky in Abe's pack. I have some protein bars. Abe had a booklet in his backpack with information about edible plants. I'll figure it out."

Ike's chin tremored. "I wish..."

"I can handle it." Ben attempted to sound more confident than he felt. "I will do my best to care for Abe." Ben swallowed hard. Neither one mentioned the bears.

Ben handed the paper and pencil to Ike. Ike wrote his name, age, address, and Annie's phone number on a piece of paper. On the back, he wrote the general location of Abe and Ben. Then he tucked the paper into his front shirt pocket and passed the rest of the paper and pencil to Ben.

"Do I want to ask what that's for?" Ben asked.

"No, but...it doesn't hurt to do the same for you and Abe. At least put your names and the numbers of your closest kin."

In case something happens to us and our bodies are found... Ben stopped there. He nodded and wrote his name and Abe's. He put the same contact name for both. Marianna Sommer. Tears sprang to his eyes as Ben wrote her name. *Please, Lord, get us out of here. For her sake.*

With a quick wave, Ike turned to head up the trail. Ben could tell he was trying not to limp, maybe so that

Ben wouldn't worry. How could he not worry? How could he not go through the next few days with fear tightening around his heart like a guitar string binding in the nut slot, unmoving? Then a thought hit him.

"Ike!" Ben's voice caused his friend to turn. Ben jogged to him. "Why don't we pray?"

Ike's eyes widened. "Ja, of course." He reached his hand to Ben's and squeezed. Ben knew for someone raised Amish, this was not a natural response, but Ike—like Abe and Marianna—had grown used to turning to God in prayer.

"Dear Lord," Ben began. "Even though we feel so helpless in so many ways, I know that You are with us, and You are strong. Give us Your strength to, well, survive. Help Ike's ankle. Touch it and heal it. I pray that You will help ease Abe's pain too. Help his body handle the shock of this injury. And, Lord, I'm completely out of my element. I don't know what to do, but You do. So help me, too, please. A hot dinner would be nice for starts. Amen."

"Amen." Ike cleared his throat. "And send the right people to help. Somehow make them aware of our situation. You can do that and, uh, other things we're not thinking about. We love You. Amen."

Then, without another word, Ike patted Ben's shoulder and turned, walking with the same limp yet with a straighter back, as if he had new hope.

Ben stood on the trail and watched as Ike rounded the trail curve and disappeared. Before today, he'd thought trying to get his music before the right people took courage. That didn't compare to this. Abe, his future father-in-law, had a severe injury, and Ben needed to keep him alive. He also had to somehow find food.

And...how would he go about preventing a bear attack?

Chapter Twenty-Two

TUESDAY, JULY 4, WEST KOOTENAI, MONTANA

Pounding on the cabin's door caused Marianna to sit straight up in bed. At Trapper's barking and clawing on the door, the hairs on the back of her neck rose on end. Marianna jumped from the bed and quickly slipped on her robe. The wood floor was cold on her feet, but it didn't matter. There was a problem. No one would pound on the door in the middle of the night if there wasn't. Since there wasn't enough moonlight to light her way, Marianna quickly lit an oil lantern and carried it with her as she rushed to the front door.

Marianna heard her mother's footsteps coming from upstairs. She swung open the door to see Annie standing there. Instead of being in its usual long braid, Annie's blonde hair poured over her shoulders. Annie's truck was parked out front, and she held a flashlight. Her eyes were wide with panic.

Immediately, Marianna knew. "Something happened," she blurted. "Is it Dat? Ike?" She couldn't say Ben's name. She couldn't.

Annie blinked twice. "Ike? No, no." She blew out a breath. "They're four days into their journey. My guess is they're heading back down from the mountains tomorrow. We should hear from them this weekend."

She stated it so matter-of-factly, Marianna knew Annie was counting down the days too.

"If it's not our men, what is it, then?" Mem asked.

Our men. Marianna pressed her lips together, trying not to smile when she heard that.

A cold wind blew through the open door. Annie stepped inside and shut it behind her. "Deborah Shelter came asking for help. Since Jenny had an early shift, she had Kenzie stay the night at Deborah's with Evelyn. Deborah woke in the night to discover the two girls weren't in bed. They snuck out for some reason, and it appears they went into the woods."

Marianna glanced out the window, listening to the wind howl. The moon was just a crescent in the sky. She wouldn't want to be out there tonight. "Why would they do that?"

"Kenzie got a new flashlight for her birthday a couple of days ago. Everyone's guess is they wanted to try it out. The Shelters have asked neighbors to help them look for the girls. Deborah and Sarah came and woke me up, asking if they could get more flashlights from the store. When they told me the story, I knew I had to come to get you." Annie's eyes fixed on Marianna.

"Me?"

"Deborah heard them talking earlier about beavers that come out of their lodges at night."

Marianna nodded. "Yes, my special place, the beaver pond. Someone must have shown them where to find it."

"Can you take me there? I have a feeling..."

"Yes, of course."

Marianna hurried to get dressed. The sound of Joy's crying could be heard from upstairs.

"I'll be praying," Mem said before heading upstairs. "I'm glad you came for Marianna, Annie." Then Mem's voice lowered. "But I'll be praying for the men too. I've had a strange feeling all day that something's wrong."

Marianna shut her door to change before Annie responded, but both of their voices were low. *Is this what being directed by God is like? Having an inner stirring that doesn't come from your natural senses?* She was still learning about how to know God and follow Him. If Mem had a bad feeling about their men, it was worth praying for.

Ten minutes later, she and Annie were walking side by side to the beaver pond with flashlights in hand. The night was dark, with just a sliver of moon. Even with the flashlights lighting the way, they seemed slow going. Marianna's ears were perked to every noise, and she again thought of the men way up in the Bob Marshall Wilderness. She knew she could turn and be back home in ten minutes. What would it be like to be so far from civilization?

"The beaver dam is just ahead." Marianna angled her flashlight in that direction.

Annie carried her flashlight and a can of bear spray in one hand. "It's quiet out," she said. "Maybe if we called for the girls?"

"Kenzie, Evelyn!" Annie's voice rose, and Marianna joined in.

They called and then paused to listen. As they reached the water's edge, Marianna held up a hand. "Did you hear that?"

The softest whimper came from the other side of the pond.

Annie tilted her head. "Sounds like a cat meowing to me."

"It's a child. I know it." Marianna motioned her forward.

They hurried to the other end of the pond, and Marianna caught a flash of red. Kenzie sat on her knees behind a log in a red nightgown, holding a small, pink flashlight. Evelyn hunched down beside her in her white nightgown and sleeping kerchief.

Marianna stood before them, shocked that they were hiding. "What are you two doing? Why didn't you answer us when we called?"

"Because we're gonna get in trouble." Kenzie folded her arms and pouted.

"Well, is getting in trouble worse or a bear finding you?" Annie asked. "Do you know there are bears out here—and other creatures?"

At Annie's words, Evelyn began to cry.

Marianna stepped forward to comfort her, but Annie grabbed her arm. "They need to learn," Annie said between clenched teeth. "If they're living in Montana, they have to learn. This isn't a game."

Marianna motioned them to come out from behind the log.

"Marianna"—Annie pointed in the direction they came—"let's walk to your house, since we know the way. And then I'll call the Shelters with your house phone. I left my cell phone with them."

"Yes, of course." Marianna reached to take the girls' hands, and Annie shook her head.

Annie jutted out her chin. "They walked this far without help and can walk back without it too."

It was a quiet walk back to her house. When they arrived, Annie motioned for the girls to get into the truck. Then she went to the phone shed to call the Shelters.

Marianna climbed into the truck with them, waiting for Annie to return.

Kenzie's lower lip quivered. "Annie's mad at us."

Evelyn's large eyes were round, scared.

"Annie knows the dangers around here more than anyone. She wants you to know how serious this is. She loves you—we all love you—and we want to ensure this doesn't happen again."

"It won't," both girls promised just as Annie showed up.

Marianna climbed from the truck, and Annie stood before her, crossing her arms over her chest.

"I know why the Amish do what they do. They believe that the telephone invades the family unit, but this is Montana. It would have been easier if the Shelters could have just called everyone. Time was wasted."

"Ja, yes, that makes sense." Marianna had a feeling she knew where this was going.

"Tomorrow, if you don't mind, I'm going to send someone over to feed a phone line into your house. With your dat away, you need to be able to call for help."

Marianna nodded. "I'd appreciate that." She moved to the porch and watched as Annie left. Then she said a quick prayer, thanking God that the girls had been found. It could have turned out so much worse. And Annie knew that. She'd no doubt seen a lot and had come to the end of her rope. Amish rules might work well in other locations, but not here. Marianna just wondered what Mem would say about Annie's plan.

A sad smile curved on Marianna's lips when she remembered how Ben had called her on one of the first days in the cabin to see if she'd needed a ride to town. Oh, how conflicted she'd been when the phone rang in the shop—and not out in a phone shed—and she'd answered.

She missed Ben. An ache in the pit of her gut told

her that she didn't want to live without him. No matter their differences, they could work it out. No traditions or rules she'd grown up with were worth missing out on the man she loved with all her heart.

Trapper's whining inside the door reminded her she needed to go in and tell Mem that the girls had been found. More than that, she needed to get to bed. She needed to rethink the old traditions that were tripping her up.

And she needed to pray.

Chapter Twenty-Three

WEDNESDAY, JULY 5, SCAPEGOAT WILDERNESS, MONTANA

Ben looked at the sleeping Abe. Was it a good sign or not that he didn't stir? After Ben had fed him a simple dinner of beef jerky and water, Abe had tried to sleep but wouldn't settle. That had lasted for hours, him moaning in pain. Even two of the pain relief tablets did little to help. Yet somehow, in the last hour—and long after midnight—as Ben prayed by his side, Abe had stilled and fallen into a deep sleep.

"Please, Lord, let him rest. And keep us safe." Whereas the wilderness had seemed so quiet the first three nights, after the encounter with the grizzly, Ben hadn't rested at all. Understanding that the bear was out there was unnerving. The fact that the bear knew where they were made it even worse.

"I need rest, Lord." Ben snuggled under half of the sleeping bag and scooted closer to Abe to feel his slightest movement. Because of the wickiup strung over them, he couldn't make out the stars, but it gave him peace knowing they were there. He thought of Ike out there alone on the trail. Would Ike stop to rest, or would he keep going? Ben sent a prayer up for him too.

He listened to the sound of the creek and thought of the still waters. Of Marianna. Ben rubbed his brow and remembered his last time at the beaver pond. What could have been a beautiful moment had gone so wrong. Why?

What had they even argued about? Marianna was concerned about the wedding. She was worried about how to make everyone happy. And his mind had been on the news he'd heard from Stacy Cannon—how their community would be invaded by the media, and all because of him. He also thought of Jason and the text from Hannah. Her anger was justified. She'd lost her brother. Yet should guilt keep Ben from marrying and planning a promising future with Marianna?

He closed his eyes, thinking about Marianna and what he'd say now if he saw her. He'd listen as she shared her heart about the wedding. And then he'd take her hands in his and tell her that what mattered most was the marriage to follow. All the days of their life together.

Ben sighed, imagining their cabin, sitting before the fire and watching the snow fall outside. He thought about next spring and planting a garden together. He considered the joy in her eyes when he told her the next addition he was already planning—a nursery for a baby or two.

One image settled him most—the thought of dancing around the living room, trying to be quiet as their babies slept. Then, finally, his eyes drifted closed.

Ben yawned and stretched his arms from under the sleeping bag, feeling sunshine warm his face. Slowly, the memory returned of their trail ride and—Ben sat up with a start. The bear. He glanced around, heart pounding. It was morning, and he'd fallen asleep. He hadn't stayed up in fear, and they were all right.

Abe lay beside him, and his eyes fluttered as if he were trying to open them. A low moan escaped Abe's lips.

Ben tried to keep his voice low. "Abe. How are you doing?"

The sound of the creek in the distance caused Ben to smack his lips. His mouth was dry, but the idea of having to walk to the creek for water again caused goosebumps to rise on his arms. Still, he had to get water. He had to take care of Abe until Ike brought help. He couldn't allow his fears to overwhelm him and shut him down. He was all Abe had right now. Yet, to walk to the creek meant he could stumble across that grizzly again. Or even more. He'd also be leaving Abe alone.

"Whose idea was this—to go four days into the Bob Marshall Wilderness?" Ben muttered to himself.

Abe's lips parted. "God's." The words were no more than a whisper.

Ben narrowed his eyes as unexpected anger rose within him. He pulled his shoulders back and lifted his face to the sky. Really, this was God's plan? How could this be God's plan? Abe hurt. Ike alone and hiking out with an injured ankle. Ben was more scared than he'd ever been in his life. If God loved him—loved them—how could He let this happen? It made no sense. It didn't make sense that God had let Jason or Marianna's sisters die.

It was so much easier to have faith when things were going right.

Ben pushed the sleeping bag to the side and stood. "This is God's idea, huh? Then I suppose I'll just have to see what comes next. Either I'm able to get water, or I get eaten." He moved to his small pile of supplies, thankful for the water bottles with filters. He picked a couple up and walked toward the creek, scanning the trees. The forest was quiet, peaceful even. Yet nothing in Ben's heart felt peaceful. The familiar ache grew, expanding from his heart and taking over his chest. It moved upward, causing his throat to grow tight. Ben squeezed his eyes shut to keep the tears from coming.

He kneeled at the side of the creek and filled the bottles with water. A familiar phrase filled his mind as he tried to keep the bottled-up emotions from spilling. *Sometimes God requires us to face hard things, Ben. If you cry, you're telling God you don't trust Him,* his father had said more than once when leaving for a trip.

The words haunted him even here, on the top of a mountain. He was far from California, but he still told himself he couldn't cry. He had to have faith.

Ben's eyes stung. He rubbed them, rose, and hurried back to Abe.

Abe's eyes were open, and he allowed Ben to lift his head as he drank from the water bottle. Abe drank hungrily, and Ben drank from his own water bottle when he was finished.

Then, without hesitation, Ben moved to his small pile of supplies again. Somewhere overhead, a bird sang, but the ache inside didn't release.

Do you trust God, Ben? he chided himself. *I'm so quick to tell everyone at my concerts about God, but what about now? Do I really believe it?*

He pushed those thoughts from his mind too.

They didn't have much to eat, and Ben knew that it was more critical that Abe eat. He pulled one of the granola bars from the stash Ike had left and took it out of the wrapper.

"I have breakfast for you, although it's not as good as what we'd get from the Kraft and Grocery."

"Don't mention the wonderful food..." Abe moaned.

"You're right. Let's not think about the..." *Cinnamon rolls and the biscuits and gravy.* His stomach growled, but the ache in his heart pierced even more. "Yes, let's not think about that."

Ben felt strange feeding the granola bar to Abe, but it was clear the man didn't have any strength.

Abe took a bite, chewed it, and swallowed. "What about you?"

"Me?" Ben shrugged as if the hunger didn't bother him. "I'll eat later."

Abe narrowed his gaze.

Ben nodded. "I promise, later."

After Abe ate the granola bar, Ben checked the bandages on his leg. The blood still hadn't soaked through, which was a good sign. Since they didn't have more bandages and the only extra shirt was the one on his back, Ben decided it was probably better to keep the bandages like they were rather than mess with them. The break caused his mouth to grow dry and his stomach to constrict. It was splinted, but was that enough? He hoped it was.

"How's the pain?" Ben dared to ask.

"Doesn't bother me much unless I try to breathe. I definitely don't want to try to move."

Ben smiled. "Don't move, but keep breathing, please. You have some womenfolk at home that want you back."

Abe's eyes fluttered closed. "I'll do my best. But I need to ask...what's going on?"

Ben stilled. His shoulders tightened, and he knew Abe was no longer talking about the food or the pain when he moved. But worries about Ben were the last thing Abe needed.

"Nothing's wrong. Everything's fine."

"Ja, well, it's all right for you to be mad at God for letting this happen."

"Excuse me?"

"We..." Abe adjusted slightly and winced. "We were just trying to have a nice adventure." Abe sucked in a deep breath and released it. "I was just trying to enjoy time with my family—we were coming home from an ice-cream social when we lost my daughters, you know."

Ben nodded but couldn't speak. His lower lip trembled. The tension in his chest increased, and everything within him told him to run. Run from this conversation. Run from the pain. The only problem was there were bears out there—and other dangers he didn't want to think about.

They sat in silence as the minutes ticked by, and then the tears started to come. Maybe he didn't have faith, and perhaps now Abe would see that he wasn't a good fit for Marianna after all.

"My dad works in the state office for our church denomination," Ben finally said, his voice flat. "He travels a lot supporting missionaries. He has since I was young. My mom travels with him. She always traveled with him, but I stayed behind because I was in school."

Abe's eyes were open barely a slit. "Does not seem much of a childhood."

"Or adulthood. I can count the days they've been around on one hand."

"When your friend died?"

Ben shook his head.

"When you were put in jail for your involvement in—"

"Jason's death. No, but they managed to call." Ben shrugged. "And they're in Southeast Asia and won't be able to make it for the wedding either." His lip curled up. "I guess God cares more about lost souls out there than me or what I need."

"Is that what you think?" Abe's eyes were closed now, and his breathing was steady.

"It's pretty obvious, isn't it?"

Abe opened one eye. "It's okay to be angry at God at times," Abe repeated. "He can handle it. But sometimes we place the failings of men and women—their poor decisions—on God."

"Are you saying God didn't ask them to leave me behind?"

"I'm saying that it no doubt hurt His heart to see you hurting and alone—then and now."

A low gasp escaped Ben's lips, and tears broke through. *It really hurts God's heart to see me hurting?*

"I bet all those times you were crying, He was crying with you, Ben," Abe said just before sleep overtook him.

Ben's eyes burned, and he curled to his side, letting the pain he'd bottled up inside for most of his life seep out of his heart like sand sifting through one's fingers.

God, You're here. You care... Ben had told himself for years he believed that. But as the waves of release moved through him, stuck here high in the mountain, he really felt it.

For the first time in his life, he truly believed it.

Chapter Twenty-Four

THURSDAY, JULY 6, WEST KOOTENAI, MONTANA

Marianna yawned wide as she pulled the muffin tins from the commercial oven, breathing in the aroma of apples and cinnamon. As hard as she tried, she couldn't shake the feeling that something was wrong on the mountain. Worries filled her mind, and although she prayed, she couldn't just sit. She couldn't watch the clock and wonder if any minute bad news would be coming. Instead, she'd come in early for her shift and decided to bake some of Annie's favorite muffins. Still, it was hard to think about anything else.

Did she have to wait three more days before hearing anything from Ben, Dat, and Uncle Ike? The other night, Annie's sternness with the girls reminded Marianna they lived in a wild, untamed, and sometimes unfriendly place. How much more so up in the wilderness?

"Take a break and enjoy some of the fruit from your labor," Annie said with a smile, interrupting her worries. "I'm not sure you noticed—you've been so lost in your thoughts—but I've already eaten two." Annie rubbed her stomach. She was the same, carefree Annie that Marianna always knew, but she'd seen a different side of Annie Tuesday night. *I'm sure she's seen so much during her years as an outfitter. Annie was right. Children need to learn.*

"Thank you, I think I will." She removed her flour-spotted apron and washed her hands. "My stomach has been rumbling, and I could use some coffee."

Grabbing an apple cinnamon muffin, Marianna was pleased to see Millie Arnold sitting in the dining room area and enjoying a cup of coffee. Even though Millie had to be older than Marianna's Aunt Ida, she moved with the energy of a much younger woman.

Returning to their conversation at church, Marianna thought again how different Millie's life had become after living in Seattle. Somehow the city girl had made a home for herself in the rugged country of Montana, and she'd stayed married through the ups and downs of life's challenges. Marianna poured herself a cup of coffee to go with her muffin and hurried in Millie's direction.

"Sweet girl, what are all those worry lines I see across your forehead?" Millie cooed as Marianna sat across from her. "Are you thinking about your wedding? I know all the decisions can be so much."

Marianna nodded. Yes, it was easier talking about the wedding than about worries about Ben in the wilderness, entertainment reporters, photos, and stories of her and Ben all over the internet.

"Oh, Millie, the more I think about our wedding, the more I'm afraid I'll make the wrong decisions."

Millie took a sip of her coffee. "How can marrying a godly man who loves you wholeheartedly be wrong?"

"I'm not talking about marrying Ben. That is the good part. The hard part is figuring out how to mesh our Amish ways with Englisch ones. No matter what we choose, someone's going to be disappointed."

"Someone?"

"My parents—or more specifically, my mem. The other Amish women." Marianna sighed. *And maybe I'm disappointed in myself too,* she wanted to say. *Perhaps I wouldn't have had to deal with this if I hadn't fallen in love outside my culture.* But instead of focusing on that, she narrowed her gaze on Millie. "Then there is Ben to think about. He doesn't understand Amish tradition, and he's experienced things differently."

"And what's the worst thing that can happen if you make a decision that someone doesn't like?"

"I suppose they'll be disappointed." Marianna

took a bite of her muffin, feeling her shoulders relax. She had a feeling she knew where Millie was going to go with that answer.

"Well, darling, in my opinion, this isn't an Amish or Englisch problem. No matter what you decide, someone will always be disappointed. I guarantee that. What I'm more concerned about is why it matters so much to you that someone is disappointed."

"Why it matters?" Marianna let the words replay in her head. "Well, it should matter, shouldn't it? I mean, I want everyone to enjoy the day. I don't want Mem or our Amish family to feel uncomfortable. Then there's the idea that it will be written up in *The Budget*. Or worse, no one will mention it and just shun us."

"Oh, then many people will be disappointed, won't they? Or...will they just be curious? Will they be hurt by your decisions, or will it just be something for them to chatter about when they meet up for Sunday church?"

Marianna had to think about it. "Well...I don't know."

"Will anyone actually be hurt by your decision? In the end, I feel your mem will find joy in the fact that her daughter is happy and a good man's wife."

Marianna watched a group of Amish children entering the store with their mem. They walked behind her calmly, looking at the items on the shelves but not daring to touch anything.

We are an example of God's ways to a watching

world. She'd been told that a dozen times if she'd been told that once.

"All my life I've been taught to be concerned with what others think," she explained to Millie. "The Amish have certain standards. We learn to do what we ought because we're told someone's always watching."

"They may be watching, but in my opinion, we ought not always be concerned about what they think." Millie smiled. "When Ben gets home, talk to him...and listen. That's the important part. Then the two of you decide on how you want your wedding to be. Then the rest of us...well, that day, we'll all be so thrilled by you two coming together that it won't matter if we get our way."

"Thank you, Millie. I'll take that advice. I promise, when Ben gets back, we'll sit and have a long talk about what really matters. Just me and him."

~

THURSDAY, JULY 6, SCAPEGOAT WILDERNESS, MONTANA

AS ABE SLEPT, BEN KNEW HE NEEDED TO FIND food. He didn't have any idea how long it would be before help came, but the two granola bars they had left wouldn't tide them over.

Ben pulled out the booklet of edible plants. Not once when they'd been coming up the trail had he looked at a plant and thought, *That looks good. I want to eat that.*

The truth now was that the purpose of food was survival. He flipped through the pages and looked at the color illustrations, trying to see if anything looked familiar. From the descriptions, he saw that most edible plants were helpful for tea or herbs to use for cooking. As Ben's stomach growled, he knew he wanted more than tea.

Abe's eyes opened, and Ben thought it wouldn't hurt to ask for help. Surely Abe knew more about finding food in the wilderness than he did.

"Do you need more water?" Ben reached for Abe's water bottle. Abe nodded and allowed Ben to hold the water bottle to his lips as he took a long drink.

Abe glanced around. "How long has Ike been gone?"

"He headed out two days ago, but his ankle was in pretty rough shape." Ben forced a smile. "The good news is we've made it this long. The bad news is we're out of jerky and only have two granola bars left." He held up the booklet of edible plants. "I looked at this, and unless we want a cup of tea, I don't think it'll do much good. I was wondering if you could tell me how to fish without a pole or make a rabbit trap."

Abe rubbed his brow. "Have you seen any rabbits?"

Ben shook his head. "Well, near the truck, but not up this far."

"Then it might be hard to trap something you haven't seen."

Ben's shoulders slumped.

"Are you sure all you had in your backpack was granola bars? That doesn't seem like Annie to me. I mean, as much as she packed everything else for you. In fact, she's the one that gave me that jerky."

Ben thought of the torn pack. "But I turned it over and dumped it out."

"Did you check the bottom zipper?"

Ben scurried over to the ripped-up backpack. "Bottom zipper?" He laid it out flat, and as he did, he noticed an exterior pocket he hadn't seen before. Quickly unzipping it, laughter spilled from Ben's mouth. "Abe, you're right. And I will give Annie the biggest hug when I get back." He pulled out two food pouches and waved them in the air. "I thought I would have to learn to skin a rabbit, but look here. This pouch has peanut butter and oatmeal. And this one, red beans and rice." He turned the packet over to look at it. "All we have to do is add hot water to the pouches."

Ben pulled out something that looked like a foldable dog dish. Still, when he opened it, an illustration showed that it was a collapsible kettle with a handle to heat up water for the food pouches. "And look at this. Annie's going to get more than a hug. I'll name my first child after her...if it's a girl, of course."

Abe's eyes fluttered closed, but a smile curved on his lips. "That oatmeal sounds good to me."

"Yes, of course, coming right up." Ben moved to the fire, poking it to bring the embers to life. The last time he'd been this excited was the day that Marianna had agreed to be his wife.

"Thank you, Annie," he whispered as he pulled a dozen more small packets from the bottom of the pack. *Thank You, Lord, for keeping us safe and providing for us through friends. And, Lord, be with Ike... bring him a miracle even now.*

Chapter Twenty-Five

Thursday, July 6, West Kootenai, Montana

The apple cinnamon muffins were a hit. The last one was sold during the lunch hour. Marianna was thankful for the chance to talk to Millie, and as the hours ticked by, she hoped she'd get an opportunity to speak with Annie too. Millie was right. Marianna needed to focus on what she and Ben wanted...

The thing was, things hadn't ended well between her and Ben before he left.

As the cooks prepped for dinner, the store smelled like roast beef and gravy. Marianna smiled, realizing that she knew the day of the week by what was being cooked up from the dinner menu. She sniffed and also detected the sweet aroma of oatmeal cookies, realizing that Sarah must have also come in to do some baking. And even though it smelled amazing, Marianna's face fell when she noticed the concerned look on Annie's face. Then Annie walked to the front of the store, where Edgar sat behind the checkout counter. Was something wrong with Edgar?

Even though Annie's main job was running the Kraft and Grocery, her other job included being a mom to everyone at the store. Today, Annie wore a light-pink plaid shirt, and her high ponytail flipped as she talked.

"Maybe you should go and put that foot up, Edgar. Sit in my office. I'm going to get you an ice pack."

"You sure do a lot of mothering for someone half my age," Edgar mumbled.

"You need someone to take care of you." Annie crossed her arms over her chest and leaned against the back counter. Behind Annie were shelves filled with camping supplies for tourists who came to town: lanterns and oil, rope and tent stakes, flashlights, and batteries. All things often used by Amish folks in these parts too. Annie narrowed her gaze at the older man. "Either you sit in my office, or I'm going to drive you home for the day. If you don't get off your foot, it's going to get worse, then you'll be stuck home even longer. Alone." Annie's brow puckered threateningly.

"Fine."

Annie glanced at Marianna. "I'll be right back."

"No problem. If you have time to talk..."

"Yes, of course. Why don't you get some coffee for the both of us, and I'll be right there."

Then, with short, slow steps, favoring his right leg, Edgar hobbled to Annie's office. Their footsteps echoed on the wooden floors. The television clicked on, and the sound of the noonday news filtered out from the office. Marianna poured two cups of coffee and listened as Annie moved some things around so Edgar could elevate his leg. Then, with a satisfied look, she exited the office.

"Finally got him to listen?" Marianna kept her tone light, pretending her upcoming conversation about Ben didn't weigh on her heart like the wooden beams overhead.

Annie nodded and then approached the table where Marianna sat with two steaming cups of coffee before her. "I'm sorry that took a minute. Edgar sure can be stubborn at times, as you know."

"Yes, but I missed that when I was in Indiana. Baking is not as fun when you don't have someone pestering you for a sample every five minutes."

Annie settled into the chair across from her. Jenny approached as if also knowing this would be more than a five-minute conversation. Jenny had been thankful for Annie's and Marianna's help finding her daughter Kenzie, along with Evelyn.

"There's two pieces of apple pie left. Hold on while I snag them. It's on me." She winked.

"Thanks, Jenny," Marianna stated simply. Jenny was a pretty woman, and Marianna had sometimes wondered why Ben hadn't pursued her instead. However, deep down, she was glad he hadn't.

Annie took a sip of her coffee. She nodded her thanks to Jenny, making it clear that this wasn't a social time that Jenny could join in. Instead, with a sympathetic smile, Annie reached over and placed her hand on Marianna's. "You're not having second thoughts about your wedding dress, are you?"

The image of the white dress and her reflection filled her mind. "No, Annie, not at all. What I want is to figure out how to make things right."

"Right?"

"With Ben." She shook her head and tucked a strand of hair behind her ear. "Things weren't left in a good way when he headed out. And that's the worst part. I want to talk to Ben and apologize. I was just letting my worries block out the truth that I knew. I wish Ben was coming back tomorrow. I know I shouldn't think this, but sometimes my worries get the best of me. I hope Ben doesn't think I don't love him or I don't want to marry him."

"Well, let me think about that... Ben, if I can remember, is someone who clings to hope. He hung around when Aaron was around. Even though you made it clear that you wouldn't leave the Amish faith, he kept hanging around. Do you remember that?"

"Yes, of course."

"Well, I don't believe for one second that he thinks you're giving up on the two of you. I guess Ben knows you're worried about the wedding and all. But he also knows that you'll be together on the other side of these hurdles. For life." Annie smiled. "I think that's something that you need to—"

A loud crash from Annie's office caused them to sit up straighter.

"Annie!" Edgar's voice called.

Without hesitation, Annie rose and hurried to the back room. Another minor crash sounded, and Marianna rose and followed her.

They entered the office at the same time. Edgar was standing, pointing at the television. A stool was tipped over, as was a plastic mug. Coffee had spilled on the floor.

Annie rushed to his side with Marianna following close behind. "Edgar, what's wrong?"

"There, on the news. A reporter was up in Ovando, interviewing someone from the Forest Service about the upcoming tourist season, when a report came in that a riderless horse had been found on the trailhead near the parking lot, along with a mule."

Annie glanced at the television, but it had moved on to the following report. "A riderless horse?" She looked back to Edgar.

He cleared his throat. "And a mule. And not just any horse and mule. They were Ike's."

Marianna sucked in a breath and moved to Annie's desk chair to sit. *Please tell me this isn't happening... Oh, Lord, please.*

"Wait, wait." Annie held up her hands. "This is a big state. There are lots of horses, lots of mules."

"But you don't understand. They showed them on video." Edgar's eyes were wide. "I recognized Ike's horse and mule." Edgar pointed to Annie's phone. "Look at that smartphone of yours and go to the news page. I bet they have a picture posted."

Annie's fingers moved over the phone in ways Marianna didn't understand. Soon she pulled up a picture. A gasp escaped her lips.

"That means something's happened to them. Why would the horse and the pack mule have come back without Ike, Abe, and Ben?" Annie nibbled on her lower lip. "And do you see that pack mule?" Annie held up her phone for Marianna to get a closer look. "The mule's loaded down."

A sinking feeling came over Marianna. "It means they're stuck up there without supplies."

"That's not the worst part. I think you need to sit down too, Annie." Edgar pushed the chair he'd been sitting on closer to Annie.

"Edgar, please. This is no time for games." Annie's voice was sharp.

Edgar folded his hands in front of him and shook his head. "I need both of you to sit."

Marianna's legs trembled like wildflowers in the wind. "It's serious then."

Annie sat in the chair with a huff and turned her head to Edgar. She lifted her eyebrows as if saying, *Satisfied?*

Edgar sat on the edge of Annie's desk with a

somber look. "The news reporter said that there was blood on the saddle."

"Blood?" Marianna gasped. "At least one of the guys is hurt."

Annie eyed Edgar blankly as if she was trying to take it all in.

Then, with a fierce determination in her eyes, Annie rose. "I'm going down there." And without hesitation, she moved out of the room.

"What do you mean?" Marianna followed Annie with quickened steps.

Annie moved to the shelves behind the counter and took down two flashlights and an extra package of batteries. "Ike told me what trail they were taking. I know where they are."

"Shouldn't you call the authorities?" Edgar's voice called as he hobbled out from the office toward the front checkout counter.

"Yes, of course, but it's going to take them a while to pull a search team together. Time the guys might not have." Annie moved to another shelf and grabbed a tarp and some waterproof matches.

"Shouldn't you have someone go with you? If they're in danger, what can..." Marianna let her voice trail off.

Annie's gaze narrowed. "What can one woman do?"

"I didn't mean it like that. You'll be putting yourself in harm's way."

Annie pointed to her office, where Edgar had watched the news report. "If the horse and the loaded pack mule were found, they'll be up there without many supplies. The blood on the saddle means at least one of them was hurt. I can bring them supplies. I can bring them aid. I know where they are. I know how to get to them."

Marianna nodded. "Yes, of course. But can I help you pack things up?"

"You'll just slow me down," Annie snapped. "I know where things are, and I already have some emergency packs prepared. I've learned to be prepared. One can't think well in an emergency. I've learned that from, uh, situations before. It will not take long to pack up my horse and mule. I can load my animals and get down there before dark. Thankfully, it's a first quarter moon tonight—enough light to ride by."

Marianna felt her body stiffen. The thought of Annie riding at night into the mountains, along dangerous trails, filled her with fear. But at the same time, she knew that it was important for Annie to get there as quickly as possible. Lives could be hanging in the balance right now. The faces of Ben, her father, and Uncle Ike filled her mind. *Please, Lord, be with them. We don't know what's happening, but You know.*

Annie's gaze softened. "And I will call authorities and tell them what I know." She blew out a long breath. "I just can't sit here when he's—they're—out there. Not again." Tears rimmed Annie's lower lashes, and she quickly turned and wiped them away. Clearing the emotion from her throat, Annie turned back to

Edgar. "Can you call Sarah and tell her I need her to help Jenny cover the store and restaurant? If she can't cover it all, just put a Closed sign up. I'm sure everyone will understand."

Edgar nodded solemnly as if he'd just been punched in the gut and all the spunk had been knocked out of him.

Annie took a step closer to Marianna and grasped her hand. "I think you should find a ride down to Missoula or even Ovando. It's closer to the trailhead than here. Your mem will probably want to come too. See if Deborah Shelter can round up some women to watch the kids. You'll need to be down there..." Annie didn't finish the sentence, but Marianna knew. Whether good news or bad, she needed to be close.

"But should I go with you? I know how to ride—"

"This is not a ride through a meadow, Marianna. It's not an easy trail, and I will not take it at an easy pace. If you want me to get to them—"

"I understand. Yes, of course. We will work it all out about getting a ride to Ovando. You just go."

Annie didn't need to be told twice. Without another look around the store, she rushed out. She lived only a half mile down the road behind the store and always walked home from work. Today she ran like a woman half her age. Seeing her hurry, Marianna knew how serious the situation was.

"Lord, be with Annie. Help her find them. And be with the guys until help gets there. Protect them." Her whispered words caught in her throat. "Bring back my uncle, my father, and...my husband."

Yes, Ben would be her husband. She knew that within the depths of her now. Marianna didn't want to picture life without him. What a fool she'd been with all her concerns about the wedding. It no longer mattered if they married in a simple ceremony in the field beyond the store, at her parents' house, or anywhere else. All that mattered was that they'd be married and she could spend the days as Ben's wife.

Fears filled Marianna's mind over thoughts of losing him. Dat and Uncle Ike were more used to the rugged environments. But Ben... No, she didn't want to think of that. Couldn't think of that. Ben would come home. She'd marry Ben. She'd love him for who he was and for how God was using him, even if that meant through his music, on the road, working with his manager...

Marianna thought about Roy, Ben's manager, who also helped to produce his music. She'd met him only a few months after she and Ben returned to Montana from Indiana. They had gone to lunch, and Roy had been kind. It had surprised Marianna, since Ben had told her he'd once dated Roy's daughter, Carrie. But Ben had explained that Roy was truly happy for them, especially since Marianna had been Ben's muse for his biggest hit. Roy was closer to Ben than most, and she needed to tell him what was happening. Marianna pulled in a deep breath. She also knew she needed to ask for his help. The problem was how could she get ahold of him?

"Edgar, do you know how to use Annie's computer? I need to find a phone number for Ben's manager."

"Well, I'm not too hot with that thing, but Jenny can probably figure it out. We can ask her to help us."

After listening to Edgar state that they had an emergency, Jenny hurried into the office, wearing the restaurant apron and her short blonde hair pulled into a ponytail. The single mom had been a stranger to their community last year. Now Marianna couldn't imagine West Kootenai without Jenny around. If anyone could help her, Jenny could.

Worry filled Jenny's face as Marianna and Edgar explained the found horse, mule, and missing men.

"Do you think you can help me find someone on the internet?" Marianna asked the question as if she knew what she was talking about.

Surprise widened Jenny's eyes. "Yes, of course."

"Ben has a manager, Roy someone. I'd like to contact him. He needs to know what's happening, and I need to ask for his help too." Marianna wrapped her arms around herself, telling herself to remain calm and not allow fear to overcome her. "The thing is, I need to find him quickly, but I don't even know his last name and have no idea where to look."

Jenny nodded and pulled her cell phone from her pocket. "Okay, let me see." Jenny held the cell phone to her mouth. "Who is Ben Stone's music manager?"

After a tiny ping, information popped up, but after a few minutes, Jenny seemed frustrated. "IMDb and these other sites want me to pay for this information." Jenny tapped her lips with her finger. "But didn't you say that Roy produces Ben's music too?"

"Ja, he does."

Jenny lifted the phone to her mouth again. "Who produced 'Every Warm Cabin' by Ben Stone?" The phone dinged again, and Jenny scanned the page. "'Every Warm Cabin' is a song by American country music singer Ben Stone. The song was written by Ben Stone and produced by Roy Knight." Jenny's voice rose with excitement. "And this link takes me over to Roy's website where, bingo...here is a phone number for his production company. Hold on."

Jenny pushed her screen again and held her phone to her ear. Marianna could faintly hear a woman's voice answering. Then she explained the situation, gave Marianna's name, and offered her number.

With a sigh, Jenny lowered the phone. "She sounded upset to hear what was happening with Ben. She said she'd have Roy call immediately." Jenny tucked her phone into her pocket and then moved to the nail on the wall where a notebook with an attached pen was kept for leaving notes. Taking them from the nail, she wrote down what Marianna assumed was her phone number. She'd just added her name to the number when her phone rang. Jenny quickly answered it and then handed it over. "It's Roy. He wants to talk to you."

Marianna took the phone. "Hello?"

"Marianna, this is Roy Knight, Ben's manager. My assistant told me there's been some type of accident in the woods, and Ben and his friends were involved. Are you all right? You must be scared."

Maybe she hadn't expected Roy's first concern to be about her, but tears tumbled out before she could stop them. Jenny quickly handed her a tissue from the box on Annie's desk, and Marianna blew her nose and tried to compose herself. "I'm so sorry. I didn't mean to do that."

"You don't have to be sorry. I know you must be scared. I saw the news report, but I had no idea that Ben was involved."

"You saw the news report?"

"Yes, my daughter, Carrie, is one of the news anchors in Missoula. Call me a proud dad, but I try to watch her every day during lunch. The report of the horse and mule came in this morning. She happened to be close in that area anyway, interviewing a rafting guide about the upcoming season over at the Stray Bullet restaurant. When one of the locals arrived with the news of the mule and the horse, Carrie got to the trailhead where the two men who found the creatures were waiting for the sheriff and brand manager to show up."

"Brand manager?"

"Yes, the horse and the mule were branded. The brand manager can match the brand to the owner and give him a call."

"I know the owner. It's my uncle Ike, but he was up there with Ben in the mountains, along with my dat—father."

Roy was quiet for a moment. "I'm taking notes. I can call the brand manager down in Powell County and tell him he can confirm ownership with the manager up in Lincoln County. What is your uncle's name again?"

"Ike—Isaiah Sommer, actually. My guess is that Uncle Ike would have put down the phone number for the Kootenai Kraft and Grocery, or maybe his friend Annie Johnson, as the contact information. A lot of people do."

"I'm glad you called, Marianna, but I have to ask again—how are you doing?"

"Right now, I'm just trying to figure out what to do, and that's why I called."

"Let me know how I can help. Seriously, what do you need?" There was tenderness in Roy's tone.

"A ride down to Ovando? I'd like to be close."

"Good idea. You don't have to ask twice. Can you be ready to leave in an hour?"

"Yes, of course."

"Then maybe your mother wants to come?"

Mem. Marianna hadn't even told her yet. Annie had left quickly, and then Marianna had reached out to Roy. Now she had to go home and tell Mem that Dat was missing. Worse, at least one of the men was injured.

"I have five younger siblings, including a baby sister, but maybe we can find someone to step in and care for them. Yes, I do believe my mother will want to come."

"Wonderful. I'll be on my way up to West Kootenai soon. I'll call Carrie. Might as well call the sheriff, too, and see what search and rescue efforts are being made. Don't worry, Marianna, you're not in this alone. Between the authorities and the news reports, we'll get the help we need to find them."

And Annie, Marianna wanted to add but didn't. She had no idea how long it would take for search and rescue to get on board, but Annie she could trust.

"Thank you, Roy. I'll make sure Mem and I are ready when you arrive. Do you need directions to our place?"

"Nah, Ben pointed it out last time I was up that way. He's been talking about you for a while, you know. Nearly from the moment he met you."

"That's good to know. I'm glad that God brought us together."

"You should be." Roy chuckled softly. "I've never been a man of faith, but I love Ben, and I'm going to throw up some prayers that everyone makes it down from the mountains all right."

Marianna smiled at that as she said goodbye. Then she handed the phone back to Jenny. Many times she'd heard Ben pray for Roy. It warmed her heart to know that Roy was now praying for Ben.

Jenny held up the phone. "I want you to take this

so Roy can contact you. I'll let Annie know you have my phone too."

"You don't have to do that."

"It's no problem, really. It's just a flip phone, and I know you don't know what that means, but it's just for calls. You're going to need it. I can be reached at the store and my house. Everyone's number is in here. I'll show you how to get them." Jenny placed the cell phone into Marianna's hand, and she nodded. "We're all here for you, all of us."

God has a plan in all this, Marianna told herself as she hurriedly walked home. *He will bring good, not destruction, and maybe even lead others to faith.* She needed that reminder. She couldn't think of anything other than three men coming down from the mountain alive. None of the things she and Ben had been squabbling about not too many days ago seemed to matter now. *Lord, just bring home Ben, Dat, and Uncle Ike. And protect them even now. I'm thankful You do, even when we don't know where they are or what they're facing.*

Chapter Twenty-Six

THURSDAY, JULY 6, WEST KOOTENAI, MONTANA

Mem was in the garden pulling weeds when Marianna hurried around the house into the backyard. Ellie sat in the small, square patch of dirt that Dat had set up as a garden just for her. *"Better to have her digging around in her own garden than yours,"* he'd told Mem weeks ago when he'd tilled the gardens.

Today, Joy sat in a small playpen under the shade of one of the pine trees. Marianna attempted to slow her steps as she approached Mem. Yet from the way Mem's head quickly lifted and her eyes widened with alarm, Marianna knew she hadn't done a very good job concealing her worry.

Mem rose and wiped her hands on her garden apron. "What is it? What's wrong?"

Marianna paused before Mem. She grasped her hands behind her back. "Mem…"

"Marianna, what is it? Spit it out."

Glancing at her sister, Marianna smiled. Ellie's eyes were fixed on them both.

"Ellie, can you help me?" Marianna walked over and squatted in front of her four-year-old sister.

Ellie stood with an uncertain look on her face. "Ja."

"Can you get me one of those cookies you and Mem made last night?"

"Ja." Ellie nodded. Yet she still didn't move.

Marianna reached forward and touched her arm. "You can get one for yourself, too, but wash your hands first."

A tentative smile touched Ellie's lips, and she hurried to the house. It was only then that Marianna turned back to Mem.

"Please, Marianna." Mem gripped her hands in front of her. "What is going on?"

"Edgar saw a report on the news today. A horse and a pack mule showed up at the trailhead near Ovando—just where Ben, Dat, and Uncle Ike were going."

Mem gasped. "And any sign of the men?"

"No, none." Marianna folded her arms over her chest, unsure if she should tell Mem the rest of the news report.

"And they are sure those were Ike's animals? Surely there are many outfitters in those mountains."

Marianna grasped her mother's hands. "Mem, it's them. Annie confirmed it."

"Ja, she would know." Mem's voice was flat.

"Annie is heading down to Ovando. She's loading up her things."

"She's going into those mountains? Please tell me she's not going alone."

"She refused to take anyone with her. But she was an outfitter for many years. She knows those mountains. Annie believes taking someone else will just slow her down."

"Are they sending others in to find them?" Mem's desperate voice cracked with emotion.

"Annie said she'd call the authorities and report what she knows. She thinks it will take time for them to pull a search team together, and Annie doesn't want to wait."

As if Mem's legs could no longer hold her up, Mem sank onto her knees, just as she'd been sitting when she'd been pulling weeds. She looked down into the new sprouts poking from the soft ground as if the answers she sought were there.

"Mem, there's something more. The saddle—"

"Cookie, Mari, cookie." Ellie ran from the house with clean hands that clutched three cookies.

Mem's face lifted to her happy daughter, and she stretched out her hand. "Thank you, that looks delicious."

"Mem..." Marianna felt she should not tell her mother about the blood on the saddle. Not yet. At least one of the three men was injured, and her heart ached to know that.

"Mem," she repeated again. "I called Roy. I'm not sure if you remember, but he is Ben's manager." Seeing the blank look on her mother's face, she guessed nothing was sinking in, but she had to try to explain. "Roy works with Ben's music. He's coming up here to pick me up. He's going to take me down to Ovando. I'd like to be there...when they are found." Or to hear any news. Emotion tightened her throat, and she refused to entertain that thought.

"Ja, of course." Mem opened her arms and pulled Ellie into her lap, squeezing her close.

Confusion filled Ellie's face. "Cookie?" She pointed to the cookie in Mem's hand.

Mem nodded but didn't take a breath, and from the look in her eyes, it appeared that Mem was sinking. Falling into the disbelief, the depression, the despair that had no doubt plagued her when she had lost her two daughters over two decades prior. It was as if Mem's heart was held together by thin threads, and with one pull, they came out, allowing her broken heart to open and spill.

Marianna kneeled beside her mother, touching her hand again. "It may be hard to face all this at once, but Roy suggested you come too. We can ask Eve Peachy or someone to care for Joy. And maybe Deborah Shelter can help with the other kids."

"No." The word shot from Mem's mouth. "These are my children. My children. They need me. They can't lose me too."

"Mem, but don't you want to be close?"

"I can't leave them home with all these worries... and the baby, she's so young yet."

Marianna nodded, knowing she'd be going down to Ovando alone. Mem was right. She needed to be with her family. Yet Marianna also didn't want to leave Mem alone in her fragile state. Marianna's mind raced. Eve Peachy could help with the baby, but Eve was just a young woman. She wouldn't know what to do to handle Mem's emotions or to offer advice. Also, Deborah had her own young daughter, and she helped to care for Kenzie. She didn't have time to be an aid and a comfort to Mem.

A different name popped into her head. Millie Arnold. In her late seventies, Millie had faced a lot in her years. Millie had lost her husband in recent years. She'd also, no doubt, faced many hardships. Millie was also a no-nonsense type of person. For some reason, Marianna believed that was just what her mother needed at this moment, because no matter what news Mem got, she would have to hold herself together.

Knowing what she had to do, Marianna rose. Her mind raced as she tried to think how she could get ahold of Millie. Then she remembered that she had Jenny's phone. Even though Mem still had a far-off look in her eyes, she was now nibbling on a cookie as Ellie chatted on her lap.

Marianna looked over at the playpen and saw that Joy had curled up with her favorite blanket and had fallen asleep. Her mind raced thinking of what she had to pack, but first, she needed to get ahold of Millie.

Marianna's satchel was on the back porch where she'd left it. She took out the phone and clicked on the button that showed the contacts, just as Jenny had shown her. Then she found Millie's name. Pushing it, she could soon hear a ringing from the other side of the line.

"Hello."

"Oh, Millie, I'm so thankful you answered." Shaky laughter spilled out.

"Marianna? Is that you? Whyever are you calling, darling?"

"Oh, it's hard to say, but something has happened to Ben, Dat, and Uncle Ike. They went up into the mountains—"

"Oh no, oh no." Millie's voice sounded far off. "Please don't tell me that it was their horse and mule that showed up on that trailhead today. I saw it on the news."

"I'm afraid that it was. I am heading down to the area now, so I'm calling. I know you don't know my mother that well—at least, not as well as you know me. But I'm heading down to Ovando, and I need someone to stay with Mem and the kids."

"Me, of all people? Of course I'd be happy to, but I haven't been around kids for many years."

"It's actually not the kids I'm worried about. It's

Mem. I saw something in her eyes that scared me—as if, facing something painful and familiar, she was going to get lost in it all. I'm almost afraid that this will crush her if..." Marianna paused, not wanting to finish.

"I see. I see." Millie seemed to understand even without Marianna saying it. "Yes, of course. I'll pack a bag and head right over."

"Thank you, Millie."

Marianna was just hanging up the phone when Mem came into the house with a sleeping Joy in her arms and Ellie trailing behind. Marianna hadn't thought to ask where the boys were. Her guess was they were down the road playing with friends. She watched as Mem moved to the living room and set Joy in her cradle. Then Mem glanced up with intensity in her gaze.

"Did you change your mind? Did you want to go?" Marianna asked her.

"Ne. But I thought I'd need a way for you to get ahold of me." Mem sighed. "We have a phone in the shed. Maybe there's a way we can bring it into the house?"

"I have to tell you something." Marianna motioned for Mem to follow her to her room. She opened the curtains so that more light would come in. Then she opened her closet, and there on the shelf was the telephone that Annie had wired in for her.

"What is that?" Mem pointed.

"It's the telephone from the shed."

Mem took a step back like it was a snake sitting on the shelf. “What is it doing here?”

“After what happened the other night with Evelyn and Kenzie—and with Dat being gone—I thought a phone in the house could be useful. If something happens, well, it’s easier to get help.”

Relief flooded Mem’s face. “And you’ll call if you hear any news?”

“Ja, Mem.” Marianna took a step closer. “I will call.”

Before Marianna processed what was happening, Mem opened her arms and pulled her into her embrace. Marianna felt her body stiffen, uncertain, and she knew why. Mem was always loving and caring but rarely physically affectionate with Marianna. For most of her life, Marianna had assumed it was because one girl could never replace two in Mem’s eyes. But it was only recently that Dat had confessed the truth. Marianna had been so treasured after the loss of her two sisters that Mem had hardly ever put her down as a baby. It became so obvious how spoiled Marianna was that people started to talk. And instead of allowing herself to be comforted by young Marianna, Mem had pushed her away.

Mem’s hug was warm and gentle, and Marianna sank into it. “It’s all right, Mem. Dat will be all right.”

A soft sniffle sounded in Marianna’s ear. “They’ll all be all right. They’re all coming home. God is with them. We must believe that, daughter. God is with them even now.”

Chapter Twenty-Seven

THURSDAY, JULY 6, HIGHWAY 83, MONTANA

Marianna had never ridden in a vehicle as excellent as Roy's. More than that, it was odd to be alone with a man in a car, especially one who was not a driver for the Amish.

The interior smelled like leather and oranges, and she guessed the citrus scent was from some type of air freshener he had inside the car. She tried to relax as they drove down to Ovando. As they drove along the east side of Flathead Lake and down through the Swan Range, the view gave her something to focus on. The drive was beautiful, and after answering Roy's questions about growing up in Indiana and farm life, she wasn't sure what else they would talk about.

Roy had the satellite radio turned on, and they both turned and looked at each other when one of

Ben's songs came on. Tears filled her eyes as she heard Ben's voice. *Lord, please let him be all right. Let them all be okay.*

Glancing over, Roy cast a compassionate smile. "They're going to be okay," he said, as if reading her thoughts. "I have a feeling they will."

Older, with hair graying at his temples, Roy was thin, fit, and had a strong confidence about him—just as she pictured Ben would be at his age. "I've always liked this song," he said with a smile.

"Ja. I mean, yes, me too."

His eyes were fixed on the road ahead, watching for the deer that loved to dart into the roadway. "Have you ever been to one of Ben's concerts?"

She folded her hands on her lap. "Just local ones."

Roy ran a hand down his clean-shaven chin. "I think you'd like it."

Marianna shrugged. "Loud music and crowds, all those bright lights. I'm not so sure about that."

Roy chuckled. "I think you'd be surprised."

"Well, other than Indiana, Montana, and the train ride in between, I haven't been to too many places."

"It's a part of Ben's world, you know." Roy's tone grew serious. "I mean, he loves being in Montana, and even though the travel and all the interviews are hard at times, something changes when Ben steps upon that stage. He was meant to be a performer. Maybe you should know that part of him before the wedding."

With one hand, Roy opened up a video on his cell phone and handed it to her. Marianna smiled to think what the bishop in Indiana would think of this—her watching a music video of Ben on an electronic device, driving in an SUV that no doubt cost more than Dat made in three years. Then again, this was the man she was to marry. Roy was right. Shouldn't she know this part of Ben's life?

The concert started, and Ben sang some of his older songs. Marianna found herself smiling and mouthing the words as he sang. Then the lighting changed, and Ben told the audience he was going to sing a song that many of them knew but didn't give much mind to. With a joy-filled outstretching of his arms, Ben launched into a hymn that Marianna had sung a few times at church. Then her jaw dropped with amazement as many of the crowd started to sing along.

Marianna glanced over at Roy. "I didn't realize... This is beautiful."

"Yes, well, keep watching. It gets even better."

As the song ended, one of the stagehands brought out a stool. Ben sat down on it, holding his guitar, reminding Marianna of his appearance when she first saw him play at the Kraft and Grocery.

"My grandma used to sing that song, but I didn't think much of it growing up. Not until I found myself facing the lowest of lowest times when my best friend lost his life because of my negligence. Facing that, I didn't know if I wanted to live. I saw that the path of music, women, and parties wasn't leading anywhere good. That's when I headed to Montana to get away and figure out where my life was heading. On a whim, I packed the Bible my grandma had given me, and I started reading it. God met me there, and He changed everything."

Ben strummed as he talked, and Marianna listened as a hush came over the crowd. The camera scanned their faces, and Marianna saw many lowered heads. Others had tears in their eyes.

"Maybe you're at the place where you're wondering where your life is headed. Maybe you already know it's headed where you don't want it to go, and you know that things need to change. If you have a Bible, I'd suggest you start there. If you don't have a Bible, I have some on my merch table. They're free if you'd like one. I'll also be around after the show if you need someone to talk to about what a relationship with God means."

The strumming continued, and Marianna's heart doubled in her chest. Emotion filled Ben's face, and he tilted his head to the lights above him, almost as if he were waiting and listening for what to do next.

"If you've come to hear some music, we'll be getting back to that. But first, I'd like to pray for you." Ben lifted his audience up in prayer. He prayed for their relationships and their futures. He prayed they'd find hope and peace. He prayed that they'd understand how loved they were by God and him.

Tears filled Marianna's eyes, and she brushed them away. The highway took them through the mountains again, and the video started breaking up.

Roy reached out his hand. "I think we're losing reception."

"That's all right. What I saw was beautiful. Amazing, really." She handed him back his cell phone.

"I just thought you'd like to know. I know I'm biased, but I think what he's doing is worthwhile. He's giving people hope. And, well, his music is important."

"I believed that, but at the same time, I didn't really understand. He's different, isn't he? And I suppose people are noticing..."

Roy nodded and pressed his lips into a tight smile before glancing over at her and then back to the road. "You know, some people always think that the media flocks around the angst and drama, but they forget that people look for what's good too..."

"And maybe that's part of what's bringing them to Montana?" Marianna thought of Linsey Ledbetter. Deep down, did she long for a bit of hope too?

"I think so," Roy commented. "And that's why I know Ben will make it out okay. There's more good work for him to do—for both of you to do."

Chapter Twenty-Eight

THURSDAY, JULY 6, SCAPEGOAT WILDERNESS, MONTANA

Pain shot up Ike's leg with each step. Even though he'd gone on many solo hikes, he'd never felt as alone as he had over the last two days trying to make it back to the trailhead. Guilt weighed him down, ten times heavier than the pack. Over the miles, he'd replayed how he could have done things differently. He'd gone on enough trips into the Bob that he should have remembered how the bears could always be found where the tree line met the creek. He should have gone first on the trail. Then again, he doubted that anything could have stopped Flint or Shadow from bolting once they spotted a grizzly.

While he trudged along, Ike also thought of things

he should have done differently in other parts of his life too, especially concerning Annie. While Abe and Ben had thoughts of the women who loved them to carry them through this ordeal, Ike only had longings and what-ifs.

"It's not like I want to remain a bachelor my whole life," he whispered into the night breeze. Leave it to him to fall in love with the one woman he could never be with. Not only was Annie Englisch, but if she loved him back, she'd have to leave everything she loved behind—namely, the Kootenai Kraft and Grocery and her role in the community.

If he dared to ask Annie to marry him, Ike would have to walk away from the Amish faith. To do that, he'd be shunned. And marrying Annie would cause her to be shunned too, which meant that none of the Amish in the area could buy from or sell to the store. They couldn't work there either.

Marianna had to deal with the poor opinions of some, but even liberal Amish drew the line at buying or selling with those who'd left the church, or their spouses. There would be financial consequences for Annie. She'd lose everything. As much as Ike dreamed of Annie becoming his wife, he could never ask her to give up all she had for him.

The sun hovered over the mountains, yet the scent of pine needles, fresh air, and wild grasses urged him on. Ike's heartbeat quickened when he spotted a sign on the tree ahead. He remembered that sign—he was only a few miles from the trailhead and, hopefully, help.

Then again, what if there were no others in the area? How far would he have to hike out before he found someone who could call in for help? He should have thought about getting the truck keys from Ben before he'd left. Why hadn't he thought of that?

The sound of a horse's hooves caused Ike to pause. Then, like a vision or a dream, a horse and rider were climbing up the hill. Ike waved his arms and then gasped when he saw it was a lone woman who rode toward him. Not just any woman, but Annie. His heart leaped to his throat, and he couldn't believe his eyes. Was it possible to see a mirage in the mountains, or was that only in the desert?

He rushed forward and pulled his hat off his head, waving it to get her attention. "Annie!" Laughing, he replaced his hat and started to limp toward her. Ike smiled when he saw her horse start to canter.

"Ike!" Annie called to him. "Ike, are you all right?"

The horse stopped before him, and Annie swung down from the saddle. Before he knew what was happening, Annie leaped into his arms. Ike took a step backward as he got caught off balance.

"Ouch." He didn't mean to call out as he caught himself from tumbling, but he did.

Annie pulled back. "I'm so sorry. Did I hurt you?" She held him close, helping him catch his balance. Ike put his nose to her cheek. She smelled clean, like soap and lilacs.

"Hurt me? Annie, I've never been so thankful to see another person in my life. And the fact that it's you—there's no one I'd rather see." He placed a soft kiss on her cheek. Against her cheek, he said, "Thank you, Annie. Thank you for coming for us."

When he pulled back, they studied each other's faces. If Ike wasn't mistaken, he could see love in her eyes. Love for him.

It took his breath away.

He rubbed his beard growing in. Some bachelor he was. "I must look a mess."

She shook her head, battling tears. "Are you kidding?" Annie seemed to be out of breath. "You're a sight for sore eyes."

All the things he'd been thinking about this very woman across the miles, and here she was. He rubbed his brow, trying to make sense of it. "What are you doing here?"

"Shadow and Flint were found, and a reporter happened to be in the area. It was on the news, and Edgar saw it."

"And you knew they were my animals?"

"Yes, of course."

Ike ran a hand down Annie's cheek, wiping away a tear. "And you came."

"As quickly as I could."

Annie looked behind Ike, brows furrowed as if for the first time she remembered that it wasn't just Ike who she was looking for. "Where is Ben? Abe?" The color drained from her face. "They're not..." She sucked in a breath. "Are they still alive?"

Ike sat on a nearby log. His shoulders crumbled in defeat. "When I left, they were. That was two days ago." He pressed a hand to his forehead. "It happened so fast. Abe was riding. There were some bear cubs ahead on the trail. We were walking into the wind, and Shadow must have smelled them at the same time he saw them. Flint did too. Shadow tried to run up a near-vertical hill and flipped back. He landed on Abe."

"The blood on the saddle." Annie covered her mouth with her hand.

"What?" Ike jumped to his feet again.

"When Shadow was found, there was blood on the saddle. That must have been Abe's."

"It was. He has a broken leg and a huge gash. It's pretty bad, Annie."

"And Ben?"

Ike peered up into the darkening sky. The urge to go back to help his brother and Ben overwhelmed him. "He was attacked by the mama bear."

Annie leaned against Ike for support. "Oh no. So..."

"He's fine. He'll most likely be bruised, but not a scratch."

"How could he be fine? That doesn't make any sense."

"The backpack he was wearing. The bear got ahold of that. Swung him around pretty well. That's what the bruises will be from—the straps. Mama tore up the pack but not Ben."

"That's a miracle," she whispered.

"It's only part of the miracle. The wind shifted just as I got out the bear spray. The wind had been hitting our faces all day, but then...it just shifted and blew the bear spray into the bear. She ran off."

Annie peered down the trail. "But they're still out there?"

"Yes, and we need to get help for them. I hope they're still okay. Abe's leg...and the bear. I hope she didn't come back. I had to come out. To get help."

"We just have to trust that they're both all right." The lines around her lips grew tight. "And that Ben was able to care for Abe."

"They had so few supplies. All we had left on us were the few things I had in my pack and a little from Ben's pack that was salvageable."

"You must be starving." Annie hurried to her saddlebags on the horse. She pulled out a paper bag and handed it to him. "Here. Eat this." She smiled. "And we're not far from the trailhead and parking lot. Search and rescue should be assembling there soon. They're gathering volunteers, and the sheriff is tracking down the brand manager to confirm who the animals belong to. I called him on the way down from West Kootenai, and he was glad for the information I gave them. I can take you back—"

"No. Go ahead. See if you can get to Ben and Abe. I know it's going to take a few days."

Annie pulled a map from her saddlebag. "Can you tell me exactly where you left them?"

Ike sat down with the map and focused on the trails. His eyes were dry and tired. All he wanted to do was eat the food from Annie, take a hot shower, and climb into bed. But at the same time, he felt guilty that he could now do those things but his brother and friend were still in the elements.

His finger traced the path they'd traveled. Finally, Ike pointed out where he'd left them. "Ben and I set up a camp for them. Settled Abe in the area of the creek but not too close."

"Good. I'll get started. You'll be amazed at how quickly I can go alone, even with a pack mule."

"I have no doubt."

"And when search and rescue come, tell them what you told me. Also, I know that area well." Annie pointed to the map. "There is a meadow near here. Maybe a quarter mile away. It might be a good place for a medical helicopter to land. Tell them to send the helicopter, that Abe needs to be airlifted out."

"I'll let them know."

Ike grabbed Annie's hands. "Lord, be with Annie. Keep her safe. Continue to be with Abe and Ben. And, Lord, be with search and rescue, too. If it's possible, let them get a helicopter to my big brother."

Ike finished praying, and Annie clung to his hands. "You did the right thing, going out to get help. It's what I would have done. So either way..."

Either way. The words replayed in Ike's mind.

They could be fine, but there was a chance they weren't. Ike didn't know how he'd handle it if they weren't all right.

"Look at me." Annie's voice was firm. "I'm going in there. I'm going to do my best. But you did the right thing, Ike. You should not feel guilty about this. None of it."

Chapter Twenty-Nine

FRIDAY, JULY 7, OVANDO, MONTANA

Marianna opened her eyes, taking a minute to remember where she was. Red numbers shone from an alarm clock on the nightstand. She reached over and clicked on the bedside lamp. The room was simple, with a four-post wooden bed and a red-and-white checkered quilt on the bed. Then she remembered she was at the Ovando Inn, and Roy was just two doors down.

She moved to the bathroom and ran a white washcloth under the cool water, pressing it to her face. Why was she trembling? Marianna looked into the mirror, and a memory surfaced. No, not a memory but a dream. She'd been at one of Ben's concerts. He'd been playing his music, and he'd looked at the crowd earnestly when the stool was brought out. *"I usually pray for my audience, but today things are different. I need you to pray for me."*

Marianna returned to the bed and kneeled beside it. The rug's texture pressed into her knees, and she rested her face on the sweet-smelling sheets. Her fists clutched them, and nausea rushed over her at the thought of losing any of those men who meant so much to her. "I'll do anything, God. What do You need me to do? I'll do anything. Just bring them back to us," she muttered through clenched teeth.

The image from her dream stirred in her mind. *Can you pray for me?* Ben had pleaded with the crowd. *I need the prayers of all of you. As many prayers as I can get. Can you pray?*

Marianna gasped as she sat up, knowing this was the day she'd hear something. And that though Ben needed her prayers, he needed even more. He needed the prayers of many—those who loved his music. Loved him. But how could she get the word out and urge others to pray?

Marianna thought of Carrie, Roy's daughter who had dated Ben once. Did Carrie have any hard feelings against Ben? Would she be willing to interview Marianna so that she could ask Ben's fans to pray?

As she considered this, another face filled Marianna's mind, and she knew Carrie wasn't the answer. Carrie was a local reporter. Yet there was someone else who Marianna knew with a much greater reach. Marianna's photos all over the internet had confirmed that.

A tendril of panic seized Marianna's chest as she

remembered the way that entertainment reporter had filmed her without permission. Linsey had caught Marianna off guard and then twisted her words. Yet even as pained emotion squeezed Marianna's heart, a gentle whisper filled her mind. *Forgive your enemy.*

Forgive her? Could Marianna forgive her? Could she trust her?

Marianna squeezed her eyes shut. *Lord, I can't do this.*

Forgive her, and she will be my instrument.

Marianna opened her eyes and lifted her palms to the ceiling. *I give my hard feelings about her to You, Lord. Help me to be strong to do what I have to do.*

With trembling hands, she stood and found her purse on the desk. She opened it and pulled out her wallet, brush, and other things she'd shoved into it when packing. In the bottom she found what she was looking for. The card with *Linsey Ledbetter* on it. Marianna picked up Jenny's cell phone and dialed the number.

"Hello." The woman's voice sounded scratchy.

"I'm so sorry. I didn't mean to wake you."

"Marianna?" Linsey's voice became clearer.

"Yes, how did you know?"

"It's a Montana number, and I saw a short news report stating that Ben Stone is missing. Someone called and let the authorities know that a horse and mule that were found belonged to the man Ben was traveling with." Linsey sounded as if she was concerned about him, as if she cared.

Emotion caught in Marianna's throat. "Yes, that is true."

"And I recognized your voice. You have that Amish lilt." Linsey's voice was gentle, more like a friend.

"Again, I'm sorry to bother you, but I was wondering if I could ask you a favor."

"A favor?" Linsey's voice perked up.

"Ja, I mean, yes. There has been some type of accident. I'm not sure who's injured. It could be Ben, my father, or my uncle, but I know many people care about Ben. I would just like to ask them if they can pray."

"You would like to ask them? Like on video?"

Marianna paused. She closed her eyes and remembered her dream, remembered Ben's plea. "Yes, I don't mind getting on video."

"Are you still in West Kootenai?"

"No, I am at a town near the trailhead. Roy, Ben's manager, brought me."

Linsey's voice grew excited. "Can you give me the address?"

Urgency tightened Marianna's chest. "You're going to come up?"

"Yes. I can be there by this evening."

Marianna looked at the clock. Seven o'clock in the morning. "But what about now?"

"Now?"

"Can videos be made such as over a computer? I've seen people creating them when I work at the restaurant."

"Well, do you think Roy could help you?"

Marianna tucked a strand of hair behind her ear. "We're supposed to be meeting for breakfast in thirty minutes."

"Okay, wonderful. When you meet, call me back. Then we can figure something out. I'm sure Roy has Zoom on his phone."

"Perhaps." Marianna nodded. She didn't know what that was, but it didn't matter. All she knew was the urgency within her to get as many people as she could to pray for Ben and the other men she loved.

"I'm also going to catch a flight, so if you can get that address?"

Marianna paused, truly understanding what was happening. She was inviting the enemy to come. Hopefully, it wasn't a mistake.

Marianna gave Linsey the address, telling herself that it didn't matter if she was uncomfortable if it would help Ben.

After dressing and pinning up her hair in a simple bun, Marianna hurried downstairs to find Roy sitting in the small breakfast room. She poured herself a cup of coffee, placed a muffin on a plate, and then joined him.

He leaned forward, resting his arms on the table. "Good morning, how—"

"Do you know how to Zoom?"

Roy's jaw dropped. "I wouldn't be more surprised if you had told me you were a driver for NASCAR."

She added a sugar cube to her coffee and stirred. "Is that an auto race?"

"Yes."

"And Zoom?"

"Zoom has nothing to do with an auto race." Roy chuckled. "It's a way to talk over video. Why?"

Marianna pulled Linsey's business card from her skirt pocket and laid it on the table. "This is the reporter who came up to West Kootenai to make a video of me. And I thought she could help."

"Help?" He shook his head. "You can't be serious, right?"

"Well, I have been thinking a lot about that video you showed me. The audience really cares for Ben, and he cares for them." She folded her hands on her lap, wondering what Roy would say about what she had to say next. "Last night, I had a dream. It was Ben on the stage. Instead of praying for the audience, he asked them to pray for him."

Roy sat up straighter. "That happened...in your dream?"

"Yes, and I know the word has gotten out that Ben is one of the men who's missing. I bet a lot of people are waiting to hear something. And maybe, well, I thought I could ask them to pray."

"Over Zoom?"

"Linsey said you can talk to her about it—that you'd figure it out."

"Yes, of course." Roy leaned forward, still resting his arms on the table. "But Marianna, are you sure you want to do this? I've talked to Ben a lot. I know how you feel about...well, his career, the media, all the changes."

"That's one thing I feel bad about. I really didn't understand it." She sighed. "Ben left, and Ben came home. I loved his music and songs, but...I wasn't even allowed to watch television or go to a concert in my community...so I couldn't imagine. But I see how Ben would think I didn't want any part of it."

Roy took a sip of his coffee, listening.

"But I know now that to love Ben is to love every part of him, even parts I don't yet understand. And when he comes down out of those mountains, I will tell him that. And until he does return, I'm going to do my best to reach out to his fans and ask them to pray. So can you help me?"

Roy reached over and lifted Linsey's card from the table. "Yes, I'll call and chat with her. Like you said, we can figure something out."

Then, as if just realizing what she'd asked, feelings of anxiety somersaulted through her. The music filtering out from the lone speaker overhead swelled as if punctuating the moment when everything changed. Whether she liked it or not, she would no longer be a former Amishwoman who didn't understand the world. Marianna understood more of it now, at least Ben's world beyond West Kootenai. Through this choice, she was entering it in a way she'd never expected or planned.

Only an hour later, Marianna was sitting in front

of Roy's laptop computer, which he'd brought along. Roy clicked a link on an email, and soon Marianna was on a dual screen with Linsey on the other side.

"Hello, Marianna. We're going *live* on our website in two minutes. As promised, you will have the floor after my introduction."

Marianna fixed on Linsey's broad smile. "I have what?"

"You can say anything you like. Just look at the camera, and don't worry if you don't say things perfectly. Just speak from your heart."

She nodded. "Yes, all right."

Marianna looked to her left. Roy nodded and smiled. "You know what you want to say."

"Okay, we're going live now," Linsey said.

Marianna's throat grew tight. It took everything within her to sit there and look at the computer. Her instinct was to leave, to hide, but she instead smiled.

"This is Linsey Ledbetter with *Entertainment Weekly*, Los Angeles. A news station in Missoula, Montana, reported that a horse and a pack mule showed up at a trailhead with no sign of the men traveling into the Bob Marshall Wilderness. One of the missing men was also reported as music artist Ben Stone, who we all adore. Today, I'm thankful to have Ben's fiancée online, and she has something she wanted to tell us." Linsey offered a sad smile. "Marianna, go ahead."

"My name is Marianna Sommer. Many of you know I am engaged to be married to Ben Stone. I—"

Emotion caught in her throat. "As you may have heard on the news, Ben was on a trip into the Bob Marshall Wilderness. Yesterday the two animals being used showed up, but there was no sign of the three men. If you have been to any of Ben's concerts, you know he always prays for his audience. And now, I'm asking that you pray for Ben. Please..." Tears filled Marianna's eyes. "I love him, and I know you do too. Can you please pray for Ben? Can you pray for his safety and that of my father and uncle? Can you pray that Ben makes it home to me...to us? Thank you."

Linsey wiped a tear away. "Thank you, Marianna. This shows how much you care for Ben. It means a lot. Thank you."

A minute later, their live broadcast ended, and Linsey fidgeted in her seat and leaned closer to the camera. Compassion radiated from her gaze. "Thank you for doing that. I know it will mean a lot to Ben. And if it's all right, I'd like to still come up. I'll sign off now."

"Yes, of course." Marianna looked at Roy. "Do you know how to turn this off?"

"Sure." Roy rose and moved to the computer.

"Wait." Linsey's voice came across louder than it had before.

Marianna turned her attention back to the computer.

Linsey cleared her throat. "I also want to apologize. I know I shouldn't have done that—just stuck a camera in your face."

"And then posting the photos?" Marianna tilted her head and cocked one eyebrow.

Linsey nodded. "Yes. I need to apologize for that too."

Marianna pressed her lips together. She sat silent, unmoving. Then she shot up a silent prayer, knowing what she had to do. "I forgive you, Linsey." A warmth filled her chest that hadn't been there a moment before. Warmth rimmed with peace. "And I know God has a plan in all this. I'll be looking forward to seeing you soon."

Roy stepped forward and turned off the computer. Just as Marianna leaned back in her chair, she heard a phone ringing and realized it was Jenny's cell phone. Marianna quickly grabbed it from her satchel. The name on the phone said *Millie*. She promptly answered it.

"Hello?"

"Marianna, this is Mem. Edgar gave me your number. They found Ike. He was found at the trailhead by search and rescue last night."

A vise squeezed around Marianna's heart. "Wait, only Ike?"

"Dat and Ben were still alive when Ike went out for help."

"Were alive?"

"Dat has a serious injury...and there was a bear attack. It was amazing. Ike said that no one was hurt when the bear attacked."

"And Ben?"

"Ben was fine. He stayed to take care of Dat."

Marianna moved to the window overlooking the ridge of mountains that led into the Scapegoat Wilderness. Ben and Dat were still out there somewhere.

"Where is Uncle Ike now?" she asked.

"They took him to the hospital in Missoula. He was dehydrated and exhausted. He has an ankle injury too. I don't think he rested much in the days he took to hike out."

"So what about search and rescue?"

"They're going to try to send in a medical helicopter if the weather cooperates."

"And Annie?" Marianna blew out a sigh. "Have you heard anything about Annie?"

Mem's voice was silent on the other end of the phone. Roy stepped forward and placed a comforting hand on Marianna's arm.

"Ike saw her. She went in alone to help your dat and Ben. I talked to Millie, and she's sending word for everyone to pray, Amish and Englisch." Mem chuckled. "I've been talking to Millie a lot, in fact. She's helped me to see the peace in letting go of so much pain and worry from things past and things to come." Mem sighed. "God will bring them out, Marianna. God led them to the wilderness, and He will bring them out."

Chapter Thirty

FRIDAY, JULY 7, SCAPEGOAT WILDERNESS, MONTANA

It happened so fast Ben didn't know what to think. He'd just helped Abe eat a packet of peanut butter oatmeal when a loud roaring filled the air. Ben's first thought was that the grizzly mother had returned and was bearing down on them. Then he realized it was an unnatural roar. A mechanical roar.

Overhead he saw a helicopter skimming over them, bending the trees. It was going beyond them. *Does it know we're here?*

Ben stood as the realization hit him. "Ike must have gotten out. He's sent help!"

He glanced down at Abe, looking too thin and pale on the mat.

"Go." Abe's word wasn't much more than a whisper. "Go tell them we're here."

Ben scurried up the hillside to the trail. And it wasn't until he reached the trail that he remembered the mama grizzly and the cubs.

Fresh bear tracks brought him pause, and the torn pieces of fabric they'd left there were scattered even more. Ben eyed the helicopter's direction, and he guessed it had landed. He couldn't see around the next bend—didn't know if help or the mama grizzly awaited him.

"I don't have a choice." If it was just him, he could most likely hike out, but he had to get to that helicopter. He had to help Abe.

Ben shot up a prayer. "Lord, I need you now." And then he started running down the trail. As he ran, Ben pulled his whistle around his neck and blew. Over and over again. He needed the rescuers to know they were here.

He raced down the trail, rounding one corner and then the other. Then he saw it. In a vast meadow, the small helicopter rested, and two paramedics climbed out with a stretcher.

Ben waved his arms and shouted.

The men hurried toward the trail.

"Are you Ben Stone?" one of them asked.

Ben didn't know why, but that caught him as funny. Maybe because he'd been asked that many times when a fan recognized him. And maybe because, how many other men were lost in the wilderness? But most likely because it meant Abe would be getting help—more help than he'd been able to give.

A soft laugh slipped out of Ben's mouth. "Yes, that's me."

"Are you hurt?"

Ben shook his head. "No, it's a miracle, but I'm not." He motioned up the trail. "C'mon, I'll take you to Abe."

Within a few minutes, the medics had retrieved Abe. Ben followed them to the helicopter, expecting that he'd be given a ride too.

"I'm sorry, buddy." There was both humor and compassion in the man's gaze. "This is a medical helicopter, not a taxi service. But even if we wanted to give you a ride, we can't. There's only room for one."

"But what if I had been hurt?"

"We would have had to make a second trip and hope that the weather held. It's not like we have a surplus of medical helicopters around."

"Yes, of course."

The man patted Ben's shoulder. "The search and rescue team is on their way in to help you. If you start heading back the way you came, you will run into them." The man gave him a thumbs-up. "Don't worry. You've got this."

Ben walked back onto the trail, not knowing what else to say. He'd been so relieved that Abe would get the help he needed that it wasn't until the helicopter had lifted off that Ben realized he was alone.

Ben sighed, knowing that Abe would be getting the help he needed.

As Ben walked up the trail alone, the weight of all that had happened over the last three days—or had it been four?—hit him. The sighting of the bear. Tending to Abe. Ike's determination that one of them get out and get help. Going hungry. Finding food.

Ben thought of the bear, feeling his legs grow heavy with the burden of it all. The grizzly would have bitten into him if it weren't for his pack. With trembling hands he covered his face. "Jesus, thank You. I don't know what else to say. You protected us. You brought help. You..."

Marianna's face filled his mind, and love and longing filled his heart. He'd been overwhelmingly drawn to her from the first moment he saw her at the train station. He'd known the obstacle to his growing affection that day at the quilt auction over a year ago when he'd been helping her display the quilts and she'd asked him to leave her alone.

"Single men and women do not spend time together like this unless they are courting," she'd curtly told him.

"Well, maybe we should start courting," he'd declared, much to her horror. Yet all these months later, she'd agreed to be his wife and they were engaged to be married. Until he'd let doubts, worries, and regrets fill his mind—pushing her way.

"Lord, please keep her heart soft toward me," Ben spoke into the crisp mountain air. "And get me back to her, God. I'm as green as green can be in these parts. But I know You'll help me find the way..."

Follow Me.

The words were like a gentle whisper to his soul.

"I'm not alone." He lifted his face to the sunshine. "I've never been alone. Will never be alone..."

With quick but sure movements, Ben made it back to the campsite and packed anything worth keeping into Abe's backpack. He had the map. He also had a memory of the way they'd come. He still had the two granola bars left, and thankfully he knew he'd be able to find water on the way back. And he should be able to walk faster than the three miles an hour they'd been going with the horse and mule.

Although fear tried to jump on him, making the burden he carried on his heart even heavier than the one he bore on his back, Ben pushed those thoughts away. There were bears and other wild creatures. There could be weather problems and other dangers on the trail, yet God was with him.

Through the hardships, God had proved Himself faithful. And Ben knew He'd continue being so every step of the way.

Chapter Thirty-One

FRIDAY, JULY 7, MISSOULA, MONTANA

With quickened steps, Marianna rushed into the hospital room. Her dat looked so small and frail in the bed, unlike the strong man she'd known her whole life. His eyes were closed in sleep. His leg was in a large cast, suspended above the bed. What exactly had happened? She wanted to know the answer. More than that, she wanted to know about Ben.

Her father must have heard her enter the room, because his eyes fluttered open. "Marianna?"

"Hey, Dat." All the emotion she'd been holding in spilled over with those two words. The softest sob escaped her. Her lower lip trembled, and the tears she'd been holding back refused to be confined any longer.

"Marianna," he said again. Sadness and compassion filled his gaze. Was he thinking about Ben still out there alone? Surely he was.

"It's so good to see you, Dat." Without hesitation, she leaned forward and kissed his cheek. Then she reached for the box of tissues on the bedside table and quickly wiped away her tears. "You're okay."

"I'm here because of Ben." Her father's voice was scratchy and filled with emotion. "Well, and because Ike went for help." Dat winked. "But Ben stayed beside me. He tended my wounds. He brought me water and fed me. I'll never forget that."

"He's a good man."

"Have you heard any news?" Dat asked.

"Not yet. Roy's been talking to search and rescue. They started up the mountain this morning."

"And Annie?"

"She headed in last night. I'm not sure how long it will take her to get to Ben..." Tightness constricted Marianna's chest, and she blew out a breath, praying with it. "I heard there was a bear attack?"

Dat's eyes filled with tears. "It was right after the horse fell on my leg. Ben covered me with his body, and the bear grabbed him up by his backpack. It was a miracle that he wasn't seriously hurt."

Marianna sat on the side of his bed. "So you're saying that you're fine with me marrying an Englischman?" She presented a lopsided grin.

Laughter spilled from Dat's mouth, and he winced as he adjusted himself on his pillows. "Ja, Marianna.

And if any man or woman, bishop or elder has anything to say about it, I'll ask them when's the last time their future son-in-law saved them from a bear. Let them put that in *The Budget*."

When the nurse came in to tell Marianna that Dat had to rest, she made her way into the waiting room where Roy sat.

He rose when she entered. "So, how is everything?"

"Dat's doing well. He's going to be fine. And right before I went in to see him, Mem called. It seems she's heading this way."

"Oh, so she found a driver?"

"Millie Arnold." Marianna smiled. "Millie's bringing her and Joy down. Friends are stepping forward to watch my other siblings."

Roy ran his hands through his hair. "You have quite the community, you know."

"Yes, I know."

"As Ben would say, there's nothing like a warm cabin, a good wife, and friends." Roy winked.

"Yes, especially a friend like Annie who goes in after him."

"Do you want to go back to Ovando to wait?"

Marianna crossed her arms over her chest and sat. "I've been thinking about that. Leaving Dat is hard, but I want to return to the trailhead. I want to be there. I have to know." She rose.

"Your father will understand. I know he will." Roy pulled his keys from his pocket. "I think it's time for us to head back to Ovando. I'm sure the first thing Ben wants to see when he emerges from those woods is your pretty face."

~

Friday, July 7, Scapegoat Wilderness, Montana

Ben hadn't thought much of crossing the Continental Divide earlier in the week. He'd been walking in the back, and they had stopped to take in the view, chat, and laugh. He'd been focused then on the beauty and the accomplishment of their hike. But now, on the way back, he was so focused on getting up and over the mountain pass he almost forgot to look around at the mountains and the Chinese Wall, named for being as tall and vertical as the Great Wall of China, stretching as far as the eye could see.

His burning legs felt like rubber as he walked the trail. The sun bore down, and the wind whipped along the mountain path as if he were in a wind tunnel. His stomach growled, and his water bottle and Abe's were getting low. Yet he couldn't stop. The farther he got along the trail, the closer to safety he was. Hadn't they passed a cabin along the way? Ben tried to remember just where that had been. He also hoped that search and rescue were making their way to him. Why hadn't he asked more questions of the men in the medical helicopter when he'd had a chance?

Ben continued to focus ahead, and his eyes burned from the sun and the wind. Every noise, every movement, caused him to jump. He continued to look around for more bear tracks, but what good would it do if he spotted them? It wasn't like he could turn around and head back in the other direction.

I'm gonna make myself crazy. I need to think about what's ahead. I need to stop letting the fears lead.

God has a promising future for me.

God has never failed.

He walks with me.

Then, as if remembering again that he didn't walk alone, Ben let the words of the old hymn roll off his tongue. The refrain punctuated each step.

> "'*And He walks with me, and He talks*
> *with me,*
> *And He tells me I am His own,*
> *And the joy we share as we tarry there,*
> *None other has ever known.*'"

Another familiar hymn followed that, and then another. And soon his eyes lifted from the ground and the search for bear prints. Instead, he focused on the landscape of the sky and mountain ranges before him. Of the beauty of God's creation as it surrounded him alone.

As he reached the top of the Divide, he paused. Ben felt a peace wash over him for the first time since

Abe's accident. The day's warmth suddenly paled to the warmth filling him.

God had done so much already. God had saved Abe. God had directed Annie to provide all the extra food and survival gear before they left. God had already saved him from a bear attack.

Kneeling at the top of the trail, Ben determined to continue the walk in faith down this trail. Faith he'd make it to safety. Faith Marianna would be waiting for him. Trust that he could look forward to their wedding, but more than that, all their years together.

And as Ben quickly moved down the trail, he had a new song on his lips. A song about his future with his bride. A future he could hope for because God was by his side.

The following two hours went quickly as a refrain for a new song ran through his mind. The scent of pine filled the air, and Ben's steps felt lighter as he walked down the trail. He was just about to round a corner when he remembered the pencil and paper he had in his waist pack.

Whistling the tune of his new song, Ben found a large boulder to sit on. He pulled out the pencil and paper and wrote. He filled a page and then turned it over.

"In a world that always changes, rocks, and whirls—girl, you're always the center of my universe," he said aloud as he jotted down the words.

Ben was so lost in thought he almost didn't hear

the clomping of a horse's hooves. And just as he realized that he did, a woman's laughter split the air.

"Ben Stone, I've come to rescue you, and you're—" Annie cocked her head.

"I'm writing a song."

"Oh." Annie threw up her hands. "You're writing a song." She laughed again. "That is the last thing I expected."

Ben jumped to his feet. "Annie, you're here. You've found me." He took a few steps toward her.

"Is it just you?" Worry filled her face.

"They got Abe. The medical helicopter." Emotion caught in Ben's throat at the sight of her. "And Ike? Did you see Ike?"

"Yes." Pink rose to her cheeks, and she quickly looked away. "I saw him at the trailhead. Ike is fine. Wonderfully fine."

Then he noticed the pack mule behind her. "Wait. Do you have food?"

She smiled again and slid off the horse. Then she rushed up and gave him a quick hug. "Yes, I have food. I have a tent and a camp stove. I have everything that we'll need to camp for the night."

Relief loosened his shoulders, and Ben suddenly realized how tired he was. Not just today but from all the previous days of staying up and watching over Abe. He didn't have to do that tonight. Knowing that Annie was here, he could sleep with a full stomach, and soon he'd see Marianna.

"And then tomorrow?"

"If we get up as soon as daybreak hits, we can make it to the trailhead before nightfall."

It was with those words that Ben smiled. "It's really happening, Annie. I'm going to make it back...to Marianna."

"Yes, you're going to make it back." Annie pointed to the horse. "Why don't you ride a while. I know the perfect campsite not too far back. Although, we might come across search and rescue on the way." She paused. "Oh, you don't know about the horse and mule making it to the trailhead, do you?" Annie moved to the saddlebag, pulled out a paper bag, and handed it to him.

"No. I don't know anything except that Ike left, and he must have made it out, because the medical helicopter came for Abe." He glanced down at the bag. "And what's this?"

"It's your lunch, although it's almost dinner time. I packed it this morning because I figured you'd need it. I would usually say don't eat it all because you'll ruin your dinner, but today that's not going to be a problem." She laughed.

"So, as I eat, will you tell me about Shadow and Flint making it to the trailhead?"

Annie nodded. "Oh yes, and you'll never believe how we found out about them. To say it caused a stir is an understatement."

Chapter Thirty-Two

SATURDAY, JULY 8, OVANDO, MONTANA

Marianna tapped her fingers on the table at Trixi's Antler Saloon where she sat with Roy and Carrie. She tried to be patient as Roy finished his rib eye steak and potato. Even though search and rescue had told them they'd come across Annie and Ben and it would take them until dark to get out, she had a hard time waiting. She just wanted to be there. She needed to run into Ben's arms and see that he was all right.

"You know, my dad has always been a slow eater." Carrie winked at Roy. "I'm sorry, Marianna, that you have to wait. I know you're ready to get to the trailhead."

Carrie smiled broadly, and Marianna guessed she displayed the same smile when she hosted the news on television. Carrie looked out of place in the saloon, with her red blouse, styled hair, and perfect makeup. So did the other woman sitting next to Marianna.

With excitement and compassion in her gaze, Linsey reached over and gently touched Marianna's arm. "It makes sense that the local news will broadcast that Ben—the missing hiker—has been rescued. But are you sure you want me to be there?"

Marianna gave a weary smile and nodded. "As much as I'd love a private moment with Ben, I know I'll get that later. I asked all his fans to pray for him, and I want them to see their prayers are answered." She shrugged. "Who knows, maybe this is their first answered prayer."

Roy placed his fork and knife on his plate. "I think Ben's going to be surprised by the change in you, Marianna. Happy too. He hasn't often said it, but I know he's worried about how the media will affect you."

Marianna looked first at Carrie and then at Linsey. "The truth is I'm going to have to count on friends to help me know what to do and probably what to say at times. Like I learned in the West Kootenai, we all need each other. It's a wild place out there, and no one will do well if they attempt to face it alone."

Roy's phone buzzed, and he looked at the text. "I'm glad you feel that way. Search and rescue said he should be out of the woods in an hour." Roy glanced at Carrie. "I suppose I'll go ahead and alert the media." He smiled.

"It'll be a great story. Lots of rejoicing," Carrie said

as she placed her napkin on the table. "And I think everyone's ready for some good news by now."

Less than an hour later, the small crowd that gathered at the trailhead saw Annie on her horse heading down the trail.

Where's Ben? Marianna's heart sank. *Did something happen?* Then she saw Ben walking just behind Annie.

Annie halted her horse, and Ben rushed around her. He didn't seem surprised by the cameras set up, but he looked past all of them, finally locking eyes with Marianna.

A paramedic took a step forward, likely to check if Ben needed assistance, but Roy placed a hand on the man's arm. "Give them a minute, will you?"

Not able to hesitate any longer, Marianna rushed forward. A broad smile filled Ben's face as he ran toward her. They met just as the trail started into the woods. Without hesitation, Ben swept her up in his arms.

He bent down and kissed her once and then pulled back slightly as if remembering where they were. "I didn't know the media would be here, although I should have guessed. Are you okay if I give you a decent kiss? We are engaged, after all."

Marianna smiled at him, taking in the blue of his eyes and knowing that she truly loved this man with all her heart. "I'm good with it, Ben. In fact, I'm the one who invited some of those people out here."

"You? What do you mean?"

She smiled. "There's a lot to tell you, and we'll have time, but first, I'm waiting for that kiss."

Ben's smile softened, and tenderness filled his gaze. His lips touched hers, and a thousand fireworks exploded inside.

When he pulled back, Marianna knew there was only one thing she wanted to say. "I love you, Ben Stone, and nothing about the wedding matters. What I want most is to just be your wife. Hopefully sooner rather than later."

"I was hoping you'd say that. But are you sure, Marianna? I'm not a perfect man, but I love you with all my heart. Trusting God and thinking of you—that's what got me through."

She dared to look into Ben's face and see him—the complete Ben. All of him. Through all the ups and downs, she knew this was the right choice. Ben was the right choice.

"When I was first in Montana, I longed for Indiana and the area I grew up in. When I was in Indiana, I could only think about Montana, my friends, and my family. And over these last few days, my heart has settled. Ben, I love you and cannot wait to become your bride. God has brought us together. Our love, together in Him—that is my home."

"I'm so glad, Mari, because I prayed two things out there. That I'd be able to get your dat home to your mem and that I'd be able to come home to you. You are the one I love, and I know if Jason were here, he'd tell me not to let you go." The softest smile tipped up his lips. "More than that, I feel God saying the same."

"The worries of losing you..." She pressed her lips together and looked away. "It was almost too much to bear."

His hand stroked her chin and tilted it up until her eyes met his. "But I'm here, Marianna. We made it out. God brought us through."

Chapter Thirty-Three

SATURDAY, JULY 22, KALISPELL, MONTANA

As Marianna stood in the bedroom window overlooking the backyard, she couldn't have imagined a more beautiful spot for a wedding. When Roy had suggested his property near Kalispell, she knew it was the right decision. Especially when he offered to provide drivers for any of the Amish in West Kootenai who wanted to attend.

Mem and the other women couldn't have been happier preparing food in Roy's gourmet kitchen. Many of their guests had arrived the day before and filled all of Roy's guest rooms. And while the women cooked, the men set out the white wooden folding chairs and erected a large arch for the focal point of the ceremony.

Even though both Ben and Marianna had thought

the view of the Swan Range was beautiful enough, Carrie had insisted on ordering flowers. Flowers filled every corner of the expansive yard. Soon, in this beautiful place, Marianna would be marrying Ben.

She turned away from the window toward Mem, who was wearing a new Amish dress and kapp. Mem smiled, but her eyes also glimmered with unshed tears. Marianna knew she must be thinking of the two daughters she'd lost, even as she celebrated Marianna's marriage. And that was all right. Having joy and sadness at the same time was possible. Marianna felt the same. Even as she celebrated the new—the future—there was a bit of an ache of all that was left behind. She had Ben and this new life, but she'd never live the Amish one again.

Thank you, Lord, for the past years and the ones to come. Salty and sweet. Light and dark. Longing and hope.

Tucking one of her light-brown curls behind her ear, Marianna looked to Mem. "I still can't believe that Aunt Ida came. Can you imagine taking the train all the way to watch her niece marry an Englischer?" She mimicked the chatter she'd heard her whole life around sewing circles and church gatherings.

Mem chuckled. "Ja, well, what would she have to write about in *The Budget* if she stayed home? You can guarantee that next month her column will be the first that everyone turns to—just so they can shake their heads in shock."

Marianna looked out the window again. She

watched Aunt Ida arrive with some of the other women. Aunt Ida looked around and then chose her seat on one of the white wooden chairs that faced the floral arch with the mountain behind. Aunt Ida didn't have to sit there alone very long. Soon Wyatt, the Amish driver, joined her on one side and Edgar on the other. Marianna covered her mouth with her hand to hold back her smile. No, Aunt Ida hadn't ever attended a wedding like this. And yes, she'd have plenty to write about.

Marianna turned back to the room just as the door opened.

Annie entered. "Land sakes, woman! What are you doing standing there and not even dressed yet?"

Marianna looked down at her slip and then back to Annie. "I've been waiting for you to come and help me with the dress, Annie. You're the one who saved the groom, and you're used to all those buttons."

Pink rose on Annie's cheeks, and a smile lit her face. "You should have told me sooner. I would've asked one of the bachelors to do the chores so I could have got down here sooner." Annie whistled as she looked around the room. "It's mighty nice of Ben's friend to let you use this place. Do you think the media's gonna be mad that they weren't invited?" Annie approached and took the dress from the garment bag.

"Oh, we have some media here. Linsey Ledbetter came. We promised she could share clips from our wedding if she was discreet. Said she could come, but she couldn't let on that she was one of those fancy entertainment reporters from Los Angeles."

Annie looked at Marianna and nodded. "That's mighty nice of you. Ben's fans will appreciate that." She sighed. "I know you would never want to go through what you did again, but I think you're entering your marriage at a better place. It's not going to be easy mixing the old with the new. The simple with the flashy. But I feel the two of you will work it out just fine. Now, get over here and climb into this dress. I don't like being late for anything, especially my best friend's wedding."

Thirty minutes later, Marianna stood alone at the end of the grassy aisle. Instead of walking her down the aisle like Englischers did, Dat sat near the front in a wheelchair. His leg was doing better by the day, and since walking the bride down the aisle wasn't an Amish tradition in the first place, he didn't feel like he was missing out.

Marianna's brothers, and even Uncle Ike, had offered to walk her down the aisle. After praying about it, she decided on another way. Her walk down the aisle alone was a dedication. To God and to Ben. She was becoming a wife today. But more than that, she became a woman learning to trust God with every part of her life.

With towering mountain peaks as the backdrop, Marianna walked down the grassy aisle with Ben waiting for her in pressed jeans, a white shirt, and a black jacket. Marianna carried a bouquet of white and pink roses surrounded by sprigs of greenery. On both sides, Amish and Englischers sat with joyful faces.

This ceremony wasn't about Amish traditions or even Englisch ones. Instead, it was about a man who loved a woman and a woman who loved a man, and their vows before God.

They'd decided on a simple ceremony. Rather than the preacher giving a long sermon, they'd asked Pastor Kellen from Summit Community Church to share the importance of a marriage covenant and Millie Arnold to share her thoughts about marriage. After all, it seemed smart to hear from someone who had been married for almost sixty years.

Marianna couldn't help but smile when Millie shuffled to the front. "I've spent two days writing down everything I think you should know about being married, but I left that list at home." Millie winked. "I'm saving that for your first wedding anniversary. Right now, I think these are the three most important things." Millie cleared her throat. "First, be sure to taste your words before spitting them out. Arguments are best worked out before they start.

"Second, like John Wayne said—and my dear husband often quoted—'Courage is being scared to death and saddling up anyway.' Whatever comes, face it together. Work on it together.

"Finally, a wedding lasts a day, but a marriage lasts a lifetime."

With a smile, Millie returned to her seat, and the pastor asked Ben and Marianna to join hands.

For as long as Marianna lived, she'd never forget the look in Ben's eyes as he spoke his vows, their first kiss as man and wife. She couldn't help but blush. This was not something that happened at Amish weddings. Still, she knew it was right, good. Beautiful, even.

After the ceremony ended, the food was eaten, and the presents opened—part of Amish tradition—and the band played a soft melody as couples mingled on the grassy dance floor. Nothing loud or jarring. The refrain fit with the sway of the grasses in the fields beyond Roy's fence. With the setting of the sun and the strings of lights shifting with the breeze, Ben pulled Marianna to the side for a private moment together.

The air was a cacophony of voices. Around the tables was a mishmash of motion. Groups of adults talked and laughed in small huddles. Children ran and shouted playful chants and songs—some Amish, others Englisch—without awareness of their differences.

Not far from where Ben and Marianna stood, Annie and Ike sat in chairs side by side. Marianna couldn't help but watch as Ike leaned close as if to tell Annie a secret. Annie laughed and then glanced around. Maybe to see if anyone overheard.

Ben's gaze was turned in that direction too.

"So, during your trip to the mountains, did my bachelor uncle confess to not wanting to stay a bachelor forever?" Marianna asked as she snuggled against her husband's chest.

"I cannot comment one way or another. What's

discussed in the mountains stays in the mountains," he teased.

Ben pulled Marianna closer. She felt different now that she was a wife. More cherished, worthier. She lifted her face, and then her heart doubled in size as her husband pulled her into a deep, unhurried kiss. When the kiss ended, she gazed into her husband's blue eyes while his finger twisted a lock of her hair.

"There's one more thing I have for you, Mari. It's what kept me going on the trail."

"What's that? Thoughts of my apple cinnamon muffins or strawberry pies?"

Ben chuckled. "Yes, that too." He gave her one more kiss and then winked. "Although I love your baking, what helped me was looking ahead to the future. I thought about today. But more than that, I thought about our future. Of simple days. Of growing old together. I thought about putting our kids to bed at night and pushing back the sofa so we can dance." He smiled. "And so I wrote you a song."

"A song?" Her smile broadened. "You have a habit of doing that."

"I just finished it last night. But I wanted to share it with you first."

Marianna wrapped her arms around his neck and hugged him. "Thank you, but I'd really like you to share it now. Share it with everyone."

"Really?" Ben's eyes brightened.

"God gave me you, Ben. But He also gave them to you. Our families, our friends, and our fans. I bet

Linsey won't be too upset if she gets the scoop on the new song too."

The softest laugh escaped Ben's lips, and he quickly wiped away tears with the back of his hand. "I loved you before, Marianna, but I'm not sure if my heart can expand enough to share how much I love you now."

"Then sing to me of your love, Ben Stone. I want to hear it, and I want the world to hear it too."

With joy in his step and a smile as bright as the twinkling lights strung across the backyard awnings, Ben picked up his guitar and strummed a few chords as he approached the mic set up near the band.

"Well, everybody. My friend Millie gave me the best advice. She told me that if I want to keep my wife happy, the best way to do that is with a 'yes, ma'am.' So Mariannaat—yes, ma'am. I'm singing this song for you, darlin', and I'm also sharing it with those we love most. It's called 'Living Room Dance Floor.'"

We've been waiting
Been all working and no playing, baby
Yeah, we've been waiting
For the stars to align
The way you look right now
Got me thinking now's the time.

Push the sofa back against the wall
Turn the lights down and the TV off

Tell those kids don't come outside those bedroom doors
Let the country station be the band
Baby, take me by the hand
Ain't no time for waiting anymore
Let me hold you close
On this living room dance floor.

Let's just lean in
Ain't no need for talking, just breathing, baby
Feel that feeling
Been too long since we felt it
You fan that fire like no one else
Makes the world around us melt.

In a world that always changes, rocks, and whirls,
Girl, you're always the center of my universe.

Push the sofa back against the wall
Turn the lights down and the TV off
Tell those kids don't come outside those bedroom doors
Let the country station be the band
Baby, take me by the hand
Ain't no time for waiting anymore
Ain't no time for waiting anymore
Let me hold you close
On this living room dance floor.

"I love you, Ben," Marianna whispered as the last chords of the guitar faded into the night and applause from their friends and family erupted. "I love you," she said loud enough for him—and all those present—to hear. "And I'm thankful to be your wife, and I'm looking forward to our living room dance floor and whatever else God has in store."

Then, with more love in his eyes than Marianna could have ever imagined, Ben leaned down for another kiss.

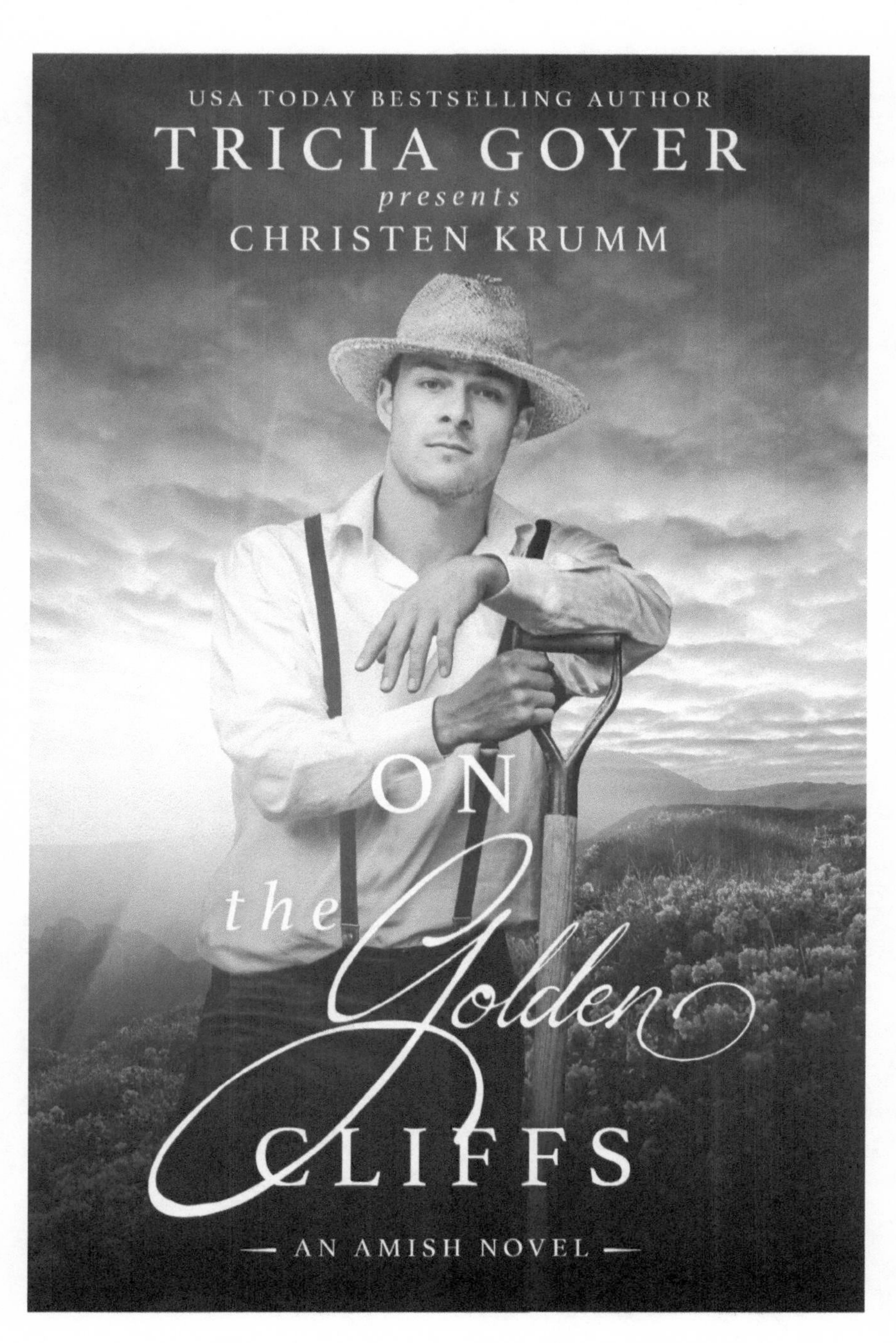

Turn the page for a sneak peek at the next Big Sky Amish novel,
On the Golden Cliffs...

On the Golden Cliffs Sneak Peek

CHAPTER 1

He, Reuben Milner, was an author. He held the evidence in his hands.

A breeze pushed up from the lake below, and the sun rose a little higher in the sky, its rays warming his face. Smoothing the pages of the book—*his book*—Reuben clutched it a little tighter so it wouldn't end up in the lake below.

It was abnormally warm for April in West Kootenai. Last week they'd had a snowstorm, evidence still sparkling on the ground, and this week they were pushing the upper fifties. Another breeze blew, sending Reuben clutching for the straw hat on his head. At least the wind coming off the Canadian Rockies was still cold, still predictable.

Cold wind, rain, a snowstorm couldn't keep him away from his cliff. It was where Reuben came when he needed to think or process or just be out of the house and away from his five sisters. Today he was here to celebrate. His gaze fell back to the object in his hands.

Hidden Hero, the title read. A real book that *he'd* written. His finger brushed the woman on the cover, who wore a long skirt similar to the ones his *mem* and sisters wore. Only this woman's hair was free, blowing in the wind as she looked into the distance. A biblical story set in an old Western town. He still couldn't believe this was what had captured the attention of a New York publishing house.

When others had told him to move away during his *Rumspringa* and experience life beyond the small Amish community located in the northwest corner of Montana, Reuben hadn't felt the need. And while the construction job had lured him away for a time, he'd discovered his true joy in the writing group that his roommate had hosted at his apartment. After months of listening to their meetings from his bedroom, Reuben had joined them. The rest had seemed a whirlwind when his work in progress was chosen by a visiting editor and taken back to publishing committee.

Even though he had turned in his final edits months ago, when his mem handed him the brown envelope last night with a grin, he'd never imagined that it held the finished book. He'd saved opening the envelope until he was in his spot. Now the wind ruffled the letter, which accompanied the book, as he pulled it out.

Reuben,

There's a whole box of these books waiting for you back at the apartment. I wasn't sure if it was okay to send them to you in West Kootenai, but I thought you needed to at least see one! A real book. You did it, brother! Can't wait for the next one. (You are writing another one, right?)

—Antony

Reuben couldn't be more grateful for his friend's discretion. He wasn't sure what his *dat* would say if he learned that his son had written a book *and* it had actually gotten published. Not exactly the makings of a good Amishman.

Reuben shook the worried thoughts from his mind. Today was one of celebrating. He flipped through the book again, breaking into a wide grin.

"Yes, Antony, I plan on writing many more books," he replied into the morning rays. Writing felt good. It felt right. Like this was what he was meant to do. Not how an Amishman was supposed to feel, but Reuben would have to worry about that later. He was proud of the work he had done, just as if his dat had made a rocking chair that turned out perfect on the first try. Dat couldn't fault him that. *Yes, but pride comes before a fall*. Reuben sighed thinking about how his dat would respond to his argument.

Below him, a fishing boat's engine revved. The sun was getting higher in the sky, and he knew he needed to be making his way back. Dat would have already started felling trees, readying them to transport to the mill. Reuben looked at his book one more time before putting it back in the envelope and tucking it under his arm. It was time to descend from the cliffs and clouds back into the valley of the real world—the land that he worked with his hands instead of spinning stories.

No matter. He grinned to himself. He'd still be spinning the stories in his head while he worked.

Something was wrong.

Goosebumps rose on Reuben's arms. He felt it before he saw anything. The silence of the woods around him was deafening. He strained, listening around the sound of blood rushing in his ears to attempt to pick out any worrisome sounds. Could it be a large animal that he was sensing? There hadn't been any bear sightings reported, but it was possible one woke up hungry. When he didn't hear anything large moving through the brush, his heartbeat slowed, but he still couldn't shake the feeling that something wasn't right.

And that's when it hit him. He should be hearing

the purr of his dat's gas-powered chainsaw. Reuben glanced at his watch. Dat had asked him to meet an hour ago. The plan was to cut down a cluster of pines for the sawmill. How had he let so much time pass?

There should be sounds of the chainsaw and Dat whistling while he worked. Or at least his dat's gruff baritone urging along Samson the horse. Maybe when Reuben had failed to show up on time, Dat had decided to get a head start on the custom furniture orders that were backing up in the workshop. *Ne.* Reuben's gut told him that wasn't the case.

Something was wrong. Yes, something was definitely wrong.

A sense of urgency came over him as he stepped over dead leaves and half-melted snow, quickening his steps down the hillside. He shouldn't be far now.

As a small clearing of trees opened before him, the sight that greeted him turned his stomach. Samson wasn't to be seen, and the logging wagon was overturned, one of the wheels broken, hanging at an odd angle. Pine logs littered the ground like his younger sisters' Lincoln logs Mem was forever asking them to pick up.

"Dat!" Reuben tossed the envelope to the side. He half ran, half slipped down the hill, sending up prayers that his dat wasn't under the mess of logs. He scanned the woods around him, looking to see if Samson had spooked and Dat had chased after him.

Just under the fresh cut pine, a flash of dark blue.

The color of his dat's shirt. The ground tilted beneath his feet, and he tasted bile in the back of his throat.

"No, no, no." Reuben scrambled the rest of the way to his dat. Part of him wanted to run home. Wished this was all just a dream. Dat would be sitting at the table with his cup of coffee, and Reuben would get a lecture about not being ready to work on time. That was what was supposed to happen this morning. Not this.

"Reuben?" His dat's voice was shaky, barely a whisper, but it meant he was still alive. Still breathing.

"What happened?" Reuben asked, not really expecting an answer. A trunk, at least three times rounder than his dat, pinned the older man's legs. Reuben pushed at the log, hoping it'd be easy to roll. His father's groans stopped him. "Why didn't you wait for me?" *Why'd I have to be so late?*

Reuben sat back on his heels, looking around for answers. He needed Samson. Putting his fingers to his lips, he let out a shrill whistle. They had been training Samson to come at the sound of the whistle. The horse hadn't quite got the hang of it. If there was any day that he needed Samson to respond, it was today. Where was that horse?

"Dat? Dat, I'm sorry—I know this is going to hurt, but I have to get this log off of you." His dat didn't answer, and Reuben prayed that he was still breathing. He should run for help, but the fear that his dat would die while he was gone rooted him.

There was no way Reuben should have been able

to lift the log, but with a mix of pushing and pulling, he got his dat free. Scooping him up in his arms, he turned toward home, the elation from earlier gone, replaced with the heavy feeling of regret.

This was all his fault.

Acknowledgments

I'm so thankful for the amazing team at Sunrise Publishing: Susie, Lindsay, Rel, Barbara, and Sarah. Thank you for your guidance on this story and making me look good. Also, thank you for allowing me to dive into the Big Sky world once again. Also, thank you to my husband John and my family for all your love and support.

I'm thankful for my agent Janet Grant, who has been my co-laborer for over twenty-five years. I'm grateful for my family for their love and support with every book I write. God has surrounded me with amazing people.

Thank you to Geneva Holmgren for all your help with how to handle medical emergencies.

Thank you Todd Tilghman for allowing me to use *Living Room Dance Floor*. I love this song and appreciate your friendship. Many thanks to Martha Artyomenko for reading through this story and helping with all the Amish and Montana facts. Thanks to Elly Gilbert and Christen Krumm for your amazing teamwork with these new Big Sky stories—and, Elly, your Amish song titles were the best.

Finally, this book wouldn't be possible without the expert help of my dear friend Rebecca Ondov. I knew what I was doing when I based Annie after you. Thank you for every detail on Montana culture, outfitting, search and rescue, and the Bob Marshall Wilderness. I'll never forget the moment when I picked up the phone and the first words out of your mouth were, "So, I called the sheriff." Thank you for your time, knowledge, and prayers.

Finally, thank you, God, for the honor of writing for you.

Connect with Sunrise

Thank you so much for reading *Beyond the Gray Mountains*. We hope you enjoyed the story. If you did, would you be willing to do us a favor and leave a review? It doesn't have to be long- just a few words to help other readers know what they're getting. (But no spoilers! We don't want to wreck the fun!) Thank you again for reading!

We'd love to hear from you- not only about this story, but about any characters or stories you'd like to read in the future. Contact us at www.sunrisepublishing.com/contact.

We also have a monthly update that contains sneak peeks, reviews, upcoming releases, and fun stuff for our reader friends. Sign up at www.sunrisepublishing.com

About the Author

Tricia Goyer writes out of her passion for God and her love for family and others. The author of more than 70 books, she writes both historical fiction and nonfiction related to family and parenting.

This USA Today best-selling author has won a two Carol Awards and a Retailer's Best Award. She was also an ECPA Gold-Medallion Nominee and a Christy Award Nominee and won Writer of the Year from the Mt. Hermon Christian Writers Conference.

Tricia's contemporary and historical novels feature strong women overcoming great challenges. She is a beloved author of Amish fiction, having written the Big Sky and Seven Brides for Seven Bachelors series.

Whether for fiction or nonfiction, Tricia's writing style is vivid and heartwarming, allowing readers to take home more than engaging stories, but also messages that inspire faith and hope. Her goal is to write stories that matter. Visit her at triciagoyer.com.

facebook.com/authortriciagoyer
instagram.com/triciagoyer
pinterest.com/triciagoyer
twitter.com/triciagoyer
youtube.com/triciagoyer
bookbub.com/auathors/tricia-goyer
goodreads.com/162726.Tricia_Goyer
amazon.com/stores/author/B001JP8FPC

Other Big Sky Novels

Big Sky Amish Collection

Beyond the Gray Mountains

On the Golden Cliffs

Under the Blue Skies

Big Sky Series by Tricia Goyer

Beside Still Waters

Along Wooded Paths

Beyond Hope's Valley

Beyond the Gray Mountains: A Big Sky Amish Novel
Published by Sunrise Media Group LLC

Large Print ISBN: 978-1-953783-47-9
Print ISBN: 978-1-953783-39-4
Ebook ISBN: 978-1-953783-40-0

Published in the United States of America.

Cover Design: Emilie Haney, eahcreative.com

Made in United States
Troutdale, OR
12/03/2023

15285888R00202